book club murder in kingfisher falls

the charlotte dean mysteries. book 2.

Phillipa Nefri Clark

Book Club Murder in Kingfisher Falls

Copyright © 2023 Phillipa Nefri Clark

Cover design by Kylie Sek

Previously titled Deadly Falls

book club murder in
kingfisher falls

an important note...

This book was previously published with the title **Deadly Falls.** The rights were recently returned and the author has done a light rewrite and fresh edit. The book has a new title and cover.

This series is set in Australia and written in Aussie/British English for an authentic experience.

Like to discover more about Charlotte, other titles, and Phillipa's world? Visit Phillipa's website where you can join her newsletter. www.phillipaclark.com.

To perseverance. When dreams seem out of reach, persevere. One by one, they will come to you.

prologue

'Help me! Help!'

Clinging to a post at the edge of the lookout, her body dangling over the side of the cliff, Charlotte Dean risked a glance at the almost sheer drop. If she was lucky enough to miss the jutting rocks on the way down, the river would do little to cushion her fall.

She willed her aching fingers to stay gripped, but they hurt. Her shoulders screamed from holding her weight.

Think.

Charlotte's hands were around a metal post. It was bolted into concrete and wasn't about to come loose. Could she lift herself enough to get an arm around the post? She sucked in air and tightened the muscles in her forearms. One foot found a gap in the rock just big enough for her toes.

Up. Her gaze picked a spot above her hands. That's where she had to be. Up.

Fire in her arms.

One. Big. Chin-up.

Pounding heart. All she could hear. Or was it the waterfall behind?

Her eyes levelled with the ground of the lookout. Her bag was there, its contents strewn across the lookout.

Rain began.

Her fingers slipping again, she forced her muscles to work harder than they'd ever worked. One elbow was over the edge, then the other. She rested on them for a long moment. If she let go with one hand, she'd fall.

Pushing up with her toes in the little gap below, she leaned all her body weight forward and then kicked the air. Just enough to get half her body to safety. Don't let go. Not yet.

From the waist up, she was on solid ground again.

'Aaah!' She dragged one leg, then the other to the top. Panting, she lay on her side.

'Well, what have we got here?'

No. Not you.

Charlotte released the post and rolled under the rail, back to the relative safety of the lookout. On all fours she crawled away from the edge through mud.

'Looks like you've got yourself on the wrong side of the railing, missy.' Sid stood cross-armed at the entrance to the path. To safety. 'Couldn't believe my ears when I heard a cry for help.'

'Keep…away.' Charlotte blinked the rain from her eyes, scanning the ground for a stick. Or anything. Any weapon.

'You don't want to do that.' Sid sneered as he uncrossed his arms and put one hand on the police belt. On the holster of his gun. 'Time to finish what we started.'

chapter
one

A few days earlier

'He's out there again.'

Charlotte joined Rosie at the window of the bookshop as Leading Senior Constable Sid Browne did a slow U-turn in his patrol car and cruised past. He stared in as he drove, window down, fingers tapping on the roof.

'Good. He'll eventually run out of petrol.' Charlotte was more bemused than annoyed by the man's odd behaviour. In the week since the bookshop reopened after the Christmas break, he'd been a regular passer-by. Sometimes in the patrol car, other times on foot.

'Well, if he wants to speak to us, he needs to walk through the door.' Rosie spun her wheelchair and headed behind the counter. 'All this silliness is getting to me.'

Which is what Sid wants.

'I've been expecting him to demand a statement from Christmas Eve.' Charlotte went back to stocking shelves with the first shipment of books of the year. 'If he wants the arrests to stick, he needs witness statements.'

Thanks to some help from Charlotte on Christmas Eve, Sid had arrested two young men on suspicion of burglary, property damage, and causing bodily harm. He'd taken credit for it, of course, but was keeping the town in the dark about the status of the case. And returned to his creepy habit of watching the bookshop.

'Perhaps Trev can find out what's happening.' Rosie mused. 'He'd have access to the police computer thingy.'

'Rosie. First of all, no. Second of all, I don't think it's called a police computer thingy, but I do know police can't just check up on each other using it, even if one of them is your son. And finally. No.'

Rosie laughed.

'Stop laughing at me. You know I'm right. Anyway, I'm going to ask Sid what's going on next time he goes past.'

'Then I really should call my son now and see what he can find out. He knows people.'

'I'm sure Trevor does know people, but there's no point worrying him when he's too far away to do anything.' Charlotte joined Rosie behind the counter. 'You know, when I lived in Rivers End, he talked about you a lot. Worried about you.'

Before moving to Kingfisher Falls a couple of months ago, Charlotte spent most of the previous year living on the coast along the Great Ocean Road. Rosie's son, Trev Sibbritt, ran the single police officer station in Rivers End and had become her friend. Or something.

A sigh left Rosie's lips and her smile faded. 'I know he does. Which is why he only got the edited version of the events before he arrived for Christmas dinner. I didn't tell him you were at risk, or Sid was such a pain.'

She busied herself on the computer and Charlotte took another armful of books to the back of the shop. Once or twice, Rosie had mentioned some past conflict between Sid and Trev, before he left for his first posting. But never any details, and even Trevor kept things close to his chest about it. He'd cautioned Charlotte to be wary of Sid, saying only that the man was power hungry.

He wasn't the only one. This little town had a host of people wanting to control something, from a couple of corrupt councillors, to a dodgy shopkeeper, to the book club ladies. Speaking of which…

'Rosie, what will we do with all of those books?'

Those books were ordered before Christmas for the local book club then summarily cancelled by the new president after they'd been sent to the bookshop.

Without looking up, Rosie waved a hand at a pile behind the counter. 'Those? I'd better confirm Octavia is not taking them.'

'Shall I phone her?'

Rosie looked up, over the top of her glasses. 'Let me see. 'Hello, Mrs Morris? This is Charlie—' the phone slams down.'

'Or, it might be, 'Mrs Morris, your books have arrived, and you have two days to pay for them before we bring in a debt collector.' And then the phone slams down.' Charlotte did two thumbs up.

'You are a tough businesswoman. No wonder I like you so much. However, she doesn't like you, and I think she doesn't like me these days, but let's give it a whirl.' Rosie picked up the phone. 'We might need refreshments after this.'

Charlotte agreed. Dealing with Octavia Morris, or her best friend Marguerite Browne, who was Sid's wife, was enough to drive anyone to drink. Even just extra strong coffee. She rested her arms on the counter to listen.

Rosie checked no customers were heading into the book-shop, then put the phone on speaker. It rang a few times, then Octavia answered in a pleasant tone.

'Hello, Octavia Morris speaking.'

'Octavia, it's Rosie Sibbritt. How are you?'

Over the ensuing long silence, Rosie and Charlotte's eyes met with a 'knew it'.

'Of all the nerve. How do you think I am, Rose?' There it was, the hostility both women were accustomed to. 'Publicly humiliated by you and that girl you employ at the town Christmas party. Ostracised.'

'Not quite how I recall. More along the lines of you and Marguerite attacking the Woodland family for something they didn't do. If you then chose to leave, it really wasn't because anyone forced you away.'

How Rosie ever kept her temper with this woman was beyond Charlotte. Time and again, Octavia showed a lack of manners and sometimes out and out nastiness, yet Rosie never got down to the same level.

'We both felt like outsiders. And it was your doing. What do you want?'

'The books you ordered for the book club are here.'

Charlotte held up two thumbs and mouthed 'debt collector'.

Rosie rolled her eyes. 'So, I'd appreciate you letting your members know so they can collect their copies.'

The laugh on the other end of the phone was unpleasant. 'I told you to kiss your pathetic bookshop goodbye. News-flash, Rose. It begins now.'

Click.

'O—kay.' Charlotte straightened. 'I guess that means she's not buying them.'

'She's become impossible to reason with. There has to be another way of resolving this.'

'Oh, there's always a means.' Charlotte grinned as she made her tone sinister. 'It just depends how far you're prepared to go.'

There was a gasp from outside. Veronica stood at the doorway, hand over her mouth and eyebrows raised in a horrified expression. Dressed in her customary short skirt and tank top, she wore bright orange high heels matching both her lipstick and an oversized handbag slung over a shoulder.

'Good morning, Veronica.' Rosie made no move to leave her place behind the counter. 'How can we help?

'Unbelievable! I heard that with my own ears.'

With a huff, she spun away, almost tripping over her feet, and tapped off along the footpath.

'Um…what was that about?' Something bad was about to happen. Charlotte pushed away the sense of déjà vu.

'I imagine she overheard us. Now she'll have us plotting Octavia's demise.'

'That coffee?' Charlotte reached for some money. 'Any chance I can order it with something stronger in it?'

———

Glenys Lane hobbled into the bookshop, leaning on her walking cane. Charlotte was alone unpacking another box of books. Rosie had gone out to have lunch with Lewis, her friend who owned the homewares shop.

'He's closing for a whole hour so we can sit under the trees.' Rosie had said. 'He never closes his shop and when I was running this place alone, I didn't either. So, this is nice.'

It was nice. Lewis, a widower of many years, was a delightful man who kept asking Rosie out, so Charlotte was all for their blossoming 'friendship'. Even Trev approved.

'Mrs Lane. How is your knee?'

'Glenys, dear. I think you should call me that.'

'Thank you.'

Glenys hooked her timber cane over the top of the

counter and leaned her hands on the top, letting them take her weight. 'I'm considering selling up.'

'You are?'

'There's nothing here for me. Not since Fred passed away. Well, I had the book club, but Octavia and Marguerite are running it now and I don't feel welcome.'

'But you began the book club.'

'Until they voted me out. All things change, don't they? Oh, those are the books we ordered.' She glanced past Charlotte to the back counter where Rosie had left them. 'Octavia found a supply online and the members had no say in it. I am so sorry about this.'

'We'll work it out.' Charlotte waved a hand.

'Octavia should pay for them.'

'Rosie already asked her to but she...well, she laughed at her.'

Glenys gazed at her hands. 'Rosie deserves better. I will tell Octavia to apologise.' She raised her head with a small huff. 'I might walk up there now while my car's being serviced and have a nice chat.'

'There's no need, Glenys. Please don't put yourself out.'

But Glenys had her cane in hand and off she went. Hopefully, the ladies would make up rather than continue the cold standoff since the Christmas Eve street party. The moment Glenys took a stand on behalf of the Woodland family, Octavia and Marguerite had turned their backs on the woman who'd been their close friend for so long.

'Was that Glenys?' Rosie wheeled back in, removing the straw hat she'd donned before leaving. Perspiration streaked her makeup which was not surprising with the day hot even by mid-summer standards and a rapid rise in humidity heralding a storm.

'She spotted the book club books and will talk to Octavia. I said not to, but she was insistent.'

'Oh dear. Something tells me that won't be a pleasant discussion. I'm not holding out much hope she'll succeed, so let's make a nice window display of the books and perhaps we should add a big discount.' Rosie chuckled to herself.

'You are one bad woman.'

Octavia could learn from Rosie's can-do approach to everything. That's if the grumpy woman could even still learn.

———

Charlotte and Rosie had customers as a police siren approached. Everyone stopped talking and gravitated to the front of the book shop as Sid's patrol car screeched to a haphazard halt outside.

Sid climbed out and waved his arms as he puffed his way to the door. 'Missy!'

'Oh, what now?' Charlotte grumbled.

'You're a doctor.'

'Psychiatrist, but—'

'No buts. Grab your bag. Need help.' He leaned against the doorway, panting.

'Do you want an ambulance?' Rosie asked.

'Not me. Please, Charlotte. Grab your bag and come with me.'

He never called Charlotte by name. 'Okay, but why?'

'It's Octavia. I think she's dead.'

chapter
two

Charlotte raced for the back door even as the others clamoured around Sid for information. She hurtled up the steps, key at the ready. Her long unused medical kit was in a cupboard and it took a moment to dig it out.

None of this made sense. What happened to Octavia? Why was Sid here instead of wherever Octavia was? And what about an ambulance?

'Quick, darling. Sid's waiting.' Rosie called as Charlotte rushed back in. 'Call me as soon as you know something.' Her face was white.

'I will.'

The motor was on and the passenger door open, and Charlotte slid in and closed it.

'Seatbelt.' Sid grunted as he turned the patrol car in the opposite direction and floored it.

'Tell me what you know.' Charlotte clicked the seatbelt and looked for something to hold onto. Unlike Trev's police car, which was immaculate and had all the latest equipment, Sid's was disgusting. Crumpled chocolate wrappers and squashed drink cans were beneath her feet and the stench from his cigarette habit made her want to throw up. The insides of the windows were filthy, and the radio blared country music.

'I think she's dead.'

'You said that. Is an ambulance on its way?'

'I'm not stupid. Called it first but half an hour away. The real doctor in town is out on an emergency, so you have to do. You can do stuff?'

'Medical degree says so.'

The patrol car sped through the roundabout, wheels bumping over the central gutters. Why did Sid think it safe to drive like this, sirens or not? Then, he turned down the road toward Veronica's garden centre. Charlotte had walked along here a couple of times. The homes were large and set in big gardens.

'I was heading to town after a patrol. Glenys was waving madly from the grass verge outside Octavia's house. Ran inside and felt for but couldn't find…you know.' His voice faltered.

'A pulse? Any idea what happened? Fall?'

'What makes you think that?' He shot her suspicious look through his beady eyes.

'You didn't mention any sign of blood or attack and falls are common as we age.'

Sid flicked the sirens off as he pulled into a wide driveway between graceful silver birches, then screeched to a halt near a double garage. The house was two level in red brick, an older but beautiful looking building with English style gardens.

Charlotte sprinted to the front door and it swung open. Glenys stood just inside, ashen as her hand waved about.

'I'll check you in a minute but go and sit somewhere please.' Charlotte's voice was steadier than her hands, which she doubted would let her even open her bag. But one second in the lounge room and her professional persona took over.

Antique-looking armchairs and sofa formed a semi-circle around an ornate marble fireplace. The hearth was two bricks high, finished with a marble slab. And that was where the life had ended of a woman who had once been a friend of Rosie.

Octavia lay face down with her forehead against the base of the bricks at a steep angle. Blood trickled onto the carpet beneath her body. Charlotte stepped carefully to one side of Octavia and squatted. She checked for the pulse she knew was no longer there.

'Shouldn't you get your stethoscope out?' Sid burst in.

'Stop. Please take care where you stand and what you touch. And yes, I will, but I am so sorry to advise that Octavia has passed away.'

Sid's mouth dropped open and his arms fell to his sides. To his credit, he came no further into the room as Charlotte checked for a heartbeat. From the colour and feel of her skin, Charlotte estimated the woman had died two to three hours ago but only a pathologist would be able to confirm this.

'I don't want to move her to check for injuries, Sid. Not until proper photographs are taken and—'

'What the hell? She's tripped and hit her head. No need for anything other than—'

'Leading Senior Constable.' Charlotte stood. 'I know Octavia was close to your wife and this is upsetting, but we owe it to her to ensure the area is examined. Yes, it most likely is a dreadful accident, but if someone else is involved, wouldn't you prefer to use your training and position to ensure justice prevails?'

He blinked a few times.

Too many big words?

'You don't really think…' He grabbed a radio from his police belt. 'Keep watch.' Then he was gone, heading for the front door.

Charlotte packed her stethoscope away and closed her bag. Apart from the blood from Octavia's head, there was no other sign of an injury. On a whim, she took photos with her phone. First of Octavia, then the surrounds. As many as she could. Just in case.

'Why are you doing that?' Glenys swayed in the doorway, arms wrapped around herself.

After picking up her bag, Charlotte moved away from Octavia, noting small details like the colour of the carpet, the contrasting dark blue mat which Octavia lay upon, antique-filled display cabinets, and two large bookcases. When she reached Glenys, she guided her away with a gentle hand on her arm.

'Is there somewhere we can sit?'

Glenys led her to an ornate dining room with more antique furniture.

Charlotte pulled out a chair. 'I think you should rest.'

Glenys lowered herself onto the seat and put her head in her hands. 'This is a nightmare. I'll pray for her soul.'

'Sid said you waved him down.'

'The battery of my phone is flat, and Octavia's landline didn't work. I didn't know what to do. Charlotte, why did you take photos?'

'Oh. Old habits, that's all. I was taught to treat every incident as a potential…well, crime scene. I took photos last year after Esther's window was broken and of the Christmas tree in the roundabout being destroyed.'

'Incident? Is that all she is?' Tears flooded from Glenys eyes. Charlotte rubbed her back.

'You've had a shock. I think when the ambulance comes, they need to check you over. Okay? And Sid will arrange a lift home. Or to somewhere with some company.'

'I don't have anyone.'

'We'll find someone.'

'I think I should leave now. This is all so upsetting.'
Glenys began to rise.

Charlotte squeezed her arm. 'Probably best if you stay. I
can hear the ambulance, so are you fine to sit here for a few
minutes? I'll be back.'

Once Glenys had nodded, Charlotte raced back to the
lounge room. There was one last thing she wanted to check
before the house was taken over by the appropriate
authorities.

chapter
three

Charlotte stood near the kerb outside Octavia's house. The paramedics were inside doing their job. Marguerite was on her way, despite Sid telling her to stay home. And a few minutes ago, Kevin Murdoch arrived. She'd only ever seen him from a distance at a public meeting he'd presided over. His brother, Terrance, was a local council member and Kevin was Octavia's self-proclaimed man-friend. He'd climbed out of his car as the paramedics carried her off, his eyes dazed.

Charlotte wanted to go to Rosie. Although the past few weeks had divided them, Rosie had known Octavia since high school and this terrible news would devastate her.

The bookshop phone wasn't answered and Charlotte checked her watch. Well before closing time. She dialled Rosie's phone, which rang a few times before being answered with a quiet, 'It's true. Isn't it?'

'Are you home?'

'Yes. I closed early. Everyone says she's gone.'

'I'm on my way but I'm walking. Hold on. I'll be there soon.'

After a final glance at the house, which was barely visible behind the trees and bushes, Charlotte crossed the road and hurried along the footpath. The humidity was rising fast and grey clouds approached across the top of the hills.

As grey as I feel.

Which was little. Not yet, anyway. Later, she'd unpack the events, the smells and sights in Octavia's house, the lounge room, Glenys' grief, even Sid's disbelief. The feelings would crush her if she wasn't careful. For now, her focus was on helping Rosie deal with her loss.

It didn't take long to reach Rosie's house. She tapped, then opened the front door, expecting it to be unlocked as it normally was. 'Rosie?'

'I'm here, Charlie.'

Charlotte followed her voice to the outdoor covered area.

Rosie's wheelchair was at the table, a pile of magazines to one side. She looked up from an open photo album. 'Would you believe, Octavia was once a brilliant runner? We both did track and field at school and I was good, but she was better. We used to team up in relays and won just about everything we entered despite limited coaching. She dreamed of building a place where young athletes could train.'

Charlotte sat beside Rosie and looked at the photographs. A very fit teenage twosome smiled back, arms entwined and medals around their necks.

'I had no idea. Trev told me you were into diving but never mentioned this athletic mother of his.'

'He probably wouldn't remember me talking about it. After high school, I moved to the city for university and met his father, my Graeme. It was only when I became pregnant that home beckoned, and I was lucky Graeme fell in love with the region as well.'

'What about Octavia. Did she leave and return?'

Rosie closed the photo album and raised pain-filled eyes.

'She married the school captain. Kingfisher Falls has always been her home. What happened to her, Charlie?'

'It appears she fell and struck her head on the hearth in the lounge room. It would have been instant, Rosie.'

'On the marble. Why would she fall though? She was healthy. Walked everywhere.' Rosie sighed. 'Our birthdays are only days apart.'

Charlotte took her hand. 'Until there's an autopsy, we won't know if she had some underlying problem that affected her balance.'

Or if she was pushed.

'Autopsy? Is there a chance she was…' Rosie lowered her voice to a whisper, 'murdered?'

Charlotte didn't know how to answer. Something about the death bothered her but she wanted to look through the photos on her phone before jumping to conclusions.

'Charlie, you think it's possible?'

'I don't know. Nothing looked out of place or strange. There's no reason to suspect anything. Not this early.'

The phone rang in the kitchen and Rosie went inside. Charlotte glanced at the magazines. All school yearbooks by the look of them. Reminiscing over an old friend was one way to deal with grief.

Charlotte turned a page, finding a photo of a young Rosie playing guitar. She bit her bottom lip as she closed the yearbook and ran a finger across the cover.

Rosie was on the phone.

'I wish it wasn't true, dear.' Rosie's shoulders were slumped. 'Charlie's here, but I thank you for thinking of me. If anything, Glenys needs some support, I imagine.'

Mellow and Mayhem, Rosie's cats, sat on the back of the sofa watching her. No doubt Mellow would make a beeline for her lap at some point as she was sweet and had an uncanny ability to know when a warm, furry body was required. Mayhem was less likely to do anything other than tell you off. But he had his nice moments as well.

'They have? Oh, how very generous and kind.'

Charlotte went to Rosie's small but well stocked bar and made them both a gin and tonic. She doubted Rosie would object and she had an unusual need to take the edge off after the horrible afternoon.

'That's so sweet of Doug and I won't say no. Not that I want to eat right now, but...well, thank you, Esther.'

A moment later, Rosie finished the call and met Charlotte near the sofa on the side where one of its arms was absent. She parked her wheelchair and slid herself onto the sofa. 'I understand if you want to drink both of those, but darling, I would love one.' Tears filled her eyes for the first time since Charlotte arrived. 'I think I'd like to make some toasts.'

———

'Do you know, I never asked if Kevin showed up.' Rosie stroked Mellow's fur as the cat purred on her lap. Mayhem, predictably, was stretched out on the far end of the sofa.

'He did, but I was leaving. The poor man looked distraught and in shock, so I hope the paramedics checked him as well as Glenys.'

'I didn't tell you. Glenys has gone to stay with the Woodlands.'

Charlotte's jaw dropped. Glenys was one of the people who had accused Darcy Woodland of stealing the town's Christmas trees last year and only changed her mind when the real thieves were arrested. Her property was next door to Darcy's Christmas Tree Farm. 'What a sweet gesture.'

'The minute Abbie heard what happened, she made space for Glenys. Considering her baby is due any day, I am touched and rather impressed. To Abbie, Darcy, and Lachie Woodland.' She raised her glass.

'And to new baby-Woodland when he or she makes their arrival.' Charlotte reached her glass out to touch Rosie's with a satisfying 'clink'.

They sipped. 'Nice. You've got this mix down perfectly.' Rosie said. 'How did Glenys know to go in the house? Was the door open?'

'Now whose the detective? I don't know. Sid was taking a statement from her when I left, but I didn't ask. She mentioned she'd tried to call for help using Octavia's landline but it wasn't working.'

'Strange. That was the phone I spoke to her on earlier. Should we tell Sid?' Rosie asked.

'He has no clue, Rosie, none. Before coming to get me, he'd stomped all over the living room, maybe moved the… um, Octavia, and contaminated everything. I understand Glenys maybe touching things because she's not trained to deal with these things and would have been shocked. But he *is* trained.'

'He thinks it is accidental?'

'I imagine so. It took my best 'Doctor Dean' voice to get him to stay away from Octavia until the paramedics arrived. The idea of him in charge of an actual investigation…' she grimaced.

'To no need for investigations!' Rosie lifted her glass.

'Drink to that.'

Someone tapped on the front door.

'Oops, that was the other thing I forgot to tell you. Doug is sending us dinner. Would you mind getting the door?'

Dinner was the last thing on Charlotte's mind. But when she thanked the delivery driver and took the bag from him the aroma of garlic and tomato made her stomach rumble.

She unpacked two takeaway containers and a long, foil wrapped bread.

'Why has Doug done this?'

'He knew you would be exhausted and I most likely wouldn't bother to make food tonight. There are lap tables in the cupboard to your left if you'd like to bring two over. I'd rather eat here, if you don't mind the informality.'

Charlotte found the tables and brought them and the food to the living room. 'I'll get some cutlery.'

'Thank you, darling. And another drink.'

The food was delicious. Two pumpkin gnocchi and garlic bread. 'I had this the first time I went to Italia.' Charlotte mentioned between bites. 'I told Bronnie there how much I loved it.'

'One of my favourites as well. How sweet Doug is.' But Rosie pushed hers away half eaten. 'I'll keep it for tomorrow.' Her shoulders drooped.

Charlotte picked up both plates and headed for the kitchen. She put the remains of Rosie's meal into the fridge and packed hers back into the bag it came in.

'I should go home.'

'You are welcome to stay. But I can only imagine how you feel, darling.'

Charlotte sat beside Rosie and nodded. 'I'm tired. I want to shower and sleep. Why don't you take tomorrow off?'

'I was about to suggest you do that.'

'Thank you, but I'm a believer in keeping to routines when there are upsets. Decide tomorrow, and if I see you, I see you.' She leaned over and kissed Rosie's cheek. 'I'm so sorry about Octavia.'

'Me too. Never had a chance to make things right and I'll always regret it.'

———

Charlotte let herself into her apartment, closing and locking the door before turning on all the lights. She dwelt on Rosie's words. She'd been with Rosie the day Octavia tore their long-standing relationship in two. Their teenage friendship was a thing of the past but when Charlotte first met Octavia a few weeks ago, there was still a mutual respect.

That was until the events leading up to Christmas created tension between many people in town, with sides taken and fingers pointed. Rosie tried to be the voice of reason for everyone, only to find herself turned on by Octavia and her then-closest friend, Marguerite. With a final declaration that Rosie's shop would fail, Octavia had flounced out.

She'd said the same thing this morning on the phone. 'I told you to expect to kiss your pathetic bookshop goodbye. Newsflash, Rose. It begins now.'

Newsflash, Octavia. We're here for the long haul.

Charlotte exhaled. Whatever Octavia had said, or done, it didn't matter now. Her lifeless body was in a morgue some-where. Her close friends and family were grieving. Even some not so close people. She might have become a viper in recent times, but Octavia Morris had been a long-standing member of the Kingfisher Falls community and would be missed.

———

A long shower later, Charlotte curled up on the sofa—wrapped in her dressing gown—a cup of tea beside her. She scrolled through the images she'd taken this afternoon. At the first—a full shot of Octavia's body—she drew her breath in, but then she forced the emotional response away.

There were over fifty images, not only of the body, but the lounge room and some from the adjoining kitchen. Both rooms were immaculate with nothing on coffee tables or cushions out of place. Perhaps Octavia was house-proud. Or expecting guests.

Or there'd been a struggle, and someone tidied up.

With a shake of her head, Charlotte relegated that to the "not likely" basket. There were several photographs just before Glenys had interrupted her with one of particular interest. Taken from above Octavia's upper half, it focused on the back of her head and shoulders. Octavia's silver hair was thinning a little, not that you'd notice under normal circumstances. But from this angle, there was discolouration through the silver.

Charlotte zoomed in. It might be the light in the room. Except, the more she zoomed in and out, the more obvious the difference was. Did Octavia have a birthmark on her skull? It was near the base of her skull and ran horizontally. She sent the image to her laptop.

As the ambulance had arrived, she'd run back to the kitchen to look for...well, she didn't know what. Again, a perfect, tidy room. The only sign of anyone actually living here was a teapot on the side of the sink. She'd glanced inside. Half empty, but cold. And no cups. Something made her open the dishwasher, which was partly packed and included two matching cups and saucers. Pretty ones in the same flowery pattern as the teapot.

She'd taken photos, not knowing why, and closed the dishwasher as voices approached. By the time Sid led two paramedics in, Charlotte was back with Glenys.

The quality of these photos wasn't as good but one of the cups caught her interest. Both cups had lipstick marks on the rims. One was the light mauve Octavia favoured. Charlotte had seen it on her so many times. But the other?

Bright orange.

Charlotte opened her laptop and found the image of Octavia's head. On the large screen it was obvious. This was no birthmark. Although the abrupt connection between her forehead and the marble hearth probably ended Octavia's life, she hadn't simply tripped.

There was a distinct mark on the back of her skull. She'd been hit from behind.

chapter
four

Charlotte glanced at the time. Almost nine. She believed someone killed Octavia or hurt her enough to lead to her death. And if Sid didn't think there was reason to pursue an investigation, then that someone might get away with it.

There'd be checks in place to ensure any death was noted as accidental or otherwise. But her knowledge of the processes in Victoria let her down because her medical training was in another state. And it was years ago.

If she phoned Trev, would he insist on coming up to see for himself? It was what held her back. There was bad blood between him and Sid. He had no jurisdiction in Kingfisher Falls according to Sid, so couldn't even investigate.

Charlotte opened the sliding glass door and stepped onto the balcony. A storm was close. Lightning flashed in the distance, too far away to hear thunder, but it was coming.

One thing she knew about Leading Senior Constable Trevor Sibbritt was that he was the real deal. He loved his mother and would be distraught if she kept this news from him. If she dropped in her own thoughts, then he'd explain what happened under the circumstances. She'd have a calm, non-emotional conversation about a terrible incident.

As the phone rang, Charlotte leaned against the balcony railing. The town was quiet. It always settled in the evening, but there was an eeriness she wasn't used to. As though the town itself was grieving one of its own.

'Charlie? Are you alright?' Trev's familiar, steady voice answered.

'Yes. And so is Rosie.' Calm and non-emotional. 'I'm sorry to ring so late, Trevor.'

He chuckled. 'Late? I just got in from a VIP event at Christie's beauty salon.'

'I'm sorry. Did you say you attended a beauty event? Didn't we discuss this at Christie and Martin's celebration party before their wedding? Let me see if I remember—'

'Very funny. I'll tell you all about it later. What's up. Or do you miss hearing about Rivers End?'

'I miss everyone.' From nowhere, tears prickled behind her eyes.

'Everyone?'

She tried a laugh. 'Almost.'

'What's going on. I'm listening.'

'Um. Okay. So, something happened today.' Charlotte moved to the little round table in the corner and sat. 'Octavia Morris? She died.'

'Holy…oh, my goodness. Is Mum alright?'

'She's sad. Shaken up. I've just come from her house and Rosie was going to bed and, well, I imagine she'll have a bit of a cry. She wishes she'd been able to bridge the recent distance between her and Octavia.'

'How did she pass away?'

'She fell. Hit her forehead. I went to the scene.'

'Why?'

'Sid came and got me. Wanted a doctor and was in such a panic so I grabbed my bag, but she was gone already. She was there, lying face down on her blue rug on the cream carpet with everything in place in her beautiful and perfect house and even her clothes were perfect...except she has a mark on the back...of her skull and the tea...cup has orange lipstick on it and I...I don't know what to do next.'

The words poured out, tripping over each other and Charlotte burst into tears.

There was a stunned silence from Trev. Then he made soothing noises. 'Shh. Hey. Don't cry.'

A manic laugh formed in her throat but she caught it at her lips.

Pull yourself together, Charlie.

'I should drive up.'

'No.' Sniff. 'No, this is why I wasn't going to ring you.'

'Are you alone? Can someone come and stay with you?'

Charlotte dug up a tissue and blew her nose. 'This is just an emotional response to the adrenaline coming down. I'll be okay in a moment.'

'But you shouldn't be alone, upset.'

'Stop being hysterical, Trevor. I'm fine.' There, she'd regained control. Not that she could see well through blurry eyes, but at least the waterworks had stopped.

He chuckled. 'I'll stop being hysterical, Charlotte.'

'Sorry. Anyway, I didn't ring to show how pathetic I am. I have some questions and you are the only police officer I trust.'

'I see.'

'That didn't quite come out as I meant it to.'

'I'm pleased you trust me. What questions?' Trev didn't sound the least put out by anything she said.

Wiping the last of the tears from her eyes, Charlotte told Trev about the photos she'd taken. 'So, I have two issues. One is the mark. I can't believe I didn't see it at the time so I could investigate further. If she was hit from behind—'

'Whoa. Investigate? Charlie, that's not your job.'

'Yes, I know, but you get what I'm driving at. If she was hit with something from behind, and fell forward, then whoever hit her might be responsible for her death. Yes?'

'Yes, but—'

'And then there's the orange lipstick.'

Trev sighed. A long, drawn out sigh and Charlotte imagined him sitting at his kitchen table with his head in his hands.

She giggled.

'Excuse me?'

'Adrenaline. So, the lipstick belongs to Veronica. Do you know her?'

'Adrenaline? Have you considered pouring a glass of wine?' Trev said.

'Good thinking.' Charlotte made a beeline for the counter. 'I have some red. Maybe just half a glass.' She poured almost to the rim as she talked. 'Veronica has caused some trouble in Kingfisher Falls. Opened shops and closed them quickly, then was involved romantically with one of the Christmas tree thieves.'

'What does this have to do with Octavia's demise?'

Charlotte returned to the balcony, sipping the wine as she walked to stop it splashing out. Perhaps it was more than she should have poured. Glass on the table, she sank back onto the chair. 'Veronica was wearing the same colour lipstick this morning. She was at the bookshop. Well, near it.'

'I get the feeling there's a lot more to this you could share.'

'But I just want to know what to do with the information. Do I tell Sid?'

'Much as I'd prefer you stay clear of him, you must. Has he asked for a statement about your attendance at her house?'

'Nothing. To be fair, he showed signs of shock.'

'He's a trained police officer, Charlie. Whether or not he

knows her, there are processes to follow. He should have done a door knock and made sure he followed proper procedure. Because there are questions around Octavia's death, she'll be examined—probably in Melbourne. At this point, if this mark is fresh and the death is considered suspicious, then the coroner's office will take further steps.'

'Okay. I might ask Doug to come with me to the police station.'

This time, Trev's sigh was one of relief. 'Good idea. And back up your images. Are they date stamped?'

'Yeah, and I have.' The wine was warm in Charlotte's stomach. 'Thanks.'

'Are you doing okay? Apart from this?'

'I love it here, Trev. Rosie is wonderful and the waterfalls are beautiful.'

'The pool at the bottom is special. Good for picnics.' There was a question in his voice and Charlotte closed her eyes. She would cry again, over-tired and done with the events of the day.

'Hadn't noticed. Oh, I painted the balcony and am starting work on the back garden next day off.' Anything to change the subject.

They spoke for a few more minutes. Trev made Charlotte laugh about some of the happenings in Rivers End, then they said goodnight.

A long low roll of thunder followed a flash of lightening.

'We'll have that picnic one day,' she whispered.

chapter
five

'It feels quiet today.' Rosie dusted a shelf. 'Not many people in.' She dusted the same one again.

'The town is quiet. Hardly any cars but I guess it isn't even ten yet.' Charlotte stared out of the window she'd been cleaning. The storm had come and gone overnight, leaving a fresher day with less humidity. 'And so many people said they were going away for these couple of weeks, before school begins.'

'True. But still.'

A car slowed. Hopefully there might be customers in it. Anything to break them out of the mantle of exhaustion and sadness. But it kept going.

'Um. I phoned Trevor last night.' Charlotte decided she should say something about it.

'I know.'

'You do?'

Rosie wheeled across to join Charlotte. 'He rang this morning. Wanted to check up on me and make sure I didn't want him to drive up.'

'He wanted to last night. I guess it's difficult for him being so far away from you when something bad has happened.'

'Well, I reassured him that both of us are fine.'

Charlotte found a mark on the window and rubbed at it with her cloth. 'I told him last night I was okay. He needed to know what happened though and I asked him some questions because I wasn't sure if I have to make a statement.'

'And?'

'I'm going to ask Doug if he'd mind coming with me to see Sid. Rather not go alone and Sid seems to respect Doug.'

Rosie laughed. 'Doug takes no rubbish from anyone. You saw him last year standing up for the Woodland family. Have you spoken to him yet?'

'I wasn't sure when was best. He works pretty late being a chef. What do you think?'

'I'll text Esther and get him to ring you. Is the statement about checking…um, checking Octavia for a pulse? And things?' Rosie was texting but there was strain in her face. 'If it was an accident, there's little more to do, I imagine?'

Charlotte bit her bottom lip, searching for the right words.

'Charlie? It was an accident?'

The ring of the shop phone saved Charlotte from answering and she hurried to the counter, reaching over it to get the phone.

'Kingfisher Falls Book Shop. Charlotte speaking.'

'Oh, Charlotte. It's Abbie Woodland. I'm glad I caught you.' Abbie's voice had a worried note.

'Everything alright? Baby behaving?'

Abbie laughed. 'Apart from some savage kicks, no signs of an appearance. I wondered if you've seen Glenys?'

'Today? No.'

'Okay. I'll phone around.'

'Wait a sec. Why are you concerned? I heard she stayed with you last night.' Charlotte turned to catch Rosie's eye, who was giving her a 'what's going on' expression.

'She packed a small bag and drove over early evening. I had a bad night and just got up, but her car is gone. I'm worried, that's all.' Abbie said.

'Hang on a sec, Abbie, let me tell Rosie.' Charlotte put the phone on speaker and relayed Abbie's concerns.

'Gone home, maybe?' Rosie offered.

'Darcy went over but no sign of her. And he was out on the other side of the property from dawn so didn't know she'd gone until I did.'

'Abbie, Rosie here. First, thank you so much for taking Glenys in. This was all such a horrible shock and your generosity warms my heart. Now, I would think Glenys has gone to the lookout because she does when she's sad. She'll often pray there for Fred.'

'Shall I just wait?' Abbie sounded uncertain.

Charlotte tilted her head at Rosie, who nodded. 'I might run up there now, Abbie. I'll see if she's there and let you know.'

'Please. I know she's a grown woman, but Octavia was her dear friend for a long time, and I feel we came between them.'

No, Octavia pushed everyone away.

After handing the phone to Rosie to continue the conversation, Charlotte picked up her sunglasses and phone and waved as she left. A brisk walk would clear her head anyway, and whilst Glenys might go to the lookout for spiritual comfort, Charlotte went to savour its peaceful beauty.

She turned left from the bookshop and followed the footpath until it became little more than a track in the grass verge well past the shops and houses. The first time she'd been along here was late one night. She'd run from internal demons, from sheer panic over something which she couldn't even remember now. With no idea where she was headed, she'd stumbled upon the lookout by accident.

If Glenys was there, had she left her car somewhere? There was no sign of it parked along the road. Her heart went out to the older woman. The last few weeks must have been so hard. Thinking her neighbours were criminals thanks to her own nephew's dreadful deception and actions. Then losing the presidency of the local book club she'd started and run for decades.

Lost to Octavia.

Charlotte sped up as she took the path to the falls. The lookout was high, and Rosie had mentioned some tragedies in the past of people falling to the river far below, including Glenys' poor husband, Fred. Glenys was at least seventy and using a walking cane these days. A slip might be a disaster.

The sounds and smells of the bush enfolded Charlotte. Birds chirping close by. Magpie song and the screech of black cockatoos as they soared overhead. Eucalypt and wattle. Running water.

Careful of her footing past the information area, Charlotte tried to hurry. The conditions underfoot left a lot to be desired, with gaps and cracks and all sorts of difficult terrain. She rounded the corner before the lookout.

Glenys faced the thundering waterfall, leaning against the railing, both arms outstretched.

'Glenys!' Charlotte sprinted. By the time she reached the semi-circle of the lookout, Glenys had turned.

She swayed on her feet, face drawn and dried tears cutting lines through her makeup. 'What are you doing here?'

Were you praying?

'I'm so sorry if I interrupted. Abbie is worried about you. Rosie thought you might be here.'

'I'm not throwing myself off, if that's what you all believe.' Glenys hobbled away from the railing. 'I needed some time to myself.'

'Come and have a coffee with us? We'd love the company.'

Charlotte moved aside to let Glenys past, then followed. 'Is your car here?'

'In the car park. Not up for socialising.'

Charlotte sent a quick text to Rosie.

Found her. She's fine.

'I'm sorry I couldn't stay with you longer yesterday.' Charlotte said. 'The paramedics said they'd make sure you were okay before they left.'

'They were nice but as I told them, I wasn't the one they needed to look after.'

'Oh, careful there. The rain made that spot slippery and I almost turned my ankle walking down.' Charlotte offered her arm and after a pause, Glenys took it. 'Where's your walking cane?'

'At the Woodlands. I wanted to go home yesterday but they were so kind, and Lachie is so sweet. I'll go and pick it up and my bag and say thank you to Abbie.'

At the information board, Glenys stopped to catch her breath and pointed off to the left. 'Carpark's just through there. I'm fine to get there alone.'

'Actually, I was going to be cheeky and ask if you'd drop me near the bookshop. Rosie's on her own.'

Glenys pursed her lips. But she nodded and headed along the path to the carpark. It narrowed, so Charlotte trailed her. Although she favoured one leg, Glenys was quite nimble along the dirt track, even in shoes with a small heel.

The bush gave way to a carpark. 'I didn't know this was here.' Charlotte waited for Glenys to unlock a small SUV before climbing in. 'Makes things easier if you're not a comfortable walking distance away like my place is.'

'I might stop visiting here.' Glenys started the motor. 'Too many sad memories.' She gripped the steering wheel and kept her thoughts to herself for the short drive to town. When she pulled over across from the bookshop she kept her eyes forward as she spoke in halting words. 'Charlotte. Thank you for caring. You and Rosie.'

'We're only a phone call away.'

Charlotte was sure Glenys wanted to say something more. Her face held such pain. But she just nodded and said thank you.

———

Sid's patrol car drew up as Charlotte crossed over the road. She waited for him to get out, heart sinking when he put his police hat on as if he was trying to look official.

'Are you coming to see me, or Rosie?'

'You.'

'For the statement?'

'How do you know?' Sid asked.

'I was at the scene of a death at home. You asked me to be there. These things require paperwork, Sid.'

'Leading Senior Constable Browne. Told you before, we're not friends.'

Charlotte sighed. 'I'm happy to come down to the station. But Rosie needs time to have lunch—'

'You misunderstand. We're having an interview and it's about your possible involvement in the death of Octavia Morris.'

'I beg your pardon?' Rosie had emerged from the book-shop. 'Did you say Charlie is under suspicion? I thought Octavia's death was from a fall.'

'Too early to know. But there was a complaint.' Sid wouldn't look at either Charlotte or Rosie. 'Gotta investigate.'

'Then come inside and investigate. Charlie has barely been out of my sight.' Rosie spun the wheelchair and glared at Sid. 'Are you coming?'

Charlotte took advantage of the small stand-off to rush inside and get behind the counter as a barrier of sorts..

'Oi. Get back here.'

Not likely.

Sid thudded his way in, coming to a stop with his arms folded. 'I want you to accompany me to the station for an interview, missy.'

'Nobody here named missy, Sidney Browne.' Rosie parked her wheelchair next to Charlotte. 'Whatever you want to ask, you can ask here.'

'And you're not out of the woods, Rose. The complaint also mentioned you.'

Veronica. It has to be her.

Charlotte's hands shook. The woman got herself in with all the wrong people. The garden centre was her most recent attempt to run a business after a string of failures and the only time Charlotte ventured there to seek Christmas gifts, she'd found Veronica berating a young staff member. She wasn't a nice lady.

'We're listening, Leading Senior Constable.' Charlotte lifted her chin and stared Sid in the eyes, her own—she hoped—steady and giving nothing away. 'If we get customers though, you'll need to excuse us.'

He opened his mouth as though to debate, then closed it again and poked around in a pocket for a notepad. 'Right. Yesterday morning, a conversation between you two was overheard prior to Octavia's unfortunate fall. Phrases that alarmed the complainant included you, Rose, saying Octavia was impossible to reason with and there had to be another way to get what you wanted from her.'

Sid glanced at Rosie, who said nothing.

'Fine. And you, Doctor, replied that there was a way. And it didn't matter how far you had to go to get what you wanted. In a nasty tone implying you'd murder an old woman.'

'Oh, for goodness sake.' Charlotte would have rolled her eyes but knew he was serious and wasn't about to add fuel to this ridiculous fire. 'Veronica overheard a joke between us, which was to lighten things up after Octavia said something very hurtful to Rosie.'

'You admit to threatening to harm Octavia?'

'Nobody was threatened. Not by us. All this was about were some books Octavia no longer wanted to purchase. If you look in the display window, we've taken advantage of the cancellation to create a nice offer for customers of these books.' Charlotte kept her tone calm although her stomach churned. 'Rosie and I were also here all morning. Then, you came and got me.'

'Means nothing.' He snapped his notebook shut. 'You can give each other alibies. For all I know, you injected Octavia with something when you were checking for a pulse.'

'That is quite enough, Leading Senior Constable Browne.' Rosie's face was red. 'I'd like you to leave.'

Sid smirked. 'Touched a nerve, did I? There'll be evidence once a medical exam is carried out, so I'll be back. With handcuffs.' He swaggered out.

Charlotte rushed to the front door and closed it.

'Lock it, Charlie. We're taking the rest of the day off.'

chapter
six

'The nerve of the man!' Rosie was still fuming an hour later, as she and Charlotte waited for lunch at the bistro in the pub. True to her declaration, she'd closed the register and turned off the lights at the shop, leaving a sign on the door saying, *"Back Tomorrow"*.

'He's full of bluff, Rosie. We've done nothing wrong.'

'But what if Octavia…' Rosie lowered her voice and leaned toward Charlotte. 'was murdered? He will come looking for an easy target.'

'Here we go, ladies. Are you sure you wouldn't like something from the bar?' Their waiter was Henry, manager of the bistro. He'd been into the bookshop a few times and was responsible for several donations to the Christmas giving box Charlotte had set up. Henry was in his fifties, tall and fit and grey-haired but with a love of life which made him look years younger.

'Tempting, Henry. Very tempting, but I think just another glass of cranberry juice will be enough. Charlie?'

'Sparkling water is fine, thank you.'

Henry and the bistro reminded her of the pub in Rivers End. She'd had a few meals there and shared her friend

Christie's special celebration dinner in the event room upstairs. A pang of homesickness came from nowhere. But then, Rivers End was the closest she'd had to a real home.

Until now.

'Darling? You're miles away.'

'Sorry. This looks nice.' She speared some cheese and an olive in the salad. 'I love living here, Rosie.'

'I love you being here.' Rosie broke open a bread roll and began buttering it. 'But you must think Kingfisher Falls is a den of iniquity.'

'How long have you wanted to use that term?'

Rosie smiled at last. 'Ages. Sounds more impressive than a wicked town.'

'True.' The salad was delicious, but Charlotte's appetite was small. She tried for another mouthful.

'I have a lawyer, Charlie. Perhaps we should talk to her.'

'We've not done anything worth Sid's time. He's just being a pain for the sake of it. Besides, I'm confident there'll be no trace of poison found.'

Henry arrived with fresh drinks and Charlotte waited until he'd gone before speaking. One overheard conversation was enough without risking more unwanted attention.

'There's something you need to know, Rosie. It can wait until we eat though.'

Rosie shook her head. 'Cast iron stomach. Do you think Octavia was pushed?'

'The medical examiner may well prove me wrong, but I think she was hit from behind.'

With a gasp, Rosie dropped her fork.

'Oh, I shouldn't have said anything.' Charlotte reached over the table and squeezed Rosie's arm. 'I'll get you a clean fork.'

'Here's a new one, Rosie.' Henry appeared from nowhere with a replacement. He placed it next to her plate, whisked the dropped one from the floor, and was gone again.

'That man is a ninja. Anyway, no more talk of Octavia.' Charlotte released Rosie's arm and picked up her glass.

'No. I want to know, but it gave me a little shock. If there's a killer loose, then who is next? Will there be a murder spree here?' Rosie didn't look the least bit upset. If anything, her eyes were wide with curiosity. She let the questions sit between them as she bit into her roll.

Are you turning into a sleuth?

Charlotte hid a grin by munching on a mouthful of tomato and rocket.

'Are you laughing at me, young woman?' Rosie didn't even look up. 'For the record I am deeply sorry Octavia is dead. She was a big part of my life for a long time and the thought she came to an untimely end due to interference is heartbreaking.'

'But?'

Rosie lifted her glass of cranberry juice, her eyes meeting Charlotte's. 'It is possible I've read one too many Agatha Christie novels. I do love a good puzzle.'

'Welcome to the club.' Charlotte raised her glass. 'To women who read too much.'

'And want to solve murders.'

Clink.

———

After a long lunch with much discussion, Rosie went home, saying her garden would benefit from her early return. It was a good idea and Charlotte hunted around in her own garage for gardening tools. Only a sorry looking excuse for a rake hung from a hook in a corner.

There was a storeroom through a door at the back of the

garage and although Charlotte had only been in there once or twice to find things to use in the book shop, she was certain some garden tools were on a shelf. She let herself in and turned on the solitary and dull overhead light.

The air was stale, and a thick coat of dust covered most of the surfaces. Shelves lined the longest wall and at the very end of the room, on the floor, was a tower of boxes.

Much of it belonged to the family who'd lived here before Rosie and her now-deceased husband, Graeme, bought the building and turned it from a bakery to a bookshop. Charlotte knew little about them, apart from snippets Rosie shared. The bakery was an original building in the town and several generations of the family lived and breathed it until the last of the line left.

One day she'd go through the boxes and Rosie would help her find the family if possible and ask if they'd like the most precious possessions sent to them.

Possessions such as those in the cane chest she opened once before. Undoing the clips on either end, she removed the lid. Inside were clothes, neatly folded. On top was a wedding dress made of lace and silk, and nestled in its folds, baby clothes and a teddy bear. Rose and lavender drifted in the air, improving the otherwise dank smell of the room.

'I'll find out who owns you.' Charlotte whispered before replacing the lid and tightening the clips. The clothes and teddy bear left her unsettled and sad.

Charlotte scooped up anything resembling a garden tool and locked the door behind herself. Arms filled, she stopped outside the garage and stared at the back garden which wasn't a large area, but one overgrown and hiding who-knew-what.

'Oh dear.'

Until recently, Charlotte's experience with plants was almost as limited as her knowledge of cooking. She'd never lived anywhere with a garden of any size, but adored flowers and harboured a secret wish to grow vegetables. She had a little potted pine which she'd nursed back from a near-death experience before Christmas. It was at the bottom of the steps to the apartment and sooner or later, she needed to decide where it should go.

She laid out the tools on the driveway. Several hand shovels in varying degrees of deterioration. Two hand rakes. A pair of pruning shears, a bit rusty but possibly sharp enough to do some cutting. Secateurs, also rusty.

'Oh, dear.' She repeated herself. 'Now what?'

Charlotte had hoped for a mower. Rosie paid a local person to mow every few weeks, but having one here made more sense. There were no shovels or decent garden forks. And nothing electric or powered. Apart from the shears and secateurs, Charlotte tossed everything into the bin.

Starting against the back wall of the bookshop, a narrow garden bed continued along the side and then back fences. There were some neglected bushes. She tried to identify them but apart from a couple of woody roses, had no idea, so took some photos.

The side fence was actually a brick wall between the bookshop and the other buildings between here and the corner. An extendable clothesline was attached to the wall.

The back fence was constructed of six-foot-high timber palings. A climbing plant covered it. No, two. One she recognised as a nasturtium with its cheerful flowers and large leaves. This was edible. Some long-kept memory emerged. Picking and eating the leaves as a child. She took one and lifted it to her nose. Yes, the same peppery tang she remembered. Charlotte nibbled on the leaf.

The other climber was a passionfruit and her mouth watered. It wasn't ripe yet, the fruit not wrinkling and purple, but before long she'd be able to pick some. Hopefully,

Rosie would like some as well, as the climber was covered in young fruit. What a lovely find.

She put a foot onto a cross-rail and pulled herself up enough to peek over. Expecting to see houses and a garden behind the fence, instead there was a broad dirt track separating the bookshop from bushland on the other side.

My own sanctuary!

After stepping down, she took another look at the climbers. They were planted in a narrow bed otherwise filled with weeds. She glanced up at the sun. It would provide almost all-day light to this strip.

Perfect for a vegetable garden. Grinning, she took more photos, then made some notes on her phone.

Weed (buy new tools)
Add more soil
Vegetable seedlings
Gardening gloves
Shovel and hose

That was all she could think of for now, and after a short consideration, the secateurs and shears joined the rest of the old tools in the bin. Rosie knew all about plants, so she'd ask her about what would grow in the area. And, where to buy all these items because she had no interest in visiting Veronica's garden centre.

———

Rather than bother Rosie again today, Charlotte drove up to the Christmas Tree Farm. It was mid-afternoon and traffic was light as though the town of Kingfisher Falls still wore a mantle of quiet from this morning's sad events.

She parked in the large, empty carpark. Out of her car, there was no sound of the chainsaw Darcy so often worked with, but over past the sales area, the doors of his large shed were open.

Halfway over the carpark, she hesitated. Abbie's car was parked near the two-storey house overlooking the valley, so someone was home. She should have phoned first.

'Are you returning your tree, Charlotte Dean?'

Jogging up from the house, Darcy and Abbie's son grinned as he approached. Eight-year-old Lachie had helped her the first time she'd been here, looking for a small tree for her balcony. He considered himself part of the staff and called his mother an official "Mrs Woodland" when he'd worked with her.

'I fear I must. It truly is an alien.' Charlotte kept a serious face. 'And you sold me a tree, so I need a refund.'

'Not a chance. Sorry, but you've used the tree for the purpose we sold it. Alien or not.'

Charlotte almost burst out laughing. This little game they'd begun on Christmas Eve came about after she'd mentioned the tree talking to her. It had only been minutes before Octavia and Marguerite frightened the child by yelling at his parents. A much sadder thought.

He stopped in front of her, panting. 'Whew. That was a big run. Saw you from the porch—see, Mum's sitting out there and said you're welcome for a lemonade if you want.' Lachie pointed at the house and Abbie waved. Charlotte waved back.

'Thanks, dude, but I was going to ask your dad a couple of questions about my garden. I think he knows about plants and stuff?'

'You betcha. I'll go tell Mum to keep relaxing and be right back. Dad's in the work shed.' Lachie took off toward the house, calling over his shoulder. 'Meet you there.'

Just about everyone in town loved Lachie. When the bookshop ran the giving box at Christmas time, numerous customers purchased books with him in mind, so he'd been the delighted recipient of a pile of presents on Christmas Eve. Plenty to keep him occupied when his new brother or sister arrived.

Charlotte peered into the shed looking for Darcy. She'd been here once and knew he kept his tractor, flat bed ute, and tools inside.

'Hello? Darcy?'

'Charlie?' Darcy Woodland called from the far end of the shed. 'Come on in.'

She followed the direction his voice came from, skirting around the large tractor and past benches lining the side of the shed. It went back further than she realised to an open floor space. Except, there were timber frames piled up and Darcy was making more. A nail gun was on the floor and he lifted a new frame onto the others.

'Are you building a house?'

He grinned. 'Kind of.' With a grunt, he got it into place, then grabbed a rag from a bench and wiped his forehead. 'Good timing. Last one.'

'Of? Or is it a secret?'

'Only from Veronica.' He sighed. 'She'll double her efforts once she knows.'

Double what efforts?

'Knows what? Oh, hang on, are you going to restart the wholesale nursery?'

Darcy's grin widened and he tossed the rag back onto the bench.

'So, what I know—which isn't much—is that your father used to run a successful wholesale nursery up here. Christmas trees in November and December, and seedlings and stuff the rest of the time.' Charlotte circled the frames.

'Yup. Serviced all the garden centres in the region. Some even further afield. But when things went…you know, bad for him, the greenhouses were left alone. Deteriorated. I'm fixing them.'

'How wonderful! Are you still planning on making furniture?'

'On the side. I want to get this up and running first. My mate's coming to stay for a few days soon. He'll give me a hand replacing the old framework with these and patching what we can. No money for new greenhouses so I'll make do until we see a return.'

'Lemonade!' Lachie appeared around the tractor carrying two tall glasses. 'But I spilt a bit from this one, so you have it, Dad.'

'Thanks, Lachie.' Charlotte took the other one. 'This was nice of Abbie.'

Lachie gave her an offended look. 'This was my idea. Mum can stay sitting down for a bit.'

'Sorry. Thank you then.'

'My pleasure. I have to go now.' With that, he sprinted off.

Charlotte lowered her head, not meeting Darcy's gaze in case she laughed.

'Lachie has that effect on folks. They smile around him.'

The pride in Darcy's voice warmed Charlotte at the same time as opening a small rift in her heart. She'd never had family support or love. Well, Mum loved her, in her way, but it wasn't the love Darcy and Abbie poured on their son. She sipped the cool, delicious lemonade.

'Did Abbie make this?'

'No, but she has the recipe. Glenys brought over a couple of jugs to say thanks for having her here. She has citrus trees on the far side of her property and left a bucket of lemons as well.'

There was so much Charlotte wanted to ask. Was Glenys okay after she came back to get her bag and cane? Had she spoken at all about what she'd seen? Was she still planning on selling up and moving? But none of it was her business.

'So, what brought you by?' Darcy leaned against a bench as he sipped his drink. 'Did you want me to find somewhere to plant that little tree of yours?'

'I might keep it for longer. I like seeing it grow and have moved it to the bottom of the steps. Today I've been out in the little garden behind the bookshop with is the first real chance I've had since I moved in.'

'Not big enough out there to plant that tree.' Darcy smiled.

'Not nearly. I'd like to grow vegetables and make the soil good in the garden beds and stuff. Get some tools and work out what will grow. Rosie will know a lot, but I remembered you mulch old branches and stuff?'

'I can bring you a trailer load when you want. Soil is best from a place over Macedon way. They also have a fair range of seedlings and can help with soil improvers. I'll text you their details if you want.' Darcy pulled a phone from a pocket. 'Tell them I sent you. I went to talk to them the other day and once the wholesale side is up, will supply to them.'

Charlotte's phone dinged as the message arrived. 'Thank you. I'm excited about this. I've got passionfruit growing already!'

'Good. Just do your research on pests and keep the garden as natural as possible. You know, avoid the pesticides. They're not necessary if you are prepared to spend a bit of time in the garden.'

'I am. I can't wait. Do you want me to take the glasses back?' Charlotte asked.

'Nah, I'm heading down now. Been here since dawn so reckon it's time to see the family.'

They made their way to the doors, where Charlotte held

both glasses as Darcy pulled the doors closed and locked them.

'Why would Veronica get upset if you're a wholesaler? I'd think it makes sense for her to buy her stock locally.'

Darcy shook his head and took the glasses as they walked across to Charlotte's car. 'She sees everyone as a competitor. Heard she's set up her big greenhouse as an incubator. Got rid of all her exotics and put in rows of benches to grow seedlings. Wouldn't be surprised if she's trying to on-sell now.'

'Do you need anything for Abbie? Or bubba?' Time to talk about happy things.

'You're too kind, Charlie. Between the awesome hamper we were given at Christmas—thanks again to Rosie—and what we already had before moving here, I think we'll be fine.'

'Well, if you need Lachie watched or anything, you have my number.'

'Might take you up on that sometime.'

A moment later, Darcy was wandering down to the house and Charlotte was starting the engine. It was later than she'd thought and time to go shopping and head home.

chapter
seven

Shopping packed away, Charlotte made herself an iced tea and wandered downstairs. Evening was closing in, the air cooling to a pleasant temperature. Maybe a little table and chairs out here would be nice for enjoying the new garden once she'd created it.

The talk with Darcy helped put ideas in motion. She'd go shopping on Sunday for tools at the least, and begin weeding, pruning, and turning the soil in the beds. She checked the message Darcy had sent. The link took her to a garden centre in a town she'd yet to visit, but only twenty or so minutes' drive away. Their website was inviting.

Something made her look up Kingfisher Falls Garden Centre. On the front page was an image, not of the shopfront, or plants, but Veronica. She posed in front of a giant pot, holding a colourful tray of flowering seedlings as though expecting them to attack her. And those vivid orange lips.

'No need to be judgemental.'

But it was hard not to be when the woman presented herself in such an attention-grabbing manner. In her forties, she'd made it clear she liked much younger men.

Half her age younger. Not to mention her thing about parading around listening to other people's innocent conversations.

Charlotte climbed upstairs after checking the little pine tree had enough water. Inside, she locked the door and kicked off her shoes. Thinking about Veronica took her straight back to Octavia's house with its lifeless body and heartbroken Glenys and lipstick stained teacups. Heart thudding, Charlotte lay on the floor to stare at the ceiling.

Breath. One, two. Breath...slower. One, two.

The mantra repeated as she put her palms on the carpet and dissolved the bad feelings. Twenty-four hours of unusual stress had taken its toll. Now, she was controlling the emotions and packing them away into her mental boxes.

Her phone rang. Eyes still on the ceiling she considered letting it go to voicemail.

What if Rosie needs me? Or something's wrong with Mum?

She scrambled up and answered without checking the number. 'Charlotte Dean speaking.'

The pause at the other end reminded Charlotte of the delay when a telesales operator rang, and she was about to disconnect when someone spoke. A muffled, measured voice. Male.

'Stop lying.'

'I beg your pardon. Who is this?'

'You are a criminal.'

She didn't recognise the voice.

'How did you get my number? Who is this?'

'You need to leave town now. Take care before someone seeks revenge.'

A prickle of fear crept up Charlotte's spine as the speaker continued.

'This is your only warning.'

'Wait a minute...'

The caller was gone. Charlotte checked the phone for a number, but it was anonymous.

On autopilot, Charlotte went into the kitchen and opened the refrigerator. She should eat. Or plan to eat. Instead, she took out a bottle of white wine and poured a glass. Without tasting it, she let herself out onto the balcony and stood at the railing.

With an hour or two before darkness fell, the air was busy with birdsong as they finished their fossicking for the day and sorted out their sleeping arrangements. It was soothing, the squabbling and chatter amongst the galahs and cockatoos. The magpies would settle later. They seemed to be the first birds up and last to sleep.

You're a criminal.

What was the call meant to achieve? If someone believed Charlotte responsible for Octavia's death, why tell her to leave town rather than call the police? And who would do such a thing as make a threatening phone call?

Sid came to mind. He'd shown how sneaky he was by using a fake Facebook account to troll the book shop last year. And he'd vowed to uncover Charlotte's past, so why would he spoil his own plans by chasing her out of town?

Three other men were worth considering. Jonas Carmichael and Terrance Murdoch worked as councillors for the local shire. Jonas was a nasty man with nasty methods. Charlotte saw this first-hand before Christmas, when he'd publicly stirred suspicion against Darcy and his family over the tree thefts. He was also involved with Veronica, not romantically—at least she didn't believe so—but they were buddies.

She'd had less to do with Terrance. An older man, he more or less went along with Jonas but both of them were a bit too friendly with Sid for her liking. Which brought her to Kevin Murdoch. Terrance's brother. She had no idea what he did for a living, but he was as involved as Jonas at blaming the Woodlands.

And was Octavia's man friend.

That day at Octavia's house, she'd left through the open front door once the paramedics arrived and she'd answered their questions. An expensive-looking executive style car pulled up in the driveway and Kevin had got out—more a stagger than a step. He'd stumbled past Charlotte without meeting her eyes, his own blank. A man in shock.

Perhaps, once that shock wore off, he'd decided Charlotte was somehow responsible for Octavia's death. Sid had suggested she was.

Bring on the pathology report.

Once time and cause of death was on record, nobody could blame her. She'd not left the book shop until Sid showed up and there were plenty of regular customers who could attest to that.

With a sigh, Charlotte went inside. She wasn't scared. People serious about committing a crime rarely warned their victim ahead of time. This was someone acting out of grief or spite. If Trev lived closer, she'd call or go and see him. Charlotte shook her head. He didn't need her ringing every time there was a hiccup in town. And Rosie didn't need to worry about this. It was little more than a one-off prank call.

———

Barely after dawn, Charlotte hiked up to the falls. She loved this time of day when the nocturnal wildlife still roamed and the town was nowhere near waking up.

Instead of going to the lookout, she followed the some-what difficult track all the way to the pool at the bottom of the falls. Here, the waterfall cascaded from its lofty height into a crystal-clear body of water before syphoning off into the river. She'd been to the top of the falls once. The view was spectacular, even if the climb was exhausting.

The soft grass underfoot was wet from dew, so she found a fallen tree and perched on its smooth bark to drink from her water bottle. As often happened at this time of day, a mob of kangaroos visited the pool to drink. They'd take turns at the edge, while others kept watch. Some looked at Charlotte as though curious about her, but there was never a sign of fear.

After a while they moved on, picking up speed as they vanished into the heavy bush. Charlotte was alone again, apart from a couple of rabbits nibbling on the damp grass.

She'd slept well. When she'd first arrived in Kingfisher Falls, her nights were disturbed either by storms, her own restless dreams, or the Christmas Tree thieves at work. The week off work after Christmas changed that, as she taught herself how to strip paint from the balcony, repair cracks, prepare the surfaces, sand, then paint. Each night she was too tired to do other than sleep. But the result was worth every bit of work.

Last night she'd expected to toss and turn. Instead, she'd fallen asleep after reading, and not stirred.

Country living.

Sunlight streamed across the top of the falls, transforming the water into liquid diamonds. Bit by bit, the rays filled the gorge until the air warmed. Another hot one. Charlotte needed to be home in time to shower before opening the bookshop. It was a new day and nothing would go wrong.

chapter
eight

The front door of the bookshop refused to open.

Charlotte had lost track of time after her shower, indulging in just one more chapter of her latest book which became two more chapters. With ten minutes until opening, she'd done her usual tasks. Through the back door, lights on, money in the register. No time to vacuum so she'd pick a quiet moment when Rosie arrived to do it.

Broom in hand to sweep the pavement, she hurried to the front door, moved the '*Closed*' sign to '*Open*' and turned the lock. It turned, but the door handle wouldn't.

'Come on, Charlie, you're not that weak!'

She rattled the door and tried the handle again. In both directions. Something must have jammed the door from outside. She'd locked up yesterday after Rosie left to go to the bistro ahead of Charlotte. There'd been nothing out of the ordinary when she had.

After grabbing the keys off the counter, Charlotte went out of the back door and down the driveway. The front door appeared normal until Charlotte took a closer look. A thick, clear substance surrounded the area around the lock.

Charlotte ran upstairs and collected a butter knife,

container of hot, soapy water, and a cloth. She spent the next few minutes running the knife into the crevice and wiping away the sticky goo that caught on it. It was slow work and she stopped to take photos. One day she'd make a book from all this evidence she was collecting.

Inside the shop the phone was ringing but there was little point sprinting around to get it, so Charlotte kept working away until, with a hard turn of the handle, the door gave up. She pushed the door wide open and attached it to the wall with the little hook at the back. No way was this closing again until she'd cleaned whatever this stuff was out.

This time, when the phone rang, she got to it.

'Kingfisher Falls Bookshop. Charlotte speaking.'

'Charlie? Are you okay?' Rosie's voice was strained. 'I rang before.'

'I'm so sorry. I was just…um, outside, sweeping. Didn't make it back inside.'

'Oh. Oh, that's fine then.'

'Is everything alright?'

'Yes. No. Well, I'd rather not be doing this, but I've been asked to help find Octavia's next of kin and need to make some calls before I come to work.'

'Why you?'

'I'll explain when I see you, but it goes back to Graeme's friendship with Octavia's ex-husband. Apparently, nobody knows how to find her family. I might.'

'I'm fine here. You make phone calls and I'll see you when I see you.'

As she hung up, Charlotte noticed Sid in his patrol car. He'd parked over the road and the window was down, his fingers tapping the roof. She hurried outside and crossed the road.

'You didn't look both ways.' Sid said.

'You sound disappointed there wasn't a car coming.'

'Get out of bed on the wrong side?'

'Why are you parked here?' Charlotte snapped. 'In this whole region you look after, Rosie's little shop seems to attract an unusual amount of your time.'

Sid dragged his arm inside the vehicle and turned the motor.

Charlotte grabbed the top of the door. 'Don't leave on my account. I could use some police protection.'

What are you doing?

He glared at her. 'Why?'

'Why? How about you tell me.' She pulled her hand away to put both on her hips and glared back. 'For that matter, why haven't you taken a statement from me about my attendance at Octavia's house. I have information you need.'

'Like?' He looked bored.

'When shall I meet you at the station?'

'Later. Tomorrow. Phone first.'

'And just for the record, I had nothing to do with Octavia's dreadful death. Nothing. Nor did Rosie. So, tell your friends that. Okay?'

She spun around and stalked toward the bookshop.

'Oi. Missy, get back here.'

Like hell.

'Charlotte.'

She stopped and looked over her shoulder.

'I have no idea what you mean. None.' He said. 'I don't speak to anyone about a case.'

'Then who thinks I'm responsible?'

He shrugged and drove away.

———

In between customers, Charlotte worked on the door to remove the clear, sticky gel. She tried more hot, soapy water with no success. There was nothing stronger in the book shop, so she used a straightened paper clip to work her way around the lock's cavity. It was an almost fruitless exercise. What little she extracted made next to no difference.

'Are you teaching yourself to pick locks, darling?'

'Hi, Rosie, didn't see you coming.' Charlotte straightened with a slight groan as her back cracked. 'Ouch. Do you think I'll make a good cat burglar?'

She glanced around. Nobody on the street near enough to overhear.

'Terrible, if you forget to check who might be around first.'

'I'd love some coffee if you'd like a cup?' Charlotte grabbed her array of cleaning items and led the way inside.

'Beat you to it. Thought you might need one after being on your own all morning.' Rosie had takeaways cups in the holder on the arm of the wheelchair. 'What's wrong with the front door?'

'Something is stuck in the thingy the door bit goes into.'

Rosie pursed her lips together as she passed Charlotte a coffee.

'You're laughing at me.'

'Trying not to.' Rosie moved around the counter and put her coffee down. 'If you mean the latch? What is in it?'

'I'm guessing clear silicone or something similar. It is gooey and thick but is almost dry. Real pain getting it out.'

'How did it get there?'

Let me see. Who wants to cause us the most annoyance today?

Charlotte shrugged. No point upsetting Rosie. 'Bored kids?'

'After your coffee, pop over to the supermarket and buy some methylated spirits. I think that might sort it out. If not, we might need to phone a locksmith. Anything else I need to know about?'

'Nope. But once I get this done, fill me in on your morning?'

———

Not even the methylated spirits helped, so Rosie called a locksmith, who promised to get there before closing time. Charlotte's heart sank at the tiredness on her friend's face.

'Why don't you go home, Rosie.'

'I only just got here.'

'And you look exhausted. I'm fine to manage.'

With a deep sigh, Rosie wheeled to the window. 'No Sid today?'

'He was. Until I asked why.'

Rosie's eyes shot to Charlotte's. 'Oh. Was that a good idea?'

'Probably not, but his behaviour is harassment. He needs to be investigating…other things.'

'Like Octavia's murder?'

Charlotte nibbled her bottom lip.

'Charlie, I get the strongest feeling you believe there was someone there before Glenys arrived. Glenys is hardly a killer!'

With a quick shake of her head, Charlotte picked up some books left on the counter. 'Can't believe the last customer changed their mind about these just as you rang them up!'

Rosie followed Charlotte to the back of the shop. 'Don't change the subject. Do *you* think Glenys did it?'

'Oh, goodness no. I might have given it a moment's thought, but Glenys is at the bottom of my list of who might be responsible.' Charlotte finished repacking the shelf. 'Tell me about this morning. If you want.'

'Not much to tell. Graeme was friends with Octavia's then-husband. They'd go fishing at the river and watch sport.

That kind of thing. When he ran off with Darcy's mother, Graeme kept in touch. Of course, Octavia came around more than one time trying to get information, but Graeme told her to go through her solicitor.'

That made sense. Octavia had once been Rosie's close friend. But every time Charlotte had seen them together, there was only a coldness, even rudeness, from Octavia. Rosie would have taken her own husband's side, so a friendship was another casualty of the failed marriage.

'What family does Octavia have?'

'Two daughters, both long married and living overseas. Octavia told me once—in a rather tipsy moment at a community gathering—that they cared only about inheriting her house and would likely not even attend her funeral.' Rosie shook her head. 'They were never a close family. Not like mine.'

Charlotte squeezed Rosie's arm.

'I'm alright. Really. Anyway, someone from the medical examiner's phoned to see if I knew their contact details. Even her solicitor didn't have them.'

'Do you?'

'No. But I gave them her ex-husband's number.'

'Mrs Sibbritt? Locksmith.' A cheery voice from near the door interrupted.

'I'll tell you the rest later.' Rosie turned her chair, with what Charlotte was certain was a forced smile. 'There's no Mrs Sibbritt here! I'm Rosie.'

———

After closing time, Rosie followed Charlotte to the garden behind the bookshop. Charlotte showed her the passionfruit vine and asked about what she could grow.

'That's an old vine and look how healthy it is! I can make passionfruit jam or relish if you'd like?'

'And teach me how to?'

'Absolutely. I'll have you entering your creations in the local agricultural show before you know it. What you need to consider is where the winter sun will be. Not so much on the back fence and toward the corner.' Rosie gestured. 'So, plant some quick growing summer vegetables for now, and then use that area for things like broccoli and cauliflower. Carrots will grow anywhere.'

'This is wonderful!' Charlotte said. 'I talked to Darcy about mulch and he gave the details of a local garden centre. Will they have tools, do you think?'

'Maybe. But I have so many, Charlie. Next time you come over, drive up and we'll sort out what you need. You can buy your own once you decide what you need long term.' Rosie navigated toward the back of the garage, where it met the fence. 'You know there's a gate behind the vine?'

'No way.' Charlotte pushed leaves to one side and peered behind. 'Well, look at this!'

'I'll loan you some decent secateurs so you can clear the fence there. The vine will love you pruning it. All I can say is make sure you put a lock on it, if there isn't one. If there is, I have no idea where the key would be in which case, I'll find bolt cutters.'

'Exactly what kind of tools do you not have at home?' Charlotte laughed.

'No chainsaw. Or hedgers. But there's a bit in the shed that Graeme collected. Shovels, crowbars, hoes, buckets. Lots of things. Come around for dinner tomorrow and we'll investigate. I might head home, darling.' Rosie was already on the driveway. 'I'm thrilled with your plans for the garden. Too long since it's had some love.'

A few minutes later, Charlotte climbed upstairs. She opened the door and almost stepped on a note pushed under it. Why would someone make the effort to come up the stairs rather than pop into the shop to hand it to her? Charlotte glanced at the folded, white piece of paper, then closed and locked the door. After stepping over the note, she photographed it.

You are so overthinking this.

In the kitchen were some thin rubber gloves. These on, she lifted the note by one corner and placed it on the counter. Her stomach churned as she unfolded the paper. There was no writing, just a black and white photograph, possibly a photocopy by the look of the quality.

There were two people in the image of the lookout near the falls. Glenys and Charlotte.

'What on earth?'

Charlotte turned on the lights above the counter and peered closer.

It was when she had just spoken to Glenys, who was on the move. So, they were close to each other in the moment before Charlotte had stepped aside to let her pass.

The photograph was taken from higher up and a fair distance away. She took off the gloves and got her phone, scrolling until finding some photos she'd taken last year. The angle was similar. Someone was at the top of Kingfisher Falls and took a photograph. Why? And why slide a copy under the door? What possible reason could anyone have for this?

She rushed to the door and checked it was locked. Charlotte didn't spook easily but this was creepy. Even creepier than Sid's stalkish behaviour, which at least was overt.

Or did you do this, Sid?

What to do with this was the next problem. Charlotte located a plastic sleeve and after putting one glove back on, slid the paper inside. As she did, the light caught it from a different angle, and she looked more closely. Above the lookout's railing was a drawn arrow. A small, black arrow pointing over and down.

'Right. I need a drink.'

Charlotte pulled the glove off with a pop and threw it into the sink. Then picked up its partner, which joined it. She filled a glass with ice cubes and poured some water and lemon over it. Refreshing and kept her mind clear. Soon, she'd think about dinner, but for a few minutes she wanted to sit on the balcony and think.

———

Those few minutes turned into an hour before hunger drove Charlotte to the fridge for some leftover potato salad. She added a couple of slices of sourdough and returned to the balcony, this time with a glass of wine. Plate on the table, she wandered to the railing and leaned against it.

Night sounds intruded. Birds settling for the evening. The occasional car. Distant laughter and music from the restaurants at the end of the mall. How nice to stroll down there and sit outside Italia with a glass of chianti and a bowl of Doug's wonderful pumpkin gnocchi.

One could never tire of those morsels of deliciousness. She sighed and returned to her potato salad. This wasn't bad though.

Her eyes roamed the balcony. This was something she was proud of. The apartment was old and according to Rosie, not lived in for some years before Charlotte arrived. After almost a week's worth of work during the post-Christmas break, this outdoor area was transformed from its grey, peeling walls and floor.

Light olive-green walls were cooling. The floor was covered in timber slats. She would add some hanging baskets with ferns and a herb garden once she had a chance.

It mattered. These changes were more than new paint. Warmth settled in Charlotte's heart. She was making a home. At least the first steps. Room by room, she'd strip back the old and create something new and beautiful. And a little bit of Charlotte would be renewed with every stroke of the paintbrush.

She washed up after returning the rubber gloves to their normal spot. Back in the living room, a lone bauble was in a corner, hanging from the ceiling by fishing line. It was low enough to reach so she tugged, and the line slid out of the tape holding it up. This ceiling was next on her list to repaint, so she'd leave the tape up there. Somehow this little decoration was missed when she'd packed Christmas away.

The decorations box was in the third bedroom, which she'd turned into her I-don't-know-what-to-do-with-this-yet storage place. The second bedroom was set up for a guest. Charlotte had no idea why, as she wasn't expecting anyone, but it felt nice to have a bed made with crisp sheets and a new towel folded on the foot.

In the third bedroom, she opened the decoration box, which she'd left on the bare mattress. The apartment was sort-of furnished, but some things were much better than others. This single bed, for example, creaked and groaned if you sat on it, and the mattress was so old, springs poked through the end. One day she'd buy a nice bed for in here, but for now it did a good job of holding her bits and pieces.

After closing the lid again on the decorations, she hesitated, eyes on another box. This one arrived before Christmas from the facility where her mother lived.

Where she is instituted. Stop glossing over it.

It didn't matter. The box appeared on her doorstep one day, filled with some of Angelica's unwanted trinkets and memories, as well as some things she'd kept of Charlotte's.

Things her mother insisted on keeping from Charlotte's

childhood from hell. She'd glanced inside, unwilling to do more than note there were letters, jewellery boxes, and a host of ridiculous things her mother thought important enough to keep.

Except…

She'd seen some Christmas cards in there and opened them, curious because Angelica never bothered with Christmas or birthdays. Nine unique handmade cards. One sent each year from the time Charlotte was two to eleven. All with a simple inscription.

Merry Christmas, sweetie. You are loved. Z.

When she'd asked Angelica about them, her mother had remembered the words, and who sent them, but her confusion returned before she explained, and Charlotte got no further information. It wasn't her father, whose name did not begin with Z. Plus, he was still with them through some of those years. Charlotte didn't know if they were sent to Angelica, or herself.

Yet another mystery but this one from the past. Charlotte closed the door as she left.

chapter
nine

Doug was already waiting at the police station at eleven when Charlotte jogged around the corner.

'I'm so sorry.' She puffed as she stopped near him. 'Delayed by a customer.'

'I'm early. And Sid only drove in thirty seconds ago.' Doug Oaks was head chef at Italia, and married to Esther, owner of the dress shop. The same dress shop broken into last year and its Christmas tree stolen. Doug was a fair and even-tempered man and his attendance with Charlotte at the station boosted her confidence.

The police station was a standalone stone building. Very old, it cried out for a coat of paint. Unlike Trev's station, with its small house attached, this was little more than four walls and barred windows.

'Ready?' Doug led the way.

'Thanks for coming with me. I'm not comfortable being alone with him, not while giving a statement where he might...well, misunderstand me.'

Doug laughed. 'You are so tactful. We'll get this done. So decent of you to help with poor Octavia.' He tapped on the door. 'I bet Glenys was happy to see you that day.'

Charlotte didn't answer as Sid called from inside with a muffled, 'Open.'

The door swung inwards to a small entry. The air stank of cigarettes and stale coffee and Charlotte switched to breathing through her mouth. There was a counter with a door beside it.

'In here.'

The "in here" was a brick-walled room with two desks and a cell at the far end and a barred back door. The weight of decades of interrogation and suspicions chilled Charlotte and she shivered. Sid sprawled behind a messy desk.

'Only need the doctor so you can wait outside.' Sid didn't even bother a greeting to Doug.

'He stays or I go.'

Sid rolled his eyes. 'Whatever. But not one word from him.' He gestured for Charlotte to take the sole seat opposite.

The back was sticky when she pulled it out and she perched as little of herself on the seat as possible. 'Is there news yet from the medical examiner's office?'

'All they do is harass me for a report. I'll ask the questions.' Sid tapped one finger at a time on the keyboard. 'I need your full name first.'

'Charlotte Dean.'

'No middle name?'

'No.'

'Address.'

Providing only what she knew was legally required, Charlotte answered Sid's list of identification questions. He wanted more. He always wanted more, but Trev had sent her a list of what she needed to provide after she'd texted him about it this morning.

For the next half hour, Sid typed a report. He'd started with his request for her to attend the house and they'd got as far as him leaving the house to speak with his superiors.

'Right.' Sid took his hands off the keyboard and looked at Charlotte. 'You said you have information.'

'There's a couple of things I noticed. One was to do with Octavia's body.'

'Body? Her head hit the marble when she tripped. What's to notice?'

'What did she trip on?' Charlotte asked.

'I dunno. The corner of the mat.'

'It wasn't disturbed at all. Not turned over or pushed up. And it is a big mat, so she'd have staggered a few steps before falling if she'd caught her foot on the edge of it.'

Sid sat back and crossed his arms, his expression one of disbelief. 'Go on, *detective.*'

'I'm simply sharing my observations. I would imagine whoever came and took photographs before Octavia's body was removed would tell you the same thing.' Charlotte kept irritation out of her tone. 'Are homicide detectives on their way?'

'Why? It was an accident that she fell. She wasn't young.'

'Oh, Sid. You must think there's more to this!'

'Leading Senior Constable Browne. Tell me why I should?' His hands returned to the keyboard and he tapped a few words. 'Go on, what makes this a murder case?'

'I think she had a mark across the back of her skull. One that was inflicted before she fell.'

His hands lifted and his jaw dropped.

Doug, who'd been leaning against the counter, straightened with a small intake of air. Charlotte cast him a look she hoped he understood was an apology for not warning him of her suspicions. His lips were pressed together, but he nodded.

'I took photographs, Leading Senior Constable. Lots of them.'

'Why.'

'In case you forgot to.'

The words hung for a full minute. Sid didn't blink the whole time, Charlotte was sure, but she wasn't backing down. The shrill ring of the phone cut through the tension. Sid lifted it and hung up again without answering.

'Send me every photograph you took. Understand?'

'Sure.'

'If there's a mark, why hasn't the medical examiner found it?'

'I imagine there are processes. There wasn't a break in, or abnormal activities around Octavia. On the surface it would be a terrible accident.' Charlotte mentally counted the days. There would be something soon.

'What else?'

'She'd had company that day. So, you might want to interview that person to see if they saw or heard anything out of the ordinary.'

Sid shook his head. 'How am I supposed to find some mystery visitor? Glenys found Octavia face down. She didn't say a word about anyone else being there.'

'Did you look in the dishwasher?'

'Oh, this better be good. Why were you snooping around the house?' Sid said, his customary smirk planted back on his face.

'The house looked perfect. But on the sink was a teapot. No cups. Just the teapot which was half empty and cold. Inside the dishwasher were the matching cups, so you can go and take your own photos and fingerprints and what have you. Not that you need to. The lipstick on one was a dead giveaway.'

'Lipstick. Beauty expert as well as detective. I'm over your ridiculous ideas and wonder if you might have had a hand in Octavia's death after all.'

Doug took a step forward and Sid glanced up, as though

he'd forgotten he wasn't alone with Charlotte.

'You think what you want, but I'm here to help and if you finish typing that thing up, I can sign it and get out of your hair.'

Is before lunch too early for a stiff drink?

'What's special about this alleged lipstick?'

'Bright orange. Know anyone around town who wears bright orange? I do.'

————

Back out in the heat of the day, Charlotte drew in the fresh air. 'I hope you aren't too shocked, Doug. I should have warned you.'

He scratched his head. 'Took me by surprise. But the more I think on it, the more it makes some sort of sense. Octavia being murdered, not Veronica doing it. It didn't sit right that she'd simply fallen over. Never known her to have a weak moment.'

'Thanks for being there though. I'm sorry you have to keep this to yourself for now.'

'Nah. I'm not one for gossip and speculation, so nobody will expect me to say a word. Not even Esther. She's used to me using my ears more than my mouth.'

It was a shame more people didn't do that. Doug headed to Italia to do dinner prep and Charlotte refused his offer of a lift. After the oppressive atmosphere of the police station, she needed to walk.

————

The last person Charlotte had expected to see in the bookshop was Marguerite Browne, but there she was, sitting on an armchair in the reading area, dabbing her eyes with a handkerchief as Rosie patted her shoulder.

Charlotte came to a halt, ready to backtrack in case her appearance upset the woman. There'd been very few civil words from Sid's wife to Charlotte since they first met. Marguerite believed Charlotte was Trev's girlfriend and something had once happened between Trev and Sid which was never spoken about. It had caused a deep rift and Charlotte was dragged into it without a clue why.

Last time Marguerite visited the bookshop, she'd stormed out after an attempt to dictate to Rosie where donations in the giving box should go. Or not go. Like Octavia, Marguerite disliked the Woodland family and was adamant Rosie must choose another recipient for any gifts given through the shop. There'd been further conflict at the town's Christmas Eve party.

She didn't give off a hostile vibe now, with her head bowed and shoulders slumped. Charlotte stepped inside.

Rosie glanced up and smiled. A smile that said things were under control and not to worry. Whether Marguerite would feel the same was questionable, so Charlotte slipped onto her stool behind the counter and woke the computer. The orders book was open and there were several new entries, so Charlotte added them to the order file they kept running.

The monitor blinked a few times and then turned black. Charlotte checked the connection at the back, which was fine, then dropped onto her knees to look beneath the counter. She followed the monitor cord to the back of the computer tower and tightened it.

'And I don't know what we'll do about the book club now.'

Marguerite's voice drew closer. Charlotte decided to stay

on the floor until she'd leave and avoid the risk of either a harsh word, or doing something, anything, the woman took affront to. Joys of being a retailer. Be nice to everyone.

Rosie's softer tone followed. 'I would imagine the members would want a little time to grieve Octavia's passing, dear. And you have such a nice group that the formalities could wait a little. Just until everyone feels more normal again.'

Rosie's voice of reason.

'I just don't know what Octavia would have wanted. There was no plan of succession. Just like her estate, really. No will.'

'No will at all?'

'She told me last year she'd had enough of greedy children who wanted her to drop off the perch to be handed wealth they didn't deserve. Tore up her will.' There was a righteousness, a triumph, in Marguerite's voice. 'Those two girls of hers have a fight on their hands. Octavia had plans to create her own little empire, one to rival that of her scoundrel ex-husband. She had quite a portfolio of properties and had her sights on one jewel in the crown. Pity she never got to buy it.'

'I see. Well, I am pleased you're feeling a bit better, dear. Drop by whenever you feel the need.'

'I knew you'd understand, Rose.'

The silence dragged and Charlotte stared at the light on the computer tower. Understand what? What was the jewel in the crown Octavia wanted?

'Are you intending to sit there all day, Charlie?'

'Yes.'

'I'd rather you don't.'

Charlotte climbed to her feet with a dramatic sigh. 'Fine. I'm up.'

Rosie grinned. 'I would have hidden there had I seen Marguerite approaching in time.'

'Did she want to be friends again?'

'Sympathy. And probably to hedge her bets if the book club needs our services again. Who knows? How was Sid?'

'I'm beginning to understand why he spends more time in his car than in that awful station. Anyway, he demanded all the photos I took and when I left was on the phone to someone at the coroner's office. He let slip they've been asking for his report. But he knows what I know so I'm done.' She motioned wiping her hands of him. 'I signed the statement. Unless called as a witness, there's no reason for me to involved.'

'Oh, you've popped those orders in, thank you.' Rosie parked her wheelchair in front of the keyboard. 'Did you notice how odd one of them is?'

Charlotte flicked through the orders book. 'Six copies of *Perfect Photographs of Kingfisher Falls*. Is it for a school or something?'

Rosie shook her head. 'Glenys. Wants to know if any are still circulating and to do an order. She said order any remaining copies.'

'Isn't this the book she has photos in?' Charlotte collected a copy from the far corner of the store. 'This one?'

'Yes, and yes. Her husband took many of the photographs and she did a handful.'

'I remember she told me she always wanted to be a wildlife photographer, but her profession was taking wedding photos.'

'Which she excelled in. She didn't have the patience for wildlife who don't stand where you tell them to. Fred—he was her husband—was patient with a camera, if nothing else. Bit of a temper on him, but with animals and birds he had such love.'

Charlotte flicked through the pages with their full colour images of local fauna, flora, and landscapes. 'There's the lookout. Before the railing was installed.'

'Poor Fred. He fell before this book was even published.'

Opening a bottle of water on the counter, Rosie took a sip. Charlotte returned to her stool, intrigued by the stories of this small town.

'My Graeme was working part time at the local newspaper back then. We didn't need two people here all the time and he did love his journalism. Must tell you about him one day. Anyway, he covered the terrible accident and I remember him following up a few months later when the book was released. He interviewed Glenys and it was poignant. The paper included her photos as Fred's weren't all usable.'

'She took hers at the same time?'

'They'd never have worked on it together because they would never have agreed on a shot.' Rosie smiled to herself. 'Not at all like my life with Graeme. Never a harsh word spoken and always such a gentleman.'

'I'm so pleased you're spending some time with Lewis. He is a gentleman as well.'

Rosie's eyes dropped. 'Spending time? Yes, of course. Yes, he is.'

Oh no. I've said the wrong thing.

'Why does Glenys want six of these?' Quick change of subject.

'No idea, but I don't like her chances. It was printed through a tiny publisher as a very small run and I think...' Rosie tapped the keyboard. 'Yes. Out of print. And the publisher folded some time ago. There should be two more on the shelf so let's pop those aside for her.'

After collecting those, Charlotte put all three on the back

counter. Rosie was speaking to Glenys on the phone. 'You could try some second-hand shops or look online.' Her head nodded. 'We will, see you then.' She hung up. 'Today or tomorrow. Now, are you still having dinner at my place?'

chapter
ten

Charlotte drove to Rosie's house and the first thing on the list was a trip outside to what Rosie had described as a shed.

'This is a palace for tools!' Charlotte wandered around the brick building the size of a double garage. 'From your back patio the garden looks small, but it was all those gorgeous rose bushes hiding this!'

Rosie laughed as she pushed her wheelchair to the far end. 'Graeme loved this place. We both adored the garden, but he also loved journalism. He had an area set up out here so he could work into the night without disturbing me. All gone now, except for these couple of filing cabinets worth of his published work.'

'You mentioned he worked at the local newspaper?' Charlotte followed Rosie.

'He did. But originally he was an overseas correspondent and travelled as much as stayed home. For a while he was reporting from very dangerous places and paid a lot of money for the work he did. Enough, in fact, for us to buy the building the bookshop is in.' She stopped in front of two metal filing cabinets. 'In here are newspapers, magazines, notes, all manner of journalistic bits and pieces. One day I'll sort them.'

'One day?'

'Kind of makes me feel I'd be saying…goodbye.' Rosie sighed. 'Silly of me.'

Charlotte put a hand on Rosie's shoulder. 'Not silly. But what you shared with Graeme is in your heart, not these drawers.' She squatted beside Rosie and gazed up at her. 'Oh, don't cry, Rosie. I can't imagine what it is like to love so deeply and lose that person. But when I hear you speak of him with so many wonderful memories…you created a life together and shared your dreams. And built a business. Even raised a son who turned out kind of okay.'

Rosie wiped tears from her cheeks with the back of her hand, the corners of her lips turning up. 'Kind of okay. Trev's a bit more than that.'

In volumes.

'Dunno. He is bossy at times.' Charlotte stood and kissed Rosie's cheek. 'If you ever need a hand going through these, I'm awesome at files. And stuff.'

She wandered away to give Rosie a moment to compose herself. A long workbench with a low shelf ran along one wall. Neatly packed on the bottom shelf was a range of power tools in their cases. Plastic pots were piled by size and shape.

Charlotte's foot bumped something poking out from under the bottom shelf. She pulled it out. It was a piece of long, rounded timber. A handle without its head.

'Um, slide it onto the shelf, Charlie. I have to get it repaired.'

'Sure. What is it?' Charlotte slipped it between two boxes.

'Er, um, an axe. For firewood. Once it gets a new head.'

'You don't have a fireplace.'

'No. No, I don't.'

And that was that. Rosie was still at the filing cabinets, so Charlotte crossed to the opposite wall, which was filled with hooks. All manner of tools hung here. Shovels of varying lengths and styles. Forks. Rakes. A hole digger of some type. Lower down were lots of hand tools, each with their own hook.

'You should take one of the wheelbarrows.' Rosie pointed to two. 'I only need one. And as you can see there's a comprehensive range of tools so take what you need. That shovel and that one as well. See their different ends? One will dig in the existing beds and the other will help you make new ones. And a fork. Plus, whatever small tools you need. Oh, there's some decent shears to cut back those old bushes.'

For the next few minutes, Charlotte loaded a wheelbarrow with everything Rosie suggested. But there was no way she was going to fit the wheelbarrow in her small sedan.

'What if I drop the car back, then after dinner I'll push this home?'

'If you're sure you'll manage all the way there? Or we can ask around for someone with a ute to help?'

'Nah. Not a problem at all. I might leave this around the side of your house out of view from the street.' Charlotte pushed the wheelbarrow away from the car. 'I'll be back in ten.'

'In that case, I'll put dinner in the oven and arrange some drinks. Seeing as you won't be driving later.'

True to her word, by the time Charlotte returned, two freshly made gin and tonics waited on the kitchen counter. Rosie had left the door unlocked and was in the kitchen.

'Ah. There you are. I should have asked if my baked macaroni cheese and salad is fine?'

'If that's what I can smell, then absolutely. Is there mustard in it?'

'You should be a detective. Yes, it gives it that slightly

exotic smell and tang. Shall we?' Rosie wheeled past Charlotte. 'I thought outside might be nice.'

Charlotte followed with both drinks. 'Everyone tells me I should be a detective. Sid even called me detective but there may have been some sarcasm attached.'

'You think? Hello cats.'

Mellow and Mayhem were on opposite ends of a long bench seat. Mellow stretched, jumped down, and padded to Rosie, sitting at her feet before leaping onto her lap. Mayhem growled.

'Are we intruding?' Charlotte asked him, knowing better than to touch him without his permission. She passed one drink to Rosie and they clinked them together with a "cheers". As always, the mix was perfect, and Charlotte anticipated the moment the gin would warm her stomach and ease a little of the tension she carried.

'Tell me more about the interview with Sid.' Rosie rattled the ice in her glass. 'You told him about the lipstick?'

'I did. He added it to the statement but said nothing about who it belongs to. I think he'd rather pretend none of this is happening. But he was cross I'd looked in the dishwasher and accused me of being responsible for Octavia's death, although how that makes sense, I have no idea.'

'Does he think you're blaming Veronica to deflect attention?'

'Probably.'

'But you're not.'

'The teapot was cold so assuming Veronica owns the lipstick on the cup, she drank that cup ages before Octavia died. Unless my timing is out. I guess she might have still been there. I didn't know they were friends?'

Rosie drained her glass and set it on the table. 'I don't know what to think.'

'Octavia was seeing Kevin, who is Terrance's brother. Terrance works with Jonas. And Jonas—'

'Has some sort of thing going on with Veronica. Clever girl. I wonder what that thing is though? Another drink and I'll check dinner?' Rosie didn't wait for an answer.

'Yum.' Charlotte collected Rosie's glass and headed for the small bar, while Rosie went to the kitchen.

As Rosie served their meals, Charlotte puzzled over Veronica. She'd spoken to her a handful of times but seen her from a distance far more often. Some of those times she was deep in discussion with Jonas, including at the Christmas Eve street party where Veronica's sort-of-boyfriend tried to drag Charlotte away by the throat after a series of threats.

'Now, back to Veronica and Jonas.' Rosie picked up a fork once they both were at the table again. 'I wonder if she's trying yet another scheme to go head to head with someone in town.'

Veronica had a record of setting up a shop selling the same type of products as one next door. She'd failed at shoes, gifts, and one other Charlotte didn't recall, before taking over the garden centre.

'Oh!'

Both cats—who were back sleeping on the bench—woke with a start.

'Sorry guys.' Charlotte slid some macaroni onto her fork. 'Darcy told me Veronica has set up her big greenhouse to grow seedlings with a view to become a wholesaler.'

'My goodness. That won't end well.'

Charlotte giggled and took a bite. The pasta was perfect, and the cheesy sauce had just a touch of mustardy tang. Yum indeed.

Rosie waved her fork around. 'She has no idea about plants. I think I've told you before that any I bought from her died almost immediately. But why would she do this when normally she tries to steal an existing market from someone?'

After a quick sip of her drink, Charlotte nodded. 'She will be. Darcy.'

'Darcy…do you mean he's rebuilding their wholesaling side?'

'He has a friend coming to stay to help work on the greenhouses and is so enthusiastic about his plans.'

'How wonderful!' Rosie's smile was wide. 'If he is even half the grower his dad was, then he'll do well. But how does she know?'

'And *why* does she do this? Why capitalise on the hard work and good names of existing businesses?'

'Healthy competition is good for everyone. The shoppers, the shops, the products. And had Veronica opened a shoe shop or gift shop anywhere other than next door to existing ones, nobody would have thought anything was off. But she undercut both those businesses with cheap and poor-quality products which, combined with her less than friendly customer service, put people off very quickly.'

'So, she'd close them before using her rent-free period. Didn't any landlords chase her for breach of contract though?'

'Wasn't worth their time. But she'll never get another lease in town. Do you know, for a while the shop next to the bookshop was empty and she tried to move in there. Much as the landlord wanted it rented, he wasn't about to risk it.'

'That explains the boxes in the garden centre with "books" written all over them. I wondered why she had those.' Along with packing boxes filled with "gifts", "shoes" and other products, all piled against a wall in the shop at Veronica's business.

'All very interesting, but doesn't explain how she knows

about Darcy's plan, or why she was at Octavia's house.' Rosie pushed her plate away with a small sigh of contentment.

Charlotte had a theory. 'She was quick enough to make a complaint to Sid about what she heard us say. What if she also hurried her high heels to Octavia?'

And if she'd done so, had she told someone else? A someone who might see an opportunity to cast suspicion onto another party for a crime not yet committed…and then commit it.

———

Rosie and Charlotte continued their discussion long after doing the dishes and over another drink. Or two.

Charlotte bade Rosie goodnight and steered the wheelbarrow out of the garden after a couple of false starts. Once she had it going in the right direction, she trundled it onto the street, surprised there was a chill in the air. Time to get her one and only coat out.

She spent most of her life in Queensland, in more temperate conditions than Victoria often experienced. She'd never owned a jacket or coat for warmth, only for work, and they were lightweight.

During winter in Rivers End, Charlotte had relented on a freezing cold day and purchased a beautiful red coat. She'd never been one for fashion or making herself conspicuous, but the moment she slipped it on, she fell in love with it. Before she could change her mind, she'd paid and left, still wearing it. January was a long way from winter in Australia, but she'd leave it near the back door. Just in case.

The roads were quiet and a low mist was settling. Streetlights blurred through the swirling whiteness casting eerie shadows. A dog barked and Charlotte jumped, then laughed at herself.

Octavia's death and the fallout had frayed her nerves. The photograph she'd anonymously received of herself and Glenys was intrusive. Even if Octavia's death was an accident, there was someone out there using it to create unrest.

Charlotte reached the roundabout and lowered the wheelbarrow to rest for a moment. It was easy enough to push, but bulky to navigate along the footpath. She wiggled her fingers.

A few weeks ago, she'd hidden herself across the road in a narrow space between two buildings as Sid stomped around on the roundabout. Minutes earlier, two young thugs with a chainsaw had demolished the expensive artificial Christmas tree in the middle, taking most of it with them.

Instead of doing his job by preserving evidence, Sid had stomped on baubles and parked across the tracks left by the departed ute and trailer. He'd sensed someone was watching him and came looking. A prickle ran up Charlotte's spine remembering how close she'd come to being discovered before escaping along an alley behind the shops. She was no longer afraid of the man, but his behaviour made her cautious around him.

Tonight, under the mist, the town might be one from a film set. Deserted, spooky, silent. Except, there was a crunch from somewhere nearby. A footstep.

Or your imagination.

Charlotte grabbed the handles and pushed the wheelbarrow across the road. At the other side she misjudged the narrow ramp onto the footpath and hit the kerb with force. The wheelbarrow twisted sideways, a handle jabbing into her stomach before the contents of the tub dropped out with a clatter.

'Ouch!' She released the other handle and rubbed her stomach, wincing at a spot she knew would bruise.

Tools were heaped on the road. With a grunt, Charlotte

righted the wheelbarrow and pushed it with more care onto the footpath. One by one, she retrieved the larger tools first, sliding them into the tub. Then, the hand tools. Bending down hurt and it took a few minutes to have everything back where it belonged.

No more drinking and steering.

She set off, ignoring a growing sensation of being watched. Well, any onlookers would be laughing at her inability to keep a simple garden wheelbarrow upright.

At the halfway point along the row of shops in the block before the bookshop, Charlotte stopped. Handles still in her grasp, she scanned the street. Nothing on her side. Nor on the other. She waited, listening. Her heart pounded in her ears. Adrenaline flooded her body and she tightened her grip, struggling with the flight, fight, or freeze response. There was nothing to fight, and she wasn't frozen, only waiting. So, flight it was, even if at a steady pace to avoid another mishap.

In a moment she'd turned into her driveway and approached the garage. It was dark here. Really dark.

Charlotte unlocked the garage, lifted the roller door, and pushed the wheelbarrow in beside her car. The safety of her apartment beckoned and she closed and relocked the garage. She knew the stairs well and was up them in seconds. This was a silly response to a walk home. It might be dark and quiet out there, but why panic?

Door locked behind her, she put on all the lights in the apartment. Then, she dashed out to the balcony leaving the light off. She peeked over the edge. Over the street. Along the row of shops.

'Happy now?' She asked herself. If the Christmas tree was up here, she'd have let it talk her out of her fears, but it wasn't. Charlotte took a deep breath. Most people didn't expect a tree to talk to them. But it was her personal thera-pist and she missed it being upstairs.

One by one, Charlotte turned off the lights, apart from a lamp in the living room. She double checked all the doors were secure, then filled a glass with water and collected the book she was reading. This place was her refuge. Her home. Charlotte headed for the bedroom, heart rate almost back to normal.

chapter
eleven

Charlotte hadn't even got as far as making a coffee the next morning before the dread returned, thanks to another note slipped under the door.

Maybe I need a draft stopper.

Gloves on, she unfolded the paper.

Her image stared back from another printed paper in black and white. This photo was taken on her way home with the wheelbarrow when she'd stopped and scanned the street. She'd looked into the camera without knowing it. Last night she'd put her high alert response down to having been a bit tipsy. But it was time to trust her instincts.

A lump formed in her throat and her hands shook. She dropped the paper and stepped back. Her breath came in gulps and she needed to run. Fling the door open and flee from here. Go as fast as her body would allow until she could run no more. Except she wasn't doing that anymore.

Bit by bit, she forced the anxiety into a box in her mind. It wasn't helpful so it could be locked away and replaced with good thoughts and positive feelings. Charlotte closed her eyes and imagined Mellow was here. Her soft fur and sweet face. Those big and gentle eyes. Long whiskers, some black, others white, just like Mellow was. And the purr.

Unlike her brother, Mayhem, who would growl and most likely bite Charlotte rather than offer comfort and love. As different as night and day. Perhaps Charlotte should get a cat. Most likely she'd end up with a Mayhem rather than a Mellow and they'd spend all their time at opposite ends of the apartment.

Mind clear again and the tremors in her hands almost gone, Charlotte returned to the paper. There'd been nobody on the street with her so where had they hidden? The angle wasn't from above, so not in one of the other above-shop accommodations. She glanced at the time. If she hurried, she could search for the exact location before work. But this paper wasn't going anywhere. She took a photo with her phone and slid the paper into a new plastic sleeve which then joined the other one in the bottom drawer in the kitchen.

Charlotte showered, threw on clothes and makeup, and grabbed her handbag.

Last night's mist was gone as the morning heated. The forecast was for a hot day and already there was a bite in the air. People walked their dogs while it was still cool enough, and when Charlotte wandered up and down the footpath where she thought the photo was taken, she got a few odd looks.

With lots of "good morning" and "nice day for taking photos", she smiled back at the faces of people she knew and a few she didn't. Was one of them the photographer? She stopped and leaned back against a shop window. In a town so small it was possible, even likely, she knew who it was. She fought off a sudden rush of nausea and opened the phone for another look.

The image showed Charlotte outside *Kingfisher Falls*

Frames & Photos. Its glass door was behind her and over her left shoulder a display of picture frames was visible.

She moved a little further down the street and checked again, this time looking through the camera on the phone and zooming in on the shop in question until she was certain she had the correct angle. Another couple of steps and she knew she'd found the spot. Similar to the one where she'd once hidden from Sid, there was another narrow gap between two buildings.

After a glance along the street to be sure nobody saw, Charlotte slid into the gap. She held up the phone and focused on the frame shop. At night, with mist masking the lights, a person would be invisible in here unless you knew where to look. Underfoot, the ground was dirt, with rubbish blown in from the street. Papers and empty plastic bottles, some crushed underfoot.

Where's Bernie?

A dart of panic stabbed Charlotte. Her former patient had created havoc in Rivers End before being arrested for a range of crimes. His obsession with crushing empty water bottles in his wake was like a calling card. And he was a photographer.

'No, no, no.' She jabbed at the phone as she dialled Trev and then stepped out onto the street again, heart going a million miles an hour. What if he was free? If he'd tracked her down here—

'Morning, Charlie. I'm pouring coffee. Like one?' Trev's deep, calming voice filled Charlotte with a sense of safety. He was hours away, but there was something so steadying about Trevor Sibbritt that it crossed the distance.

'I would. Haven't had one yet.'

'Not like you. Did you sleep in?'

'No. Although your mother is a bad influence with late nights.'

'Do tell.'

'Not likely.' She wandered along the footpath. 'Do you happen to know where things are at with Bernie?'

'Bernie?' The surprise was real. 'Why?'

'Um…something just reminded me of him, and I want to make sure he's locked up.'

Don't question me. Just take it on face value.

Charlotte crossed her fingers, then uncrossed them when she realised what she was doing.

'He will not find you. But I'm certain he's still locked up and will be until he faces trial. It will be months, Charlie.'

'And then I must testify, I get that. But what if he's escaped?' She forced herself to stand still, to plant her feet and control her tone of voice. Trev knew her too well and would probe. 'I mean, I'm sure he hasn't, but…well, I stepped on a water bottle and got a fright. I'm silly.'

'You're not being silly. Once I'm dressed, I'll log into the database and run a query. It won't take long to find out where we're at. Where he's at. Things will be fine.'

Heat filled Charlotte and she started walking again. 'You're not dressed?'

He chuckled, a low, deep laugh. 'Got back from a run on the beach and wanted coffee before a shower.'

'Ah. Right.'

Charlie! Stop it right now.

'Okay, well thanks. Will you text me once you know?' Her words tumbled out. 'And then when I step on a bottle I won't worry.'

There was a long silence. Was Trev sipping coffee, rolling his eyes at her, or perhaps he'd fallen asleep from boredom?

The owner of the café on the corner waved to her as he cleaned an outside table. He mouthed "coffee?" and she nodded with a grin.

'I have to go. Somebody is making me coffee at last.'

'Somebody?'

'He makes coffee for me most days.' Worry-wart Charlotte was gone, replaced by the mischievous Charlie who emerged on occasion. 'All I need to do is appear and he hurries to the coffee machine.'

'I'm well aware your mood improves with caffeine. How long did it take this poor man to figure it out?'

She giggled. 'He just knew. And I'm so nice to him when he hands over that steaming, delectable cup of goodness. I even give him money.'

'He deserves a lot.' Trev didn't sound the least bit put out by her teasing. 'Are you working today?'

'Yeah. Opening soon.'

'Are you alright? Nobody's giving you grief about Octavia?'

Only Sid. And Veronica. And the stalker.

She used her Doctor Dean voice. 'There's nothing to worry about, Trevor. I'm fine. Rosie's fine. And my coffee is calling.'

'Very well, *Charlotte.*' The humour still lurked in his voice. 'Answer the call of the coffee and I shall take what remains of mine to the shower. I'll text you soon.'

With that he was gone. Charlotte caught her reflection in the café window. She was smiling.

————

Glenys was the first customer for the day, arriving minutes after Charlotte opened the front door. She'd only had time to take a couple of sips of her coffee before doing a quick sweep outside, firing up the registers, and brushing her hair as an afterthought. Now she wondered if the funny looks she'd had wasn't from her strange behaviour with her phone, but her messy appearance.

'Rosie put some books aside for me, dear.' Glenys said.

'She told me you wanted to order a few. What a shame it isn't in print anymore.' Charlotte collected the books from the back counter.

'Oh, not really. Everything comes to an end, doesn't it?'

Charlotte blinked as she turned the top book over to scan. It wasn't long ago that Glenys made a big deal of this book, insisting Charlotte hear a story about each photo she'd taken and pointing out some special places around Kingfisher Falls. Well, her poor husband had come to his end before this book even made it to his local bookshop.

'Do you know how to do that thing when you look on a computer for an item?' Glenys leaned on the counter. 'Rosie said I should search on the in-net to locate the remaining copies.'

'Internet? Of course. Would you like me to have a quick search now?'

'Yes, please. I want to find every copy there is.'

As Charlotte typed into the search bar, she remembered Rosie's words of wisdom about smiling, no matter what. Customers had strange requests, and this was the oddest Charlotte had come across so far.

'Hm. None for sale that appears on the first few pages. I'll write the names of a couple of Melbourne bookshops who sold it so you can ring and see if they have any left.'

'But how do I find who has bought them?' Glenys' eyes were fixed on a point behind the counter and much as Charlotte wanted to turn around, she kept still, the smile planted in place.

'Glenys, here's those phone numbers.' She offered one of their "with compliments" notes with the details. 'I'll ask Rosie if she has any other ideas. Did you want them as gifts?'

The other woman was miles away, off in her own thoughts.

'Glenys?'

'Oh. Yes, thank you for this.' She took the note and slid it into her handbag. 'No gifts, dear. Who would I give them to? How much do I owe you?'

After she'd paid and taken custody of the copies, Glenys left without another word. Charlotte spun around on her stool. What had Glenys stared at? Above the long counter along the wall were a few shelves, some posters, and up high, a row of matching framed photographs. Charlotte had never taken a close look at them.

She hurried to the kitchen and collected the small step ladder. The shop was still empty of customers, so Charlotte climbed up to look. All were of the same vintage, perhaps twenty years old based on recognising an upright, brown-haired Rosie on the arm of Graeme. She'd seen a photo of him before and his kind face reminded her of Trevor. Rosie wore a long dress and Graeme was dapper in a tuxedo.

'That was a special night.' Rosie's voice, from the other side of the counter, was soft. 'A council awards evening for outstanding contribution to the region.'

Charlotte glanced down at Rosie. 'You look gorgeous in that gown. Twenty years ago?'

With a smile, Rosie shook her head. 'Twenty-three, but good guess. Graeme was presented with an award for his work as a journalist.'

The photograph beside it showed a group of four, standing on the steps of a building in their finery.

'On the left is Octavia and her then-husband, who was a land developer.'

'Seriously?'

'I know. There was initially a lot of opposition to him setting up in town, but then he helped build a primary school and put a fair bit of money into cleaning up the river. People overlooked him buying up parcels of land after that, but before he divorced Octavia, he sold most of it—I think against her will. She got the house and a pile of money.'

'To other developers?'

'Mostly to council. A couple of parcels to small developers. And Glenys bought the property where she lives now.'

'Glenys did?'

'She retired around then. Sold the pub she'd run with Fred and wanted a quieter place to live.'

'And the council land. Have they done much with it?'

'Most of it has laid idle since because of in-fighting and mismanagement. Anyway, going back to the photos, to their right in the picture is Glenys with Fred. He'd won an award for his work cataloguing local fauna and flora.'

Charlotte peered at the image. Fred was a slight man with no hair and a bow tie. He scowled at the camera and held himself at a slight angle away from Glenys. There was a sadness on the woman's face that pulled at Charlotte.

'See the table at the back? There's a young man in a waiter's uniform.'

'Is that Henry?'

'He went from school to work at the pub and was on loan to help with refreshments on the night.'

The next photo featured two men of similar build and features. 'Is that Terrance and Kevin Murdoch?'

Rosie laughed. 'Funny how the years change some more than others. If I'm not being too unkind, they haven't aged well. They were both conveyancers. And their firm sponsored the awards night.'

'Well, this has been an interesting history lesson.' Charlotte climbed down and folded the ladder.

Rosie continued staring at the photographs. 'Fred wasn't a nice man. He'd not wanted Glenys in the photograph and it caused quite an upset on the night. But the newspaper insisted.'

'Why would he be like that?'

'Said he was the one getting the award, not her. I remember giving her a hug in the ladies room when she was reapplying mascara after a cry.' Rosie wheeled behind the counter. 'Why were you looking at the photographs?'

'Oh. Glenys came to buy those books and she was staring at them. I was curious why, and now I know.'

By the time Charlotte put the step ladder away, Rosie was busy with customers. A steady trail of people wandered in over the next hour or two. At one point she felt her phone vibrate in her pocket. Until lunchtime, it was a struggle to keep an interested face with the customers when she longed to see what Trev had found out.

'Darling, you get lunch first today. I had a late breakfast and things are quieter now.' Rosie was at the corner where Glenys's books were previously displayed. 'I'll change this up a bit to fill the gap.'

Charlotte needed no more encouragement and grabbing her bag, she hurried around the side of the building. The little pine tree was in the full sun, which was hot, so she pulled it into a shady spot and promised to bring some water soon.

Once upstairs, Charlotte opened Trev's message.

Call me when you can.

Her heart sank.

Was Bernie out on bail? But he couldn't possibly know where she was, and it wasn't in his nature to be so patient. He'd have already made sure she knew he was around. She flopped onto the sofa and rang Trev. Nothing would upset her. She'd manage whatever he'd found out and stay calm.

'I was just going to call you.' There was a different note to his voice. Not the chilled, confident tone of this morning. 'Wasn't sure you'd got my message and—'

'I was working and I couldn't ring you. He knows where I

am, doesn't he?' She had as much control over her response as the weather and rolled her eyes at herself.

'Hey…Charlie, no. Bernie has no idea where you are. How could he? Are you at the shop?'

'In the apartment. I'm on my lunch break.'

'I have news. He was in hospital having more surgery on the hand he injured that day. Somebody got careless and he walked right out. At this point—'

Charlotte got up and paced. 'He's escaped? Why wasn't I told. Why didn't—'

Trev wasn't normally one to interrupt but now he did with a firm tone. 'Charlie. Stop and breath. This only happened yesterday and he's in no shape to get far. I've every confidence he'll be back under lock and key in hours. He isn't in Kingfisher Falls.'

'Then who phoned?' She halted, hand over her mouth. Perhaps he hadn't heard. Or would think she was hysterical. Which she was. 'I mean, who left the bottle I stood on? Maybe just pure coincidence but the police will arrest him again? And then he'll be back getting the help he needs, and nobody will be kidnapped or tied up and risk everyone else's life just before a wedding. Well, thanks for the info.'

The room was spinning, and Charlotte staggered to the sofa as ringing filled her ears. She lay flat on her back and raised her knees.

Say goodbye, Trev. Please, let it go.

'We need to have a proper talk, Charlotte. Are you sitting down so we can?'

chapter
twelve

'You're looking pale, Charlie. Is the heat too much? I can put on the air-conditioning.' Rosie was ready for Lewis to meet her for lunch. Instead of under the trees at the park, they'd decided to go to a café and stay out of the heat.

'I was a bit over-tired earlier, but lunch helped. Here he is.'

Lewis wandered in with a broad smile. 'Charlotte! How nice to see you, but so pale? Are you unwell?'

'Just a bit tired.'

She'd first met Lewis before Christmas in his lovely gift shop when searching for present ideas and they hit it off immediately. A widower in his sixties, he and Rosie were inching toward a relationship beyond a long friendship forged through the choir they both sang in.

'Darling, maybe close the door for a while and pop the cooling on. Better for us and the customers.' Rosie popped a sunhat on, smiled at Lewis, and preceded him out.

Charlotte did as suggested. In a moment, cool air permeated the shop and she stood beneath a vent, face up to cool herself. She knew she was pale. She'd glanced in the bathroom mirror before coming back down. A whole lot of tears and the dizziness were responsible. At least she'd hidden the worst of the damage from crying as Trev both admonished and comforted her.

She retreated to the kitchen, pulled out a stool and sat where she could watch the front door. Her legs were a little shaky and whatever brought on the dizziness was still troubling her.

Lack of food, too many coffees, and working yourself up over nothing.

As soon as Trev had told her they needed a "proper" talk, Charlotte's fight or flight response kicked in. Much as she trusted him, Trev wasn't anything more to her than a sort-of-friend. She'd pushed away the memory of a shared kiss at a wedding last year. But then he'd begun talking, his voice firm but worried. If there was such a thing.

'I know you probably intend to hang up the minute this gets too hard for you, but don't. Please, Charlotte.'

Still struggling with her ears ringing and the ground moving, she'd focused on his voice to steady herself. Her Doctor Dean side was jumping up and down telling her she was reacting to a scare, based on unresolved emotions from the time Bernie had her tied up in a cave. She knew that—at least logically. But logic and fear weren't the best of friends, so she'd held onto Trev's voice.

'In a minute, I want you to explain what you said. But first…' he'd hesitated, and she heard a sigh, 'Charlie, I'm here for you. I'm your friend, at the very least. I'm Rosie's son and I know you love her. She trusts me and I hope you do.'

There'd been a question behind the words and a stab of pain had hit Charlotte. 'I do trust you.' Saying it made it real and suddenly, the room had stopped spinning.

'Tell me everything, please.'

'Everything?' Really? A murder—well he knew about that. Sid's stalker-ish behaviour. The images of herself slipped under her door. Her own reactions to events forcing her to run, to hide, to do dangerous things like hide in a narrow space when an untrustworthy law enforcement officer roamed? And the mistakes in Queensland with a patient. And her mother.

Filter, Charlie. Filter.

But it had been hard to do with Trev determined to uncover her secrets.

'Let's start with your comment. What phone call?'

'Some loser trying to scare me. That's all.'

For the longest moment, silence had fallen between them. 'Tell me.'

Charlotte had filled Trev in on the call, leaving out her suspicion it was Sid behind it all.

'Are there any surveillance cameras around the bookshop? I can't remember.'

'Nope. But I'm going to get some quotes. Not just for me, but to protect Rosie.'

'Why?'

'Why not? Your mother was accused of threatening Octavia, which she didn't do. Then, someone decided to fill the lock on the front door of the bookshop with silicon. I'd love to know who it was, let alone...' Against all of Charlotte's will, tears prickled in her eyes. 'I'm tough, Trevor. Not easily scared. But your mother is the most beautiful person I know, and I am worried. Okay. Now you know.'

'Sweetie. Sorry. Um, get cameras. Lots of them and make sure you get signs put up everywhere saying you have them. Do you want me to find some security firms?' There'd been a rare vulnerability in his voice.

'No. I can do that.'

'Anything else I need to know?'

Charlotte had stared at the ceiling through stupid tears

that refused to stop. This town needed a decent police presence but had Sid. Part idiot and part sleaze.

'No. Nothing.'

'Charlotte.'

'I don't know. I can't work out what is real and what people are lying about but I will. And none of that matters. Only that Rosie stays safe.' She'd wiped her eyes.

'Mum is fine. She knows to call if she needs help or advice. Do you remember a conversation we had last year in Rivers End when you were following Bernie and I asked you to help me? To trust me, Charlotte.'

She did. He'd taken her hand as she'd watched Bernie from a distance, the warmth of his touch filling her with a sense of safety and confidence. But when she'd refused his request for information, he'd been hard on her. Told her she had to make a choice before he'd left her standing alone at the gate of the police station with the instruction she wasn't to follow.

'I got the message.'

He chuckled. 'Which was?'

'Don't refuse to help the police officer.'

'Try again.'

'Don't let the police officer catch you following a bad guy?'

'Last chance.'

Charlotte rolled onto her side. 'Okay. You wanted me to know I can trust you with important stuff. And that includes sharing information that is relevant.' She'd known there was more to it, such as him needing to know he could rely on her and that was where she failed so often.

But how do I let anyone rely on me when I don't trust myself?

'I need you to accept, Charlie, there's nothing you can't tell me. Nothing. I wish I lived a whole lot closer though.'

So did Charlotte. If he had Sid's job, Kingfisher Falls would be in better shape.

'I should be able to deal with this.' Tears had trickled down her cheeks and she'd sat up. 'You have your own town to worry about.'

'Rivers End is behaving. Have you heard any more about Octavia?'

'Nothing. I did the interview and Sid included the information I had but was put out to know I had photographs and had looked around a bit. It's made him work harder.'

'You can't trust him.'

Charlotte burst into laughter.

'Better to hear you laugh than cry.' Trev had observed.

She'd stopped laughing. 'Doubt I'd cry over him. I'll write a memo. Don't trust the bad cop, only the good one.'

'Excellent. While you're making notes, add that you will take care of Charlie, stop disrespecting Charlie, and give Charlie a break sometimes. Got it?' The steel in Trev's voice had been new. Not aggressive or demanding. Determined.

It had done something weird to Charlotte's tummy and she'd realised she was nodding. Can't have that. 'Charlie says she'll consider it.'

Now, as customers pushed open the door, Charlotte stood and rolled the stool away. Trev could see through her. It was disconcerting but kind of nice.

chapter
thirteen

After the bookshop closed for the day, Charlotte was torn because she longed to visit the waterfall, but for the first time, she hesitated. Somebody with an agenda she'd yet to discover had taken a photo of her at the lookout. And although Trev assured her it couldn't be Bernie, there was no way to know whether this photographer was dangerous or simply a misguided person trying to send a message.

But the need to de-stress was too strong, and with a bottle of water, sunglasses, hat, wallet and phone, she headed downstairs. Even in shorts and T-shirt, Charlotte still melted in the late afternoon heat. Before leaving the driveway, Charlotte scanned the street in both directions. She never wanted to be caught unawares again. Every nook and cranny made a suspicious potential cover and she'd look in them all if need be.

And do what if you find someone lurking?

Good question. How about asking what they were doing? Taking their photo? Perhaps running off fast. Charlotte grinned at the image of herself snapping a pic, posting it on Facebook, then sprinting away to phone Trevor.

'He isn't your personal fixer-upper.'

She glanced around to make sure nobody heard her. Bad enough someone taking random photos. Last thing she needed was a local resident taking note of the crazy woman from the bookshop. Not great for business.

Partway along the path to the turn-off to the falls, Charlotte stopped. Something was wrong and she didn't know what. The occasional car trundled past. A couple of sweating joggers went in the other direction. Otherwise all was quiet. She was imagining things.

For a moment she considered going home. But her feet ignored her thoughts and started off again toward the path and in a minute, the quiet of the bush surrounded her. Clever feet.

At the information board she stopped long enough to sip water. If she hiked to the top of the falls she could take photos and should one be good enough she'd go to the framing shop and have it enlarged. Along the way, she snapped a couple of pictures of the poor condition of the track. In some places, steps were missing and in others, giant potholes filled the path. It wasn't safe yet was included on the network of walks on the information board.

Charlotte had forgotten how steep the climb was. Sweat trickled between her shoulder blades and her legs ached by the time she reached the top. The roar of the water filled her ears as it rushed to the edge in delight at the long descent ahead. She found a shady spot and sat, drinking more water, and letting her heart rate settle from the climb.

Last year she'd seen Glenys and her nephew down at the lookout. It was the anniversary of Fred's death and she had scattered flowers over the railing to the river below. What a dreadful way to go and how sad for Glenys. No wonder she was thinking about leaving Kingfisher Falls after so much upset.

With a sigh, Charlotte stood and opened her camera on

the phone. She didn't want to spoil what was left of the afternoon with sad thoughts. Focus on the scenery. Once the water reached the pool below, it flowed to the river, wide at the pool end and narrowing as it wound between high banks until it disappeared. She zoomed to the river and followed its progress, taking lots of images as she zigzagged from side to side. Almost out of reach of her camera's capacity was a beach of sorts. How nice to explore the river by boat. She'd ask Rosie if such a thing was possible.

Her water was all but gone and the heat was oppressive. The phone was low on battery, but she wanted just a few more photos. Back at the top of the steps, she directed the camera at the beautiful trees lining the descent. Birds erupted from the canopy. Parrots of some kind disturbed by…somebody on the path heading her way.

'Damnit.' Charlotte breathed the word as a prickle fluttered down her spine. She kept her camera trained on the trees until at last, a gap revealed the walker. A man. But who? He wore a wide-brimmed white hat, a white long-sleeved shirt, and long black pants. He powered along the path, neither holes nor broken steps slowing his progress. Charlotte kept taking photos.

Out in the open, he stopped and looked back, then scanned the area around himself.

'Come on, look up here.' She crouched to be less visible, her finger on the photo button. All she needed was one image. He was tall and thin, or at least appeared to be from her vantage and distance. This wasn't Bernie. She'd recognise that man anywhere.

He's just walking a public track. Stop worrying.

Her senses said otherwise. The way he gazed around differed from a simple walker enjoying the scenery. Who stops in the full sun when there is shade close by? Was he even carrying water? Charlotte's legs were cramping. She had to stand and as she did, his attention moved upward.

'Show me your face.'

His hat rose as his head lifted and…the screen went black as the battery failed.

Charlotte took off away from the steps, back along the river in the opposite direction of the falls. She had no idea where it led, this narrow path along the water, but something compelled her to keep going. Running. Jumping over small rocks and splashing across rivulets joining the main body of the river.

Exhaustion set in and her legs struggled in the heat. If the man was an innocent walker then he'd never know he'd terrified an otherwise strong woman.

––––––

Under the shower, logic returned.

Her legs were still shaky and she leaned against the tiles as the water ran over her until she was cooler and calm. This whole business of Octavia and the stranger sending photographs and calling was getting under her skin.

Taps off, she dried herself and wrapped a towel around her hair.

Was it the same person? The man on the phone called Charlotte a criminal. Told her to leave town before someone took revenge. On the other hand, the photographs in themselves were not threatening. They showed Charlotte she was being watched, but beyond that what was their purpose? There had to be one.

After throwing on shorts and top, she hurried to the kitchen and took the plastic sleeves from the drawer.

This time she placed them on the coffee table and kneeled to see them under lamp light. The first one had the small arrow hand-drawn near the rail at the lookout. Curved, it pointed over the rail and down to the river. Was this a suggestion? Jump off the cliff?

Which would make this part of the original threatening phone call.

Although she'd stared at the second image at length, only now did she search for another clue. Something added after it was printed.

'Gotcha!'

She'd looked at the display of frames as a reference point earlier to work out where the photographer stood. They were to one side of Charlotte in the image and there, circling the only frame that stood alone was the same black pen.

This was getting interesting. And needed closer scrutiny. She ran down to the bookshop. The other day she'd noticed a corkboard in the storeroom. Charlotte would borrow it and let Rosie know. Careful to lock up, she stopped in the garden long enough to fill the base of the pine's pot with water, then headed upstairs. It was almost dark, and she'd had enough of the heat today.

She put the key into the lock and paused. What if there was another note? Would the photographer be watching her every move and knew she'd gone downstairs? Charlotte looked over the side of the small landing, peering into the dusk. Nothing moved. Almost holding her breath, she opened the door and looked down. Nothing but floorboards. This level of stress wasn't healthy. With a firm click, she closed herself in and turned the lock.

———

'One of your better ideas.' The apartment was so quiet she needed to hear something, if only her own voice.

She'd found an empty hook on a wall in the third

bedroom and hung the corkboard. Each of the plastic sleeves was pinned with its respective contents side by side in the middle of the board. She'd written questions and pinned them with arrows pointing to the appropriate parts of the images.

Is something in the river below the lookout?

Did someone throw something over?

Is it a suggestion to jump?

She preferred the first two questions. Being told to leave town was bad enough.

Is somebody being framed?

Is there a picture I need to consider?

Is someone in the frame shop involved?

She'd never been in the shop.

There were more of her own notes scattered around the board. One detailed what she remembered from the threatening phone call. Words about Octavia's death. Sid's comments.

She was downloading the photos to her computer and would add information about the man on the path once she had more. With a sigh, she left the room. Dinner was cooking in the oven and delectable whiffs of garlic, basil, and chilli filled the air. She'd tossed them over some vegetables from her fridge with some olive oil, then started baking them. With that she'd have some crusty bread after adding feta to the vegetables. She was starving.

Over dinner, Charlotte flicked through the photographs on the computer. There were some lovely shots of the river and falls and this gave her the perfect excuse to visit the frame shop. She picked her favourites from these and saved them onto a speed stick to have some prints made up.

The photographs of the man were almost useless. At no time did she capture his face, and as he was so covered up, there was no way to see tattoos or other identifying features.

The broad hat and clothes were better suited for a cooler day. She zoomed in on the shirt. It was in the style of a business shirt and the pants were cut like suit pants. Was he a businessman?

Kingfisher Falls might be off the main track, but it still had businesses who'd have sales reps visit. Even the book shop did. There were two legal firms she knew of, a small medical centre, and the council office.

Jonas?

Charlotte zoomed as close as she could but lost clarity. In build, he was the closest to this man. Lean and tall. And sneaky and involved somehow with Veronica. But why would Jonas send her clues? The phone call she understood. He didn't like Charlotte or Rosie because they stood up for what was right. She scribbled another note to add to the corkboard.

Is Jonas the photographer?

Is Jonas following and threatening me?

Is Jonas involved in Octavia's death?

Or is he helping Veronica do some dirty work?

What if it was all the above? Charlotte scooped up the last piece of carrot, wishing she'd made more dinner. She leaned back in her chair, staring at the screen. It might be him. The man always appeared when something was going on, whether it was trying to blame an innocent man for a crime or supporting Veronica when her boyfriend was arrested. Rosie thought he was corrupt. Him and Terrance.

But Terrance was Kevin's brother, the man seeing Octavia. They all were so close with strong connections through similar interests. If only Charlotte could uncover what the links were. A grab for land was one, but what else?

Her phone rang and she jumped, almost knocking her water over in her haste to get to it. Rosie's name came up.

'Hi, Rosie.'

'Darling, I'm so sorry to be an imposition…' She sounded upset.

'Do you need me to come to the house?'

'Would you mind?'

'Are you alright?' Charlotte was on her feet. 'I'm leaving now.'

'I am. Just a bit shaken. Would you drive up? Someone broke into my gardening shed.'

chapter
fourteen

It might have been faster to run to Rosie's house. Charlotte dropped her car keys going down the steps and had to rummage around in the dirt for them. Then she backed out to the street forgetting to pull the roller door down and lock it, so parked and hurtled back. As desperate as she was to reach Rosie, leaving anything unlocked made her uneasy.

She parked in front of Rosie's place and remembered to turn the lights off and lock the car before racing through the gate.

The door was ajar. Rosie needed to be more vigilant. She pushed it open. 'Rosie? It's Charlotte.' There was no answer. Charlotte blood went cold as she stepped inside. 'Rosie, where are you?' She closed the front door and locked it.

The lights were all on but no Rosie. Charlotte pulled her phone out as she hurried through the house. The sliding door was wide open and the outside lights on.

Be there.

"There" was the garden shed. Its door was wide open and the internal lights blazed. Heart thudding, Charlotte ran inside.

Rosie was at the far end where the filing cabinets stood. Or, laid. For both were on their sides, drawers open, and contents spilled out over the concrete floor. She held a wad of papers to her chest and tears streamed down her cheeks.

Charlotte's heart went out to her but she needed to be certain the perpetrator of this wasn't still here. She looked behind the door, which was the only hiding spot in the shed.

'Rosie? I need to check the house. Are you okay for a minute?'

'Check? Why.'

'In case the person is still here. Did you leave the front door open?'

'Unlocked. But closed.'

As though every bit of breath went from her body, Charlotte froze. Rosie had been here at the same time. Whoever had broken in had the audacity to leave through the house.

If they left...

'Stay. Please. Here, take my phone. Call 000. Or Sid.' Charlotte handed the phone to Rosie, who now looked confused instead of distraught.

'I don't want him here.'

'Please do it. I'll be right back.'

Charlotte didn't wait for an answer but rushed to the door. There, she paused, looking around the well-lit garden. Nothing moved. She didn't want to leave Rosie alone.

'Police please. I wish to report a break in.' Rosie's voice, much calmer than Charlotte expected, reached her.

In seconds, Charlotte was at the sliding door and this time, she tiptoed inside. Most of the house was lit. Room by room, Charlotte peeked behind doors and curtains. With a mental apology for the intrusion, she entered Rosie's bedroom. Its door was wide open. It was a beautiful room with some clever designs and accessories to assist Rosie. Her private bathroom. The walk-in dressing room. No one was there. Charlotte checked everywhere, feeling bad she was in Rosie's personal space without invitation.

The main bathroom was undisturbed, as was the laundry. Only the second bedroom remained. The room Trev took when he visited. The door was closed, and no light shone beneath the door.

About to turn the handle, a thud from inside chilled Charlotte. Adrenaline poured into her and anger took over. Nobody would scare Rosie or damage her precious memories. Anyone behind this door was about to find out what it meant to pay for their crimes.

Another thud. This one louder. Charlotte could hear her own heartbeat.

Bit by bit, she turned the handle. As the door opened a crack, there was no light. Whoever was in here was hiding.

Wait for the police.

For Sid? He wouldn't even open the door without backup. And he'd accuse Charlotte of being responsible.

'Come out now! I have a gun.'

Yup. That'll do it.

Another thud and now, Charlotte knew what was happening. The person was trying to escape through the window.

She flung the door wide and found the light switch.

'Stay where you are!'

Absolute silence.

The bedroom was almost as large as Rosie's with a double bed and long, mirrored wardrobe with sliding doors along one side. One end was open.

So much for bravado. Come on, Charlie.

Every footstep was loud in her ears. There was someone in the wardrobe. Rustling and a bump told her so. She should retreat. Wait by the door. Wait for Sid.

She touched the edge of the door and with a small gulp, she slid it along the runners.

Two furious, hissing felines flew past her and she screamed.

———

'I thought you were being murdered, Charlie. Don't you ever do that again.' Rosie's hand gripped Charlotte's arm so hard it hurt. 'I can't lose you, darling. I just can't.'

'I promise you won't.' Charlotte put her hand over Rosie's. 'I'm sorry I screamed that way. Two furious kitty cats exploding out of a cupboard when you think it's a burglar will do that.'

A moment after Mayhem and Mellow had flown past Charlotte, Rosie appeared at a breakneck speed. But the terror in Rosie's eyes broke her heart. Instead of rushing around to look for bad guys, she'd knelt beside Rosie.

'Why were the cats in the cupboard?'

'Do they normally play in there?' Charlotte had wondered the same thing.

'Sometimes. But you said the mirrored door was closed.'

'Let's check.'

Rosie wheeled straight into the bedroom with Charlotte close behind, unconvinced they were alone. The built-in wardrobe was long, with three sliding doors. The one Charlotte had opened had nothing behind it.

'There. The other end is a little bit open and they'd have slipped in.' Rosie pointed. 'Then they'd have made their way to the other end when they heard you.'

'Can two small cats sound like a human? Thuds and rustling.'

Rosie laughed. 'Two cats can sound like an elephant if so inclined. Here, let's see.' She slid the far end open. 'Two suitcases knocked over. One suit bag pulled off its hanger. Yes, I think it was the work of two scared cats. I have to find them.'

They were on her bed, perched on pillows. Their tails swept side to side and neither were settled or welcoming of Charlotte. But both threw themselves onto Rosie's lap and Mayhem stood on his back legs, a front paw on her shoulder, to stare at her.

'We've got this, my boy. No more hissing and scaring Charlotte, who'd come to help you. Okay?' Rosie ran a trembling hand down his back whilst resting her other on Mellow's, who leaned into her stomach. 'We're safe. You're safe, May-may, and you're safe, Mellycat. And Charlie's safe and she wasn't the person who you hid from and she didn't lock you into Trev's room.' Her voice shook. 'And I'm safe.' A lone teardrop fell onto the hand on Mellow and she left it there rather than disturb the cat.

Charlotte spotted a box of tissues and slowly collected it, not wanting to startle the cats again. She took one out and dabbed the tear from Rosie's hand. 'This is a lovely room.' She had no idea what to do or say now. 'I'm sorry but I came in here before to look for…you know.'

Mayhem settled on Rosie's lap with a glare at Charlotte. Something like a soft purr emanated from Mellow, and Rosie visibly relaxed.

A siren pierced the quiet and all four of them jumped. Rosie gently moved the cats to her bed. 'We'll close the door. They're happy in here.' Charlotte closed it behind them both, leaving the light on.

The siren stopped but through the glass on either side of the front door, blue and red lights flashed.

'We need to call Trevor.' Charlotte said.

'No. Let's see how Sid does things.' Rosie went to the front door and opened it.

'Oi! Stop.'

Please don't be in a singlet.

'Sid, it is Rosie and Charlotte.' Rosie swung the door wide open.

'Come out with your hands up.'

'Oh, for goodness sake.' Charlotte muttered and stepped in front of Rosie, digging deep to find a helpless voice. 'Leading Senior Constable Brown? We need some assistance in here. Please come and protect us.'

Rosie gazed up at Charlotte. 'Are you kidding me?'

'Do you want to put your hands up?' Charlotte asked. 'Look, he's almost running.'

Sure enough, Sid lumbered at a faster than normal pace up the path, hand on his holster. The driver's door of the police car was open and the lights attracted neighbours who began stepping from their doors, or peering through windows.

Sid reached the door and stopped, panting. 'Got a report there'd been a break in. Didn't know at first it was you.' He stared at Charlotte. 'Did you do it?'

The only thing I will break is—

'Sidney Browne! How can you say such a thing when Charlotte just risked her life!'

'Whadya mean?'

'Somebody ransacked my garden shed. I came home from shopping, put everything away, then decided to do a spot of pruning. I found the mess and called Charlie. But the person was still here. They went through my house, terrified my cats, locked them in a room, and left my front door open.' Rosie lifted her chin. 'What are you going to do?'

You are my hero, Rosie.

'You ladies step outside please. Um…I mean, you—' he pointed at Charlotte, 'step out and Rosie, you…'

By the time he'd dug himself further into a hole, Rosie

was outside. 'Don't go into my bedroom. It's the one on the left. My cats are upset.'

Sid smirked. 'I can handle cats.'

'Go on, I dare you. One of them is quite a killing machine if he doesn't like you.' Charlotte followed Rosie outside. 'He doesn't even like me.'

'Huh. Well, that gives him something in common with me, doesn't it?' Sid turned his back and drew his gun.

'The robber isn't here, Sid.' Rosie sighed. 'Please don't shoot the house up.'

Sid put the gun away but kept his hand on the holster as he crept along the hallway.

Rosie shook her head and turned the wheelchair to watch the house. 'And Charlie? Mayhem adores you. He just isn't very forthcoming with his feelings.'

A little spark of warmth touched Charlotte heart. She understood Mayhem. Show too much and get hurt.

'Rosie, we need to call Trevor. I can or you, but we *need* to.'

'Why, darling? He'll drive up in the dark and it is a long and dangerous trip. And apart from my damaged filing cabinets there's been no harm.'

Charlotte bit her bottom lip. Was it only this morning Trevor had laid down the law about sharing important information? If she didn't fill him in on this, he'd eventually find out and then what? She shuddered.

'Darling? You can't be cold?'

'I'm so tired. And coming down from adrenaline. It messes with me a bit.'

'My fault. I should have kept my head and rung the police instead of putting you in danger. It's just that I…I trust you, Charlie. And I didn't know who else to call.'

'Always phone. But what about Lewis? In fact, should we—'

'He's away. So, no phoning him.'

Charlotte opened her mouth to ask where he was, but Rosie was on her way inside.

With a growing sense of unease, Charlotte followed.

chapter
fifteen

Something soft touched Charlotte's face. Eyes closed against the sunlight streaming through a window, she moaned a complaint and burrowed further into bed. A very comfortable bed with silky sheets.

Meow.

Now she was hearing things. Since when was there a cat in the apartment? And when did her sheets ever feel so nice? The pillow—if she turned her face into it—had the slightest hint of a familiar scent. A bit like…Trevor.

Charlotte's eyelids flew open, straight into two feline orbs staring back at her from the side of the bed. Mellow's whiskers twitched and she reached out her paw and tapped Charlotte's face.

'What are you doing here?'

Mellow purred as she poured herself under the sheets and cuddled against Charlotte. 'Oh…you shouldn't.' But unexpected happiness crept into her. She'd never had a cat do such a thing. Never had a cat. It wouldn't hurt to let Mellow stay for a while. Not after the scare both cats had last night.

She remembered. She was in Rosie's spare bedroom. Sid did little last night other than declare it was safe for them to be in the house. He'd stood at the door of the shed and agreed to arrange fingerprint dusting, but he had no idea when. By now, Rosie was quite over him and stayed civil long enough to thank him and see him to the door, before locking it and going straight to get a drink.

After pouring two, she'd handed one to Charlotte, who wasn't about to refuse, and they'd tapped their glasses and then sat in silence for a good ten minutes. The cats were free again, and both gravitated to Rosie.

'I might stay tonight, if you don't object. Happy to sleep on the sofa.' Charlotte said. 'Apart from not wanting to go home to an empty apartment, I'd feel better knowing you have company.'

'I have two wonderful cats.' Rosie stroked Mayhem. He jumped off her lap and stalked to the far side of the room. 'See, he's back to normal.' Exhaustion lined Rosie's face and it wasn't long before she nodded. 'I would like to have you here. But no sleeping on sofas. I always keep the spare room made up with fresh sheets.'

Too tired to debate, Charlotte checked the house thoroughly as Rosie went to her bedroom. They'd agreed to leave several lights on, and Charlotte climbed into bed with the door ajar. In case Rosie needed her.

Mellow's body heat, her trust, her loud purring, tempted Charlotte to slip back to sleep. But Rosie was up. The aroma of coffee was enticing. And work called.

Careful not to disturb Mellow, Charlotte slid from the covers. She stretched and yawned, then threw her clothes back on from yesterday. She'd shower at home and change before work. Mellow peeked out from the sheets and Charlotte dropped a kiss on her head.

———

The friendly locksmith from the other day arrived as Charlotte left the house. He'd been Rosie's first call this morning, expecting to leave a message to ask him when he could change every lock in the place. But he'd answered and when he heard what happened, agreed to meet Rosie after breakfast.

As Charlotte started her car, Rosie's neighbours from next door and across the road headed toward her house. If one of them heard or saw something suspicious the previous evening it would help.

Sid needs to go door to door.

But odds were that he would ignore the whole event. He'd commanded Rosie not to touch anything in the shed until it was dusted. What if that took a week? Rosie was beside herself last night wanting to clean up. To see if anything was stolen and put Graeme's work back in place. To undo the invasion, if only in her mind. Charlotte understood the emotions and distress Rosie felt. She'd helped many patients through similar trauma in their lives.

Back in the apartment, Charlotte checked each room. There was no reason to believe the intruder was connecting the two women, but all the upsets and unrest of the past week made anything possible. She paused in front of the corkboard. Would any of the people on her list do such a thing as knock over two filing cabinets and pull almost everything out? And hide in a house when its occupant was present?

'Mum is fine. She knows to call if she needs help or advice.'

Charlotte grimaced. Trev said that only yesterday. He believed Rosie would always come to him with problems, yet even this morning she'd told Charlotte a firm *no* to calling him. All she could do was see what the day brought and reassess whether to phone anyway.

'Either way one of you will be cross with me.'

Saying it aloud helped. Now she could shelve this problem for the moment and move onto the next one. Or ten.

———

'Please tell me Rosie is alright?' Henry hurried into the bookshop, almost bumping into Charlotte as she rounded the counter with an armful of books. 'Oh, sorry, let me.'

'All good.' Charlotte did a U-turn and put them down again. 'Rosie is fine, just staying at home while the locks are changed and security cameras are installed.' The last bit was a lie, but Charlotte wasn't taking chances on anyone seeing Rosie as a soft target. She had yet to raise the idea with her.

Henry's face relaxed from worry to relief. He wore his apron over his customary work shirt and pants and there was a pencil and notepad in his apron pocket. He glanced down. 'Oh. Hadn't even thought to leave this at work. I just heard what happened and couldn't get here fast enough.'

'I'll tell Rosie you were concerned. But truly, she's fine.'

'Thank goodness. I couldn't believe my ears when Jonas and Terrance discussed it right in front of me.'

'They did?'

Henry glanced around and lowered his voice. 'A few of them meet once a week for a private breakfast up in the small function room. I was pouring coffee and Terrance asked Jonas if he'd heard the latest gossip. Jonas winked. I mean, he actually winked! And said he sure had. Someone else asked what they meant, and Jonas said there'd been a break-in at Rosie's. He made it sound like nothing!'

Private meetings. People knowing things they shouldn't. What else is going on?

'I wonder how they knew about it.' Charlotte repacked the books into her arms. 'Was Sid there?'

'Him? No. But we live in a small town, Charlotte. News travels fast here.'

'But, Henry if Jonas—'

'Oh, look at the time!' Henry checked his watch. 'Please tell dear Rosie I'm only ever a phone call away.' He hurried to the door, where he paused and glanced at Charlotte. 'And you, you take care.'

Charlotte opened her mouth to reply, but he was already striding away. She gazed after him, puzzling over his quick departure. Did he have somewhere to be, or was he unwilling to answer her question? She shook her head and began putting the books on their shelves. Not everyone was a suspect.

Small towns were a different creature to the city she'd grown up in. When she'd first arrived at Rivers End, the close-knit community was a shock. Almost before something happened, the town would know. It was terrifying for someone who was private and wanted to be anonymous. Over time she almost got used to it. The friends she had there would be friends for life. And the way things were shaping up in Kingfisher Falls, she might have more people to add to that special list. Rosie, Lewis, Esther and Doug, Darcy and Abbie.

And Trevor?

Since the first time she'd laid eyes on him, she hadn't known what to think of the undercurrents between them, the unspoken maybe's, the yearning in a corner of her soul when she thought too much about him. What she did know was that keeping even more secrets from Trev was risking the balance they had found. He might just step off the see-saw and let her fall.

chapter
sixteen

Rosie arrived a little after one and shooed Charlotte out. 'I'm fine, darling. Locks are changed and it is time for you to take a break.'

'Have you eaten?'

'I have a sandwich with me if I get hungry. Go. Take as long as you need.'

As long as Charlotte needed would depend on her investigation into the frame shop. She popped upstairs to collect the speed stick with the images from her visit to the falls. This was her way to gain the trust of whoever worked there. She grinned.

Into sleuth mode.

A difficult time it might be, but solving puzzles was good for her, and keeping a sense of humour pushed the shadow of panic away. It wasn't as though she was really a sleuth. Just someone who believed in making things right.

She glanced into the bookshop as she passed. Rosie was with a customer, a smile on her face but the lines of exhaustion clear, even from here. Did Rosie even sleep last night? Shaking the thoughts away, Charlotte crossed the road and headed for the shop. Outside she stopped, nervous. The window was different again. Rather than the frames, there was a display of canvas images of people, pets, and landscapes.

'I wonder…' If this display had been here the other night, would the photographer still have taken the photo? She needed to work out if the clue referenced the frame, or the more cryptic concept of being framed for something.

Charlotte pushed the door open and stepped inside. At first glance the shop was empty, but then a smiling young woman waved from behind a machine. 'Please, I'll be just one minute.'

'No rush.'

The woman looked familiar.

The shop was beautiful, with elegant displays of frames of all types and sizes, as well as images in different formats. Behind locked glass doors on a wall, old cameras were displayed alongside photographs from different eras. Some had price tags, others had '*Not for Sale*' signs.

'Thank you for such patience.' The young woman approached Charlotte. 'You live above the bookshop.'

For a second, suspicion flooded into Charlotte. Where better to print images than a shop like this? She glanced around. Behind the counter was a modern photocopier.

'Rosie talks you up. Tells us you are the perfect person to take over when she retires.'

'Oh. She does?' Charlotte relaxed a little.

'She does. My name is Harpreet. May I help?'

Remembering her cover story, Charlotte dug in her bag. 'You can make prints from the speed stick?'

'Of course.'

'Um, okay, I've downloaded some photos from my phone's camera onto this.' She handed the speed stick to

Harpreet. 'I took a lot of images the other day from the top of the falls and would love to make some into prints. Maybe frame them.'

'Ooh! Lovely idea. Let me take a quick look first.' Harpreet went to another machine at the end of the counter and inserted the speed stick. 'It is so pretty up there but the walk! Oh, my goodness. I thought I'd pass out the first time.'

Charlotte laughed. 'I know the feeling. And the condition of the path makes it much harder than it should be.'

'I hear you. Council need to fix it before anyone else is hurt.'

'So, it is their problem?'

Harpreet glanced up and rolled her eyes. 'Which they want to ignore. Like so much else. These are really, really good.'

'Have we met before?' Charlotte frowned, casting her mind back then remembered. 'Did I see you at India Gate House?'

'Most likely. My parents need help on busy nights, so family is always the first call. Was your meal enjoyable?'

'I still remember it and that was last year. So delicious and now all I want is a repeat, so thanks.' Charlotte smiled as the last trace of suspicion melted away. 'Perhaps it's time I bring Rosie along for a girl's night.'

'You should. Would you like to choose which ones to print? Or all of them? I can do some in a large size and crop them in...like this one. Highlight the lovely little kingfisher you captured here.' She pointed to a zoomed in part of the image. It was a shot of the pool beneath the falls, close to where Charlotte had seen a kingfisher one time. The brightly coloured bird perched on a narrow branch.

'I'm officially stunned, Harpreet. Had no idea I'd got him in this.'

'Which is why you come to me. Our equipment is modern, and I often see things that aren't obvious on first inspection. This would suit a canvas. Shall I show you what I mean?'

Charlotte arranged to return when she noticed how long she'd already been. She left the shop with no more of an idea of why the frame was circled. But it didn't matter. She'd made a new friend.

———

Not worrying about lunch today, Charlotte returned to the bookshop hoping Rosie would take a break to eat her own sandwich. There was a car parked outside the bookshop. A sleek, dark sedan with an outline of lights inside the back window. Police. Detectives.

Rosie was in conversation with a mid-thirties woman wearing tailored pants and jacket. She was lean but Charlotte got an impression of strength from the way she carried herself. Over at the thriller section was a well-dressed man, with cropped grey hair and broad shoulders.

They had to be here because Octavia was murdered. Her instincts were correct.

Please have some answers.

'Here's Charlie now.' Rosie smiled as Charlotte went around the counter and dropped her handbag beneath it.

She straightened with what she hoped was a polite smile. 'Hello.'

'Good afternoon, Dr Dean. I'm Detective Senior Constable Katrina Mayer, and over there, somewhere, is Detective Senior Constable Bryce Davis.'

'Nice to meet you.' Charlotte said.

Bryce Davis wandered across. He was casual with his

walk, but his eyes were intense and she had the impression they didn't miss a thing. He was older than she'd first judged, closer to fifty than forty and something about him got Charlotte's hackles up. Probably played the bad cop to Katrina's good, not that she knew police who behaved the way the television shows portrayed. He stopped beside Katrina, arms crossed, and nodded.

'Dr Dean, I believe you were among the first on the scene after Octavia Morris died?' Katrina had a notebook in her hand. Closed.

'Charlotte. I was.'

'Why?'

'Because Sid asked me to attend.'

'In what capacity? Friend, family?'

Charlotte blinked. 'Didn't Sid include this in his report? He couldn't find a doctor available and the paramedics were a distance away, so he wanted me to check for signs of life.'

Katrina exchanged a glance with Bryce before continuing. 'And did she? Have signs of life?'

'No, sadly Octavia was deceased. But Sid must have included this in his report, and I have a copy of the interview I did with him. With Leading Senior Constable Browne.'

'Is there somewhere more private to continue this?' Bryce glanced around. 'We need some of your time.'

'Now? I'm at work. But afterwards I can meet you.' Charlotte lifted her chin. She wasn't about to be pressured into anything. 'I'm available from six tonight.' In her peripheral vision she saw Rosie about to speak. 'Rosie had a break-in last night at her house so I would like to make sure her home is secure when she returns.'

Bryce stepped forward. 'What was stolen?'

'I'm not certain.' Rosie clasped her hands on her lap. 'Some filing cabinets were upended but Sid told me not to touch anything until fingerprints are taken.'

'This happened last night?' Bryce frowned. 'Nobody has spoken with you since?'

Rosie shook her head. 'I'm sure he's busy investigating what happened to poor Octavia.'

Again, the odd glance between the detectives. Katrina took out a phone. 'Dr Dean, would you meet us at the police station after six please? We'll be there for a while, so if it takes longer than expected to assure yourself Mrs Sibbritt's house is… secure, still drop by.'

'Sure. I'll see you then.' Charlotte waited until the detectives were outside to mutter, 'but why at the nastiest place in town?'

Rosie laughed.

'No really, who'd want to spend any time there. I guess they have no choice. But I'd rather not.' Charlotte sank onto her stool.

'Then you should have talked to them here. You could have used the kitchen or gone upstairs. I wonder who she is calling?'

Katrina stood at the front of the car, her phone to her ears. Bryce leaned against the bonnet, listening with a grin as she laid down the law to the person on the other end of the phone. It was too far to hear, but her finger jabbed the air as she spoke.

'Probably telling Sid to clean the police station before they go there.' Charlotte said.

'Funny girl. And you don't need to accompany me home.'

'Too bad. You're stuck with me until I know you are alone apart from two cats and the doors are locked. And once you're allowed to tidy up the shed, I'll help. And don't bother arguing.'

Bryce got into the passenger side once Katrina hung up. She slid behind the wheel and a moment later, the car U-turned and cruised away.

—————

True to her word, Charlotte accepted no arguments from Rosie and walked home with her. They speculated on who else would be interviewed by the detectives. Rosie had arranged a time first thing in the morning. But who else?

'I imagine Veronica will be bursting to speak with them.' Charlotte strolled on the grass verge with bare feet, shoes dangling from her fingers. 'If she hasn't already done so. I mean, they weren't friendly, so I imagine she already told them we planned to murder Octavia.'

'They were nice to me. So, it might be you about to go to jail.' Rosie grinned as Charlotte's mouth dropped open. 'Veronica has a special dislike of you.'

'This is true. But she might keep her head down with real police officers. Sid is one thing. Easy to manipulate and fire up. But homicide detectives might look a bit more closely at her association with certain recent criminal activities.'

They stopped at a kerb to let a car turn. The evening was cooling and much more pleasant to be out in. Once she'd done this interview, Charlotte intended to have dinner on the balcony.

'What about Glenys? I hope they are gentle with her.' Rosie pushed her wheelchair over the road and Charlotte dashed across with a small yelp because the asphalt was hotter than expected. On the other side, she sank her toes back into grass.

'When I was a kid, I walked barefoot all the time. Must be getting soft.' Charlotte slid her shoes back on and caught up with Rosie, who hadn't waited. 'Are you in a hurry?'

'No, but you have an appointment.'

Charlotte caught up. 'Anyway, I'm sure Glenys will cope. She's a whole lot tougher than I first thought. Often the case with people from bad relationships.'

At the corner, both women stopped in surprise. Sid's patrol car was outside Rosie's house, and another was in the driveway. 'Forensics. Pretty sure that's what it says on the side.'

'Well, well. We'd better open the door for them then.'

chapter
seventeen

Charlotte hurried toward the police station after Rosie told her to go for the third time. She worried leaving Rosie with Sid and two forensics officers. Not for the latter, but because Sid kept sneaking around. She'd caught him in the spare bedroom, the kitchen, and poking around in the garden behind the shed.

'Unless you have a reason to be searching here, you need to stop.' Charlotte glared at him.

He'd shrugged and lumbered back into the shed. The officers were dusting the filing cabinets. Rosie sat near the door, hands clasping each other. Many of the files were still on the floor in a haphazard pile and Sid helped himself to the top one.

'Put it down now.' Rosie's voice was quiet but bore no argument. 'Those are private documents left by my late husband.'

'What if they're evidence?' He peered inside the file.

'Of what?' Charlotte put a hand on Rosie's shoulder and squeezed. 'Please respect Rosie's request. This has been traumatic for her and she doesn't need anyone making the mess worse.'

One officer lifted his head. 'Would prefer you don't touch them, Leading Senior Constable. We'll go through them and let you know if there's anything suspicious.' He glanced at Rosie. 'No offence, ma'am. I meant suspicious about whoever did this.'

'None taken. Thank you.'

Sid tossed it back and the pile slid, earning him a steely gaze from the officer and a glare from Rosie. His attention turned to the shelves. 'Nice lot of tools, Rose. Always admired your garden.'

Rosie's shoulder tensed under Charlotte's fingers. 'Please leave my things alone.'

'Not doing nuthin'. Just looking.' He smirked at them both. 'You know, for a weapon. Something long and heavy. Like a tool handle.'

Charlotte instinctively looked where she'd put that handle back the other day. The one she'd bumped into. She couldn't see it, which was odd. Unless it was stolen.

'Why don't you look around the garden? For buried bodies.' Rosie moved her chair away from the door, closer to the officers. Charlotte stayed put, enjoying the flash of anger on Sid's face for a moment.

'I was. Until missy here told me to stop. Know something, do you?' He pointed at Charlotte and she stepped aside with a wave of her arms.

'If Rosie is happy for you to play in the sand pit, then go right ahead.'

It was all she could do to restrain herself from nervous laughter as he stormed past with a red face. Rosie waited until he was out of sight and suggested, for the third time, that Charlotte needed to get going. And she had.

Almost out of breath as she reached the police station, Charlotte slowed down and sucked in air. She was here to help with a murder investigation. Not worry about Sid's appalling behaviour. The detectives' car was parked on the road and the front door of the station was propped open.

Can't stand the smell?

With a shake of her head, Charlotte stepped inside. Because the door was open, and her shoes were rubber soled, she made next to no sound. Katrina and Bryce were talking on the other side of the counter. She stopped, not wanting to interrupt. And curious.

'What kind of an idiot decision leaves a clown like that in charge of a community like this?' Katrina sounded agitated. Charlotte liked her. There was a quiet strength in the detective mixed with compassion. And she'd been sweet to Rosie, which was a big thumbs up.

Bryce was different. He had a side Charlotte wouldn't want to see. Hard. But not hard like Trev who was always tempered with fairness. No, the man carried himself like a fighter. He answered Katrina. 'He got a badge somehow. Staying out of sight in a backwater town makes sense.'

'We'll see.'

Much as Charlotte wanted to continue eavesdropping, she had no interest in being caught doing so, and tapped on the outside door. 'Hello?'

'Come in, Dr Dean.' Bryce opened the second door. 'Grab a seat, if you dare. We did wipe them down.'

'And it smells a little less horrible in here with the door open.' Charlotte perched on a seat opposite Katrina, at the same desk Sid used last visit. Bryce leaned against the other desk, arms crossed, eyes on Charlotte. She wasn't about to let him get inside her head.

Stare away.

Katrina tapped on a keyboard, watching the monitor. 'Thanks for coming along. Was Mrs Sibbritt's house as expected?'

'Better. Sid was there with forensic officers.'

'You call Leading Senior Constable Browne by his first name. Are you friends?'

Charlotte's lips twitched as she fought to control an impulse to laugh aloud. 'Um, no. And he reminds me of it every time I call him Sid.'

'So, you do it to annoy him.'

If she wasn't mistaken, the expression in Bryce's eyes was amusement, or even respect.

'Didn't start out that way, but it keeps things from getting too…difficult. A bit of humour helps sometimes.'

Katrina stopped tapping, turning her attention on Charlotte. 'I read the report Leading Senior Constable Browne lodged. When we spoke at the bookshop, you seemed surprised by my questions. Specifically, why you attended the scene and in what capacity. Would you talk us through the events of the day Octavia Morris died?'

Keeping to the main points, Charlotte repeated much of her report to Sid, emphasising his appearance at the bookshop, his failure to treat the house like a potential crime scene, and reluctance to follow up with taking her report.

'I expected the interview to be the next day at the latest.' She finished.

Katrina's eyes had never left Charlotte's face but now she stared at Bryce for a few seconds. What was going on? Had they worked out Sid was corrupt, or lazy at the very least? Or didn't they believe her?

'Octavia was murdered. Or at least helped to her death.' Charlotte said.

Both detectives turned to her and she continued. 'The mark on the back of her skull was blunt force trauma that caused her to fall forward. Whether the blow was enough to kill her only a medical examiner would know, but at the very least, the person who hit her is responsible, in my opinion, for Octavia dying.'

'And who are your suspects?' Bryce uncrossed his arms for the first time. 'You must have some thoughts on it.'

'I know who it isn't. Not Rosie, nor I, despite Sid's accusations. Probably not Glenys.'

'Why not?' This was Katrina, who leaned on her elbows, then lifted them with a grimace and grabbed a wet wipe from a box on the desk. 'Need to fumigate the place. Go on.'

'Glenys most likely hadn't had time. She walked there from the bookshop and I can estimate the time she left because Rosie returned from lunch at one thirty, and she'd noticed Glenys leave the shop as she approached.'

'And where had Mrs Sibbritt been?'

'Lunch with a friend. I don't know the time of death, but the walk to the house would take Glenys a good thirty to forty minutes. It doesn't seem likely.'

'Quite the sleuth.' Bryce grinned. But not a friendly grin, more one irritated with amateurs getting involved where they weren't welcome.

Charlotte bit her lip and stared back at him. She didn't want to put homicide detectives offside, but her frustration at the games was rising. 'Have you checked Octavia's house?' Her voice was calm. 'Had a peek inside the dishwasher?'

'For lipstick-stained teacups? Dr Dean, what we have or haven't done isn't up for discussion. What we want from you is a copy of the report you claim you have a signed copy of and copies of all the photographs you took in the house.' Bryce stood and there it was, the whole tough guy stance.

'Sure.' Charlotte opened her handbag. 'I've brought a copy of the report I claim to have, and all the images on a speed stick.' She rustled around and found both items, putting them on the desk in front of Katrina and addressing her. 'As you'll see, I've signed this and so has Leading Senior Constable Browne. He advised me this would be provided to the appropriate parties which I'm…deducing…' she snuck a glance at Bryce, 'are you two. Detectives.'

The corner of Bryce's mouth lifted for an instant, then he looked over Katrina's shoulder as she read the paper.

'Would you take a copy, Bryce?' Katrina handed it to him, and he looked around until spotting an ancient copier in a corner. 'This differs from the report the Leading Senior Constable provided.'

'Different?'

'A bit left out.'

'So where is the original?'

Katrina shrugged and gestured to the mess that was the desk.

At the copier, Bryce swore and whacked the side with the flat of his hand.

'Are you lot done?' Sid stomped in, straight past the desk and to the copier. 'Here. I'll do it. No spare money laying around to replace it.'

'Be my guest. Two copies, mate.' Bryce strolled back to his spot leaning against the other desk. His face was impassive but again, Charlotte had the impression those eyes missed nothing, and they stayed on Sid as he made copies.

Something interesting was going on. More than an investigation into Octavia's death. These detectives had Sid in their sights for some reason and Charlotte was taking in every clue and word to unwrap later.

chapter
eighteen

"Later" was long after Charlotte left the police station. Evening had closed in with the last of the light fading as she stopped at the supermarket for a frozen dinner.

Back home she turned the oven on before showering. The smell from the police station clung to her skin. Old cigarette smoke, stale air, and then there was the stickiness from the chair. Under warm water, she let her mind drift to other places.

Dressed again, hair wrapped in a towel, she put the tray of something resembling pasta into the oven. The last bit of sourdough would go in the oven at the last moment to disguise any staleness.

As she waited to eat, Charlotte pushed the sliding door wide open and stepped onto the balcony. The night air was refreshing. She set the small table, then retreated to the third bedroom. There was enough time to add some thoughts to her corkboard. Pen and notepad in hand, she stared at the images and words already forming on her little brainstorming board.

Should she have expressed her thoughts about Jonas to the detectives? And said what? That he behaved badly toward good people? That he fitted the body type of a man who may be watching her. Then she'd have to explain herself and they'd want to see the printouts.

And if she was wrong? Another innocent person would be harmed by her mistakes.

Charlotte wrote on her notepad. Sid. In big letters. This she tore off and pinned up. On another page she formed questions.

Why are the detectives interested in Sid?

Is Sid's copier the one used to copy the images?

What is Sid's interest in Rosie's place?

After pinning this page up, she looked for a connection, but today had exhausted her and nothing added up. The bell on the oven rang. Time to throw the bread in. She closed the door on the problems.

It wasn't the oven calling her. She stared at her phone on the counter as it rang. The caller ID was anonymous. Charlotte considered letting it go to voicemail and if it was important, and genuine, the caller would leave a message? Or was it the same person who'd threatened her?

She grabbed the phone and answered. 'Charlotte Dean.'

A long pause.

She knew. 'Look, I'm not into silly games so tell me what you want.'

'You were warned.' The same voice. Impossible to recognise past the muffling.

Charlotte listened, hoping for some background noise, some pattern of speech to identify the caller.

'Why are you still here, Doctor?'

'Who is this?'

'You're mixing with the wrong people. Detectives who will uncover your secrets. Time to leave town.'

'You said that last time.' Charlotte said. 'I'm not interested in talking to you—'

'Then listen. I know what you did to your patient. Leave town tonight or I'll tell the detectives. And the whole town, including your precious Rose.'

The line went dead.

Was there a way to track this call? Charlotte played with her phone for a moment until realising it was beyond her knowledge. The oven timer went off and she slid the bread next to the rather sad looking tray of pasta.

After writing what she remembered about the phone call, Charlotte poured a glass of wine. Call Trev? Or contact the detectives. Katrina had passed her a business card before she left. They might know how to find the caller. And she had a clue now. Few people called Rosie by her real name. Rose. And it was always used as a reminder they weren't friends or fans of the bookshop and its owner. Rosie didn't care, but it irked Charlotte.

Being nice takes no longer than being mean.

She frowned as she wrote the names of everyone she'd heard use Rose instead of Rosie.

Sid

Jonas

Veronica

Octavia

Marguerite

Was there anyone else? She'd pay better attention from now on. Listen to how people formed their sentences, used an expression, turned a phrase. She crossed off Octavia. And unless the women on the list could change their voices, it wasn't them. Which left the two she'd suspected all along of having a hand in this whole mess.

'So, is it you, Sid? Lazy, wilfully destructive, insulting, sleazy. Or Councillor Jonas Carmichael. Sneaky, cruel, corrupt. Hm. Such a choice.'

She checked the oven and decided near enough was good

enough. The bread was warm at least and she slathered it with butter. She didn't bother putting the meal on a plate, just adding the bread on top of the pasta and carrying it, and her glass of wine, to the balcony.

The sky was almost dark, and Charlotte checked her watch. After eight already. She nibbled on the bread and sipped wine before trying the pasta. It wasn't horrible, but this might be the last frozen meal she bought. There was nothing to stop her making up some extra meals and freezing them for nights like this.

'I know what you did to your patient.' Charlotte tapped her fingers on the table. The caller might be bluffing, hoping there was some history he could scare her with. If he knew the truth, had found the newspaper stories and social media reporting, then why not go ahead and tell the world? What point was there in threatening her?

Sid and Jonas both had reasons to want Charlotte gone. From their first meeting on the deserted street outside Esther's broken window in the dead of night last year, Sid suspected Charlotte of being something more than she appeared. He'd promised more than once to uncover her past and expose her secrets.

As a member of the local council, Jonas had his own agenda. Charlotte presumed he was interested in securing land for development and always believed he was behind the Christmas tree thefts last year, but how to prove it? Not even the perpetrators of the crimes knew who'd paid them, according to them anyway. Jonas tried to stir up hatred against the Woodland family over the thefts and was a bit too close to Veronica with her shady connections.

Laughter from the street broke the silence. A woman, then a man's deeper chuckle. Charlotte pushed her dinner away and took her wine glass to the railing. Below, a young couple stopped under a streetlight, hand in hand. They kissed. Not wanting to intrude on their moment, Charlotte stepped away.

There was a tug in her heart. A small tinge of longing for something not likely to be hers.

This caller might threaten to expose her mistake with a past patient, but her real secrets lay much deeper and weren't to be found on social media or in newspapers. They resided in her DNA and only time would reveal the truth. Until she knew what her future held, how could she invite another person into her life? She'd never do that. Not like her mother did.

'Go ahead, Sid, or Jonas. Do your best. Tell the world.'

Kingfisher Falls was her home. Her first real home of her choosing. A place of welcome and friendship and even happiness. And for however long it lasted, Charlotte wasn't about to be scared off or run out by anyone.

chapter
nineteen

Although she'd not expected to sleep, Charlotte did. Dreams of the bushland, the falls, and the tiny kingfisher followed her after waking at dawn. Her sense of being part of the environment grew with each visit to the lookout or the pool. And now she had a new place to explore, behind the bookshop's garden.

With a coffee in hand, she wandered around the garden as early sunlight peeked over the fence. The pine tree was in good health now after its shaky start, and she'd need to speak to Darcy before long to find out where to plant it.

'I'll miss you, little tree.' She touched the top which was now almost as tall as she was. 'But you will go live in the forest on the farm somewhere, or around one of the local sportsgrounds.'

Talking to a tree wasn't the least bit strange. As long as she didn't hear it answer, she was just fine.

Charlotte grinned and headed to the back fence. She perched her empty coffee cup on the corner of a fence post and stood back. If she did as Rosie suggested and trimmed some vines, she'd reveal the gate. She'd looked at a map on her phone of the town, surprised how much parkland and how many walking trails there were. Behind this fence though, no marked trails, just thick bushland.

She ducked into the garage to locate secateurs. The wheelbarrow was to one side of her car where she'd left it the other night. After work she might sort through it and find places for the mix of tools Rosie loaned her. Charlotte checked for the axe handle, wondering if she'd picked it up, but it wasn't there. She should have looked for it at Rosie's, but between Sid's bad behaviour and Rosie insisting she get to her police interview, she'd forgotten.

Did someone break into Rosie's shed just to turn over old cabinets and steal the handle from a tool? Charlotte snipped tendrils of the vine. Assuming the handle was missing, why? It once belonged to an axe, so Rosie said. Yet her house lacked a fireplace. And such a heavy handle would suit chopping big blocks of wood. Not that Charlotte was an axe expert—an axepert. She smiled at the made up word. But then she frowned.

Octavia had a fireplace.

The image of the woman face-down, forehead against the marble base, flashed into Charlotte's mind before she could stop it. The mark across her skull. The rug. Gracious bookcases. Funny what one remembers.

If she didn't know Rosie better, she'd have to add her to the suspects. Recent public disagreements with Octavia, knowledge of the other woman's house, access to a tool that might fit the mark. Good thing Rosie had an iron-clad alibi.

Something didn't sit right with Charlotte. What was she overlooking?

'Oh, whoops.' What she was overlooking was paying attention to where she cut, and now a whole branch was on the ground. She straightened it out. A ripe passionfruit. She picked it.

She finished clearing the gate with more care, moving a

couple of longer branches so they curved over the other panel, and taking off only as much as needed.

There was no lock on the gate. Charlotte took out her phone and made a note to buy one. The latch was long and rusty and took a few minutes wiggling before succumbing to Charlotte's wishes and sliding across. With a loud creak, the gate opened enough for her to squeeze through.

Charlotte stood on a broad dirt track. Rutted and worn, it led in both directions. Over it was bushland. Beautiful gum trees towered over scattered flowering shrubs. She crossed the track and stood on the edge of the bushland, peering in.

It was quiet in an eerie way. No birdsong or rustling of leaves as usually accompanied her around the falls. The thick canopy of trees darkened the ground. Perhaps with more sunlight it would be more inviting, but at this moment, nothing would make Charlotte step foot inside.

With a shiver, she turned around.

From here she had a unique view of the apartment. In the back garden she'd never thought to look up, knowing there'd only be brick walls the whole way apart from a high window in the bathroom which was also a laundry. The kitchen had no windows, being more open plan and getting natural light from the living room windows and sliding door to the balcony. The third bedroom had a window on one side, with a wardrobe on the back wall.

Except, there *was* a window on the back. The sun glinted on it and Charlotte walked a few steps further along the track to better see. Close to the corner was a large window, and she realised the back of the wardrobe was against it. How strange. The room was large enough for the wardrobe to be along a wall, yet someone blocked the view with it. Not for long. If she could move the wardrobe and gain such a pretty outlook, she might change rooms.

She glanced over her shoulder as a chill ran the length of

her spine. What on earth was spooking her? She loved forests and wild places and her own company. Was there a monster lurking in the depths of the bush? Of course not. But she hurried to her side of the fence and closed the gate with force. Grabbing a shovel, she forced it against the gate and pushed the latch across. Just until she got a lock.

———

A little earlier than usual Charlotte opened the front door of the bookshop and went outside to sweep the pavement. This was her routine. Make sure the shop was tidy and vacuum the rug. Put the float in for the day's trade. Sweep outside. Rosie appreciated the effort she made, and Charlotte found satisfaction in the simple act of preparing the shop.

Sid drove past, windows down and a scowl not improving his looks. Charlotte turned her back, not willing to make eye contact today when she was likely to ask him if he was responsible for the anonymous phone calls. Not much point doing so without evidence and some back up in the shape of a witness. One with a badge. She sighed and took the broom inside. In the kitchen she filled the kettle, wishing she'd run across to the café first.

Cup in hand, she left the kitchen and almost walked into Kevin Murdoch. She avoided spilling coffee over them both and stepped back. 'I'm so sorry, I didn't hear the door.'

'It didn't make a sound.'

Something else to fix.

'How may I help today, Mr Murdoch?' Charlotte's heart-beat was up a notch. She'd never liked the man after the way he'd treated the Woodland family. He was close enough to reek of cigarette smoke. 'Let me put my coffee down and I can—'

'No. I'm not buying anything.' He continued to block her

way, his hands clutching a sunhat in front of his stomach. 'I came to thank you.'

'Thank me?'

'For checking on…for seeing if…Octavia.' Kevin bowed his head and his shoulders slumped. 'You treated her with respect.'

'I am sorry for your loss, Mr Murdoch.'

'Kevin. Mr Murdoch is my brother Terrance. He's the one doing the hard yards in council.'

Not sure how to respond, Charlotte nodded. The minute Kevin moved enough, she slipped past. 'I really need to put this down. Thin china gets hot fast.' She made it to the other side of the counter and put the cup on a coaster.

Kevin followed. 'They won't release her body. She needs a funeral and we can't arrange it yet. The detectives say it might be another few days. Unfair.'

'I'm sure the medical examiner will do their best.'

'Well, you'd say that, wouldn't you? Being one of them.' He stared at her. His eyes were pale blue ringed with blood-shot white. Lack of sleep? Too much to drink and smoke?

'It is always upsetting for loved ones, not knowing when they can say their proper farewell.' Keep it nice. Stay calm. A customer will come in soon. 'Will the funeral be in town?'

'Why do you care? You and Rose made her life hell the past few weeks. She lost friends and felt like she was singled out at the Christmas Eve party for standing up for what was right. Then hounding her for books she told you she did not want. You might have done the right thing by going to her house that day, but it can never make up for how much you and your employer hurt her.'

Blood pounded in Charlotte's ears. Her fingers gripped the edge of the counter. He'd called Rosie "Rose". He was here to berate her. Or worse. And she was trapped behind the counter if he blocked the side. He was a big man, not heavy, but tall and imposing and she didn't know if she could stop him harming her if that was his intent.

'Did you phone me last night, Kevin?' Charlotte lifted her chin and returned his stare. She released the counter and backed until touching the long back bench. Somewhere were scissors. Her hands were behind her back, feeling. 'I'd like to know, please.'

He blinked. 'Phone you? Here at the shop?'

'You tell me.'

'I didn't phone here and most certainly not your private number. I don't have it and why would I want to?'

Her fingers found the scissors and wrapped around them. The steel blade gave her a small comfort.

Kevin leaned forward, both hands on the top of the counter, the hat dangling from one. 'Listen. I don't care for you, or Rose. But I don't harass folk so if someone is bothering you with anonymous phone calls, take it up with Sid. He's our law enforcement here. You'd be a whole lot better off leaving town because you've done nothing but cause trouble and are not welcome. And that's what I came to tell you.' He shoved the hat over his awful combed-over balding head and stormed out.

———

'It is time to get security cameras.' Rosie shook her head. 'We need to feel safe here and have proof of any more attempts to harass or intimidate.'

'Apparently, we are the ones doing the harassment.'

'And I'm tiring of how events are twisted by certain parties to make themselves look good.'

'Anyway, I'm pleased you want security cameras because I have two different companies coming this afternoon to do quotes.' Charlotte was at the window keeping an eye on the people in the street. Nothing felt safe. 'Trevor suggested it the other day and I have to agree. Plus, you can get them to put some at your house and—'

'Hold on a minute, darling.' Rosie wheeled to Charlotte and took her hand. 'Oh, you're trembling. Do you want to sit?'

'I'm angry. How dare that man speak to me like that.'

'He had no right. When did you speak to Trev?'

'The other day. The other morning.' Charlotte sighed and turned to Rosie. 'Truth?'

'Always.'

'I got a silly idea in my head that Bernie was in town. You know, the ex-patient I told you about from Rivers End?'

Rosie gasped. 'Not the one who tied you up in that cave?'

'Yup. But he isn't here. Trevor checked and although… well, he isn't here and doesn't know where I am as far as the police know.'

'But why did you think he was? Come on, let's sit.' Rosie returned to the counter and Charlotte followed, relieved to perch on the stool and sip some water before continuing.

'Bernie used to drink a bottle of water, laced with vodka, then crush it underfoot and abandon it. All part of an issue with his mother, long story. I saw a crushed bottle and it all flooded back.'

'And you called my son.' Rosie's smile went all the way to her eyes.

'Rosie. Stop that now.'

'But it's so good you called him.'

'And I should call him right this minute to tell him about the break-in at your house. He will blame me once he finds out.'

'Why? I'm the one who should call and I'm busy.' Rosie glanced around until she spotted a book, which she picked up and flicked through. 'Yes. I have to read this to recommend to buyers.'

'Another reason to have cameras. Keep you from fibbing.' Charlotte had to smile. 'On another subject, did you know the back bedroom of the apartment has a big window overlooking the bushland?'

'Of course. Have you never been in there?'

'Funny. There's a wardrobe across the back wall and it covers the window. I cleared the gate this morning and was on the other side of the track. First time I knew.'

Rosie frowned. 'I've not been in the apartment since my accident. Stairs are impossible. We rented it out for a while, not needing the housing ourselves. Graeme passed away when we still had tenants and I hired someone to check the place and clean it once the last renters vacated. How strange.'

'Do you mind if I move it then? I'd love to have the window back.'

'The apartment is yours to do what you want with. But get someone to help.'

'I will.'

'Trev would be a good person.'

'Rosie.'

'He is strong.'

'Rosie!'

'Have you noticed his muscles? He works out. Runs. Where are you going?'

Charlotte was about to burst into laughter as she headed for the front door. 'Getting real coffee for us both. Why don't you phone your son while I do?'

chapter
twenty

Rosie did no such thing, claiming to have had customers and then to have forgotten. Charlotte gave up, deciding she'd phone him herself and hope he'd understand how stubborn his mother was.

Between customers, Rosie outlined her interview with Katrina and Bryce. 'I like them, but now I'm wondering if they suspect me.'

'Of…'

'Murder, of course.'

Charlotte almost spat out the mouthful of coffee she'd just taken.

'No more deaths, Charlie. Try not to choke.'

'Thanks. Did they say you're a suspect?'

'Well, no, but they ran through a list of motives I might have. And mentioned they'd like to search my property for a potential murder weapon.'

Charlotte had no words. Not one. She stared at Rosie, realising her mouth was open, and closed it.

'I'd told them to go ahead. I still haven't cleaned up the mess in the shed, so warned them not to make it worse. They're meeting me there at three, if you are fine to be on your own. But if not, I'll let them know. In fact, we should tell them about Kevin.'

'Rosie, calm down. If you are okay to have them there alone with you, then of course, go. Or you could see if Lewis might come with you?'

As soon as she heard the name, Rosie's expression changed. She glanced away. 'No. He'll be busy.'

What was going on there? They'd had lunch a lot recently, so why would Rosie hesitate to ask him?

'Doug?'

'I think I can manage two nice detectives on my own. And then they'll see there are no potential weapons and I'll be in the clear.' Rosie's smile was small and fake.

'What aren't you telling me?'

'Not a thing. Oh, that's Darcy.'

'Don't change—'

But Rosie was on the move and a glance outside got Charlotte back on her feet. Abbie was in the passenger seat, her face red and contorted. Darcy opened the back of the hatch and grabbed a small bag as Lachie leapt out of the back seat. Charlotte caught up with Rosie at the passenger door, where she had her hand through to grip Abbie's.

'You don't worry about a thing except bringing this baby into the world. We'll have Lachie as long as you need, dear.'

Abbie nodded, perspiration streaking her face.

Lachie inserted himself between Rosie and the car and leaned in the window to kiss Abbie's cheek. 'Don't worry, Mum. I've got my key and will make sure the farm is okay.'

'Love you, baby.'

'I'm not the baby anymore.' He wiggled out again and Darcy hugged him, looking at Charlotte over his head.

'Got to get her to hospital and our friends were delayed for their stay with us. Are you still okay to watch Lachie?'

'Of course. He can stay overnight if you need him to. You look after Abbie.'

'Be a good boy. I'll phone you later, okay?'

'You need to hurry, Dad. See ya later!' Lachie took the bag from Darcy and stepped back.

Rosie released Abbie and pushed her chair back a bit. 'All the best, darling. You'll be fine.'

Darcy jumped back into the driver's side and glanced over. 'Thanks Rosie. And Charlotte. I'll phone.'

Lachie stared after the car and as it disappeared, he put down the bag and wrapped his arms around himself. Charlotte squatted at his side. 'My alien tree will be happy to see you.'

With an exaggerated sigh, he picked up the bag and glanced at Charlotte. 'Trees can do many things but seeing is not one of them.'

'Which proves it is half alien.'

'You are not correct, Charlotte.'

'But it is lunchtime. Coming inside?'

'I guess.'

Rosie was at the door. 'Lachie, I'm in need of a professional designer for the children's reading and quiet play area. Seeing as you are much more grown up than the children who'll use it, would you care to offer some ideas?'

Lachie turned with a grin. 'A professional, you say. Lead the way.'

———

Rosie insisted on going out to buy them all lunch, returning with a huge parcel of fish and chips which were hot and salty. They took turns eating in the kitchen, with Lachie perched on a stool nibbling away through both Charlotte and Rosie's lunch breaks. In between bites, he talked about being excited to go back to school soon. And how much he'd read of the pile of books he got at Christmas thanks to the bookshop's giving box initiative.

'I like reading. I might buy a bookshop when I grow up.'

Charlotte blew on a chip and watched steam rise. 'Sounds like a good plan.' She bit into the crisp outer with a little surge of pleasure. Absolute comfort food.

'Mrs Sibbritt loves her job. And you love working here, don't you?' He tilted his head to one side, watching Charlotte as she chewed. 'But you're really a doctor.'

Charlotte sipped some water before answering. 'First question. Yes, I love working here and Rosie does as well. Second? I am a doctor, but not practising.'

His eyes widened. 'But you should practise. Mum says practice makes perfect. How can you be a good doctor if you don't?'

How indeed.

She smiled. 'So, the type of practising I meant is being a doctor as a job. Funny English language, huh? And my special training is as a psychiatrist.'

'Psy-ki-trist.'

'Si-ki-a-trist. Good attempt.'

Lachie repeated the word a few times until he had it memorised, then reached for the last chip. 'What is it?'

'Psychiatrists treat the brain, and the heart, and feelings. Sometimes I help people who have had an upsetting experience and other times, I help people with diseases that affect the brain.'

'Like depressed?'

Charlotte nodded. 'Depression. Yes.'

'Dad says my grandpa was depressed and shoulda got some help. Could you have fixed him?' Lachie gazed steadily at Charlotte.

How could she answer this? Darcy's father passed away a

year ago after trying to hold together a failing business and losing his wife through divorce. He'd allowed the Christmas Tree Farm to run down and left his son with unpaid rates and a barely habitable house. She didn't know the details of his death, assuming it was from natural causes. How much did Lachie know?

'Some things can be fixed but not everything.'

'You fixed the alien tree.' There was a wobble in his voice.

'Nope. It just needed a bit of water and sunlight. And I talk to it all the time.'

Lachie digested this as Charlotte rolled the lunch paper into a ball. Had Lachie ever spent time with his grandfather? All she knew was Darcy and Abbie had previously lived on the other side of Melbourne. She wiped down the lunch counter.

'Rosie has to go out for a bit, so shall we find out what she'd like some help with first?'

'Is it hard to become a psychiatrist doctor, Charlotte?' He hadn't moved from his stool.

'You need good results from school to get you a place at university, then a lot of years studying and working with other specialists. Yes, it is hard. But if you love what you're learning, the time flies.'

He smiled. 'I might be a psychiatrist.' He hopped off the stool and left the kitchen.

'What about owning a bookshop?' Charlotte followed.

'That will be my hobby.'

It was all Charlotte could do not to laugh. He was such a smart and caring child and wise beyond his years. Whatever he decided to do, it would be to the benefit of those around him.

———

Rosie left just before three. There was little chance she'd be back today, so deputised Lachie to help Charlotte. She left him a list of jobs and hid a gift card inside an envelope. If he ticked off each job, then it was his.

Charlotte was busy with customers for most of the afternoon, including taking an order for a new childcare centre opening soon in one of the nearby towns. The buyer spent half an hour in the shop, browsing, talking to Charlotte, and placing the order. As she left, she nodded toward Lachie who was setting up the play area.

'How lovely you can bring your son here. Helps them learn a good work ethic.'

'Oh. Um, he's my friends' son, but I agree.'

After the woman left, Charlotte watched Lachie for a moment. If there was a hole in her heart, she wasn't about to acknowledge it had anything to do with him.

chapter
twenty-one

'Do you know when Dad will call?' Lachie wandered out of the kitchen, where he'd gone for a glass of water. 'I've done all of Mrs Sibbritt's jobs and… kinda wondering if Mum's okay.'

'I'm sure she is. Babies just take their own sweet time to join us. I'll tell you what. Once we close the shop, we'll go upstairs and send your dad a text message. He might have his phone off though, being in the hospital. But we can send best wishes. Okay?'

'Cool. Are we closing up now?'

'Very soon. And yes, I see you've ticked everything, and I thank you for being so helpful today.' Charlotte handed Rosie's envelope to Lachie. 'There's something inside for you.'

When Lachie found the gift card, his mouth opened in a silent 'wow'. He glanced at Charlotte and she nodded. 'You can spend that on anything in the bookshop. And you have two years until it expires.'

'Two years! Two minutes is enough. Thank you.' He threw his arms around Charlotte's waist for a second or two, then dashed off to the back of the shop.

Charlotte closed the front door and counted the cash, letting Lachie take longer than his two minutes to decide between books. She expected him to choose one of the adventure series he favoured, but it was a picture book he placed on the counter.

'I'd like to have this, please.'

Swallowing to push down the lump in her throat, Charlotte scanned the book and gift card. This was a baby's first story book. One for the family to read at bedtime with the new addition and to treasure for years. Two loving parents reading to their little one.

'Would you like it gift wrapped?'

'You can do that?'

'Here, come and help.'

Lachie ended up doing most of the wrapping and finished with a yellow bow Charlotte dug out from a drawer. 'Do you think Mum and Dad will like this?'

'I do. They'll love it. Hang on, that's my phone ringing.' It was Darcy's number. 'It's your dad. Hi Darcy.'

'Just looked at the time. Is everything still okay to keep Lachie for a bit?'

'Of course. How's Abbie?'

'She's so tough. I cannot believe how strong that woman is.' Admiration filled his voice. 'Still a few hours, they reckon.'

'In that case, Lachie and I might get some dinner soon and he can stay as long as you need. Would you like a quick hello?'

'Love it. And, well, thanks so much.'

'You can leave Lachie with me anytime.' She passed the phone over.

By the time she'd put the money in the safe and checked the front door was locked, Lachie was hanging up. 'What are we having for dinner?'

Oh.

There was nothing for herself, let alone a hungry growing child.

'Would you like to find all the light switches and turn them off? Then we'll make some plans. What kind of food do you like?'

Lachie ran off to look for light switches but threw a look at Charlotte. 'Everything.'

'So, vegetables?'

'Yum.'

'Brussel sprouts?'

'Vegetable. So it is yum.'

He zoomed past.

'Seafood?'

'We used to eat prawns on the beach at our old house.'

Of course, you did. What awesome parents you have. What don't kids like?

'Curry?'

Once every light, apart from the one out the front which Charlotte turned back on, were off, Lachie collected his book. 'Mum makes curry. Delish.'

'I'm getting hungry.'

————

India Gate House occupied a corner opposite the town's other great restaurant, Italia. Charlotte had been to India Gate House once, and as she and Lachie waited for mains, she wondered why it had been so long since her last visit.

The tempting aroma of spices and rich curries wafted from the kitchen to the outside table where Lachie had decided they should sit. He'd jumped at the chance to eat there when Charlotte suggested it and impressed her with his understanding of ordering and ingredients.

'Told you. Mum cooks curries and lots of stuff. Hey, I hope she won't stop doing that when my sister arrives.'

'Sister?'

'Think so.'

'I'm sure with you and your dad around to help, she'll be cooking awesome meals again in no time. Does your dad cook?'

Lachie leaned on the table with a nod. 'He can make omelettes. And pancakes. And sausages,' he said. 'But not like Mum.'

Charlotte grinned. Lachie's visit today reduced the stress of recent events with his innocent take on everything he came across. After leaving the bookshop they'd gone to the apartment and she'd let him wander around, asking only that he didn't go into the third bedroom. She made sure the second bedroom was ready for him to sleep in if he needed to stay before they walked to the mall.

'We might need to go to the supermarket on the way home, if you don't mind.' She said. There was nothing for breakfast in the fridge, no juice or milk, or even bread to make into toast for him. 'What do you like for breakfast?'

'Hm.' He rubbed his chin. 'I like scrambled eggs on toast best. But waffles are good. Oh, there's ours. I'm hungry. Are you?'

'Starving.'

Harpreet smiled as she approached with a tray. 'Hello again. But this does not look like Rosie?' She placed the tray on an empty table and transferred bowl after bowl of deliciousness.

'This is Lachie Woodland. He's my dinner guest tonight. Lachie, this is Harpreet, who also owns Kingfisher Falls Frames and Photos.'

They said hello to each other as Harpreet added plates and cutlery.

'Perhaps, Charlotte, we can catch up later in the week for coffee?'

'I'd like to. I have to come back to the frame shop to arrange those prints, so shall we make a time then?'

'Yes. Enjoy your meals.'

Harpreet disappeared inside.

'She's nice.' Lachie said, his eyes flicking from bowl to bowl as though he couldn't decide where to start.

'She is.'

'Mum and Dad won't believe this spread! We should take a photo.'

Charlotte opened her phone. 'What if I take some and I can send them as a message to your dad later on?' She took a couple of photos, then couldn't resist sneaking one of Lachie as he gazed, wide-eyed, at the selection. He glanced up and giggled, covering his mouth with his hand. 'Cheeky Charlotte. Can we do a selfie together?'

'Sure.'

He hurtled to her side of the table and stood behind her, his head over her shoulder as she snapped some images.

'Right, enough of that. Would you like to help yourself?'

He needed no second invitation and it was only a moment or two until both had filled their plates with steaming rice, succulent vegetable curry, chutney, raita, and naan bread. Silence ruled apart from an occasional 'ah' and 'yum'.

Over at Italia, voices from an outside table drifted over. Charlotte glanced across as a familiar voice crossed the short distance. Veronica. The woman laughed.

Cackled.

Opposite her was Jonas, not in his usual expensive suit, but a short sleeved, open necked shirt, and jeans. At his side, Terrance Murdoch had flung his suit jacket over the back of his seat and loosened what looked like a bow tie.

Terrance was bald and older than his brother Kevin by a few years.

'Do you want the last naan bread, Charlotte?'

She dragged her attention away from Italia. 'You have it. Are you enjoying the meal?'

'It is scrumptious!' Lachie added the bread to his half-eaten plate. 'I'm considering that as well as being a psychiatrist and bookshop owner, I might buy a restaurant. What do you think?'

'I think you will achieve whatever you set your mind on. Follow your dreams. Work hard, study harder, and have some fun.' Charlotte scooped a spoonful of curry.

'Where's Rosie?'

'Home. I sent her a message to ask her to join us but she's tired and wanted to get an early night.'

A couple of text messages back and forth earlier had told Charlotte little about the detectives visit to Rosie's house. Only that they'd left after looking around and more talking. And she had a headache and wasn't up to socialising but wanted to know if Charlotte heard news about Abbie tonight.

'Really? That's what you bring out?' Veronica's screech got the attention of all the outdoor diners at both restaurants, including Lachie. 'We ordered red. Not white.'

Charlotte recognised the server. Bronnie was the loveliest woman who always had a smile and kind word. But now she stepped back from the table, wine bottle in hand and a look of confusion.

'I apologise. I was certain you ordered white, but my error. Please let me get the correct wine.'

'See that you do.'

Was there no end to this woman's rudeness?

Lachie stared across the road.

'Hey, dude. Finish up. Then we'll get a tub of ice cream at

the supermarket if you like?' Charlotte kept one eye on him until he nodded and stuffed more food in his mouth, her other gaze on the table of three.

Who were laughing. All of them.

Terrance leaned toward Veronica, shaking his finger in jest. 'Naughty. I heard you order white.'

Veronica simpered and glanced at Jonas. He stared back, the corners of his mouth flicking up a little.

What on earth are they all playing at?

'They are mean people.'

Gaze back on Lachie, Charlotte pushed her plate aside and reached a hand over the table to take his. He stared at the table over the road. There was fear in his face.

'Sweetie? I think we might head off. Okay?'

'Okay.'

'No need to worry about those three. When you become a psychiatrist, you'll know how to handle those sorts.'

He looked at her. 'I will?'

'Yup. And, if you own a bookshop, you'll have lots of books to read about psychology.'

The fear changed to uncertainty. He wanted to believe.

'And you know what else?' Charlotte stood and pushed her chair in. 'Come on, let's go pay.'

She waited until Lachie placed his cutlery on the plate and got to his feet. Then, she leaned down and whispered, 'when you own a restaurant, you can throw them out! All three of them!'

His eyes rounded and he laughed. Charlotte laughed with him, relieved. She was responsible for this little boy and no way was she allowing those fiends to distress him. They walked inside to pay, and she dropped a hand onto his shoulder.

———

Shopping was fun with a kid. Charlotte gave Lachie the basket to carry and let him suggest a few ideas to help restock the fridge.

'Nope. I don't know how to cook that. Or that.'

'Mum will help you.'

'Mum is busy right now.'

Sure, I'll phone Abbie during labour. Hey, Abs. Fill me in on making waffles from scratch. Hello?

They settled on some eggs and bread as well as mush-rooms and butter and herbs which Lachie assured her would cook fast in a frying pan and taste delicious. Plus, a tub of chocolate ice cream, as promised.

Before going upstairs, Lachie insisted on seeing the tree. Under the light from Charlotte's phone torch, he inspected its branches, the soil, and the height. 'You have done remark-ably well, Charlotte Dean.'

He started up the stairs. She whispered to the tree, 'I think he means you've done well.'

'I heard you. Trees don't communicate with humans.'

She followed him up. 'Are you sure?'

'Of course. They talk to other trees. Why would they speak to a person?'

Made sense. If she followed her heart, Charlotte wouldn't speak to another human again. She'd burrow herself into a world of reading, walking, and learning how to cook.

Liar.

Fine. There might be one person she'd talk to. Maybe Rosie. And Lachie. His parents. Doug and Esther. Oh, Harpreet. Christie and Martin. And the others in Rivers End. And Trevor.

Nope. He'll never speak to me again when he finds out I've done what his mother asked and not told him about the break-in.

'Here, I'll carry your bag.' Lachie had hold of it before Charlotte could stop him. With a bag in each hand he still got there before she did. A person could get used to having a helper.

———

The evening passed with a few games of cards and a bowl of ice cream each. Lachie had a change of clothes and pyjamas but was reluctant to settle for the night, even when his yawns interrupted their game.

'Seriously, dude, why not head off to bed? If your dad calls, I'll wake you.'

'Do you think Mum's okay? They've been away so long.'

'I know. I bet it feels like forever waiting to hear but bad news travels faster than good news, so we'd have heard if anything was wrong.'

Lachie gave her one of those looks she was beginning to expect. Serious, with a touch of pity at her lack of understanding. 'Charlotte, you are a doctor. You must have studied physics so would know that all news would travel at the same speed.'

Charlotte opened her mouth to answer, then closed it. How did an eight-year-old get so clever? When she'd been his age…perhaps she'd have said the same things, had her family not been in such a mess. Her role at eight years was not that of a child but the person responsible for running to the shop and cleaning and checking her mother was in the house before locking up at night.

Not now.

She forced the memory away.

'Is it okay if I read for a bit on the sofa?' Lachie yawned again.

'Get changed first, then make yourself comfortable. I'll pack the game away.'

With a tired smile, Lachie scurried to the bedroom. Charlotte filled the kettle, ready for a hot tea on the balcony. She'd sit out there for a while and let Lachie relax with his book.

Tea made, she expected to see him, but he wasn't back yet. She took her tea and phone outside, keeping an eye on the sofa. Ten minutes passed and no little boy with a book. Charlotte didn't want to intrude if he was still changing, so stood outside the bedroom door he'd left ajar.

'All okay, Lachie?'

No sound from inside.

She peeked in. He was curled up on top of the bed, fast asleep, a book tucked under his arm. Charlotte's hand fluttered against her chest. For a moment she watched him breath, reassuring herself he was sleeping. Was this how parents felt all the time? Those earlier pangs became an insistent tempo in her heart.

Charlotte tip-toed away, leaving the light on in case he woke and forgot where he was. In the living room, she turned off all but the light beside the sofa and returned to the balcony. There, she stood staring into the night.

Why now? All her adult life she'd kept any thoughts of being a parent locked away in the most secure mental vault she had. To bring a child into the world was to expose them to the disease haunting her family.

Haunting me.

She'd decided years ago to stay single. Childless. A career woman with no time for family. Charlotte drew in a long, steady breath. Stay strong. There was no other choice.

The phone rang and she spun around and got it before it woke Lachie.

'Charlotte Dean speaking.'

'Charlie. We have a baby girl!' It was Abbie. Happiness poured down the phone.

Goosebumps rose all over Charlotte and tears prickled at

the back of her eyes. 'Abbie, how wonderful. Is she...are you...both doing okay?'

'We are. Is Lachie asleep?'

'Yes, but I can wake him.'

'No, let him sleep. Darcy is on his way back to collect him and they'll go to the farm. As long as that isn't an inconvenience to you?'

'Not in the least. Lachie was determined to stay awake, but I found him sleeping a few minutes ago. He's been such a good kid.'

'Thank you for today. You and Rosie.'

They spoke for a moment more, then Abbie said she would try for a nap while the baby slept. Charlotte sent a text to Rosie, hoping she wouldn't wake her, then watched for Darcy's car. Little moved along the quiet street and mist swirled around the tops of the streetlights. Valley life.

Rosie texted back.

So happy for them. Tell Darcy congratulations. Talk tomorrow, darling.

Charlotte wanted to talk to Rosie. Make sure she felt safe in her own home. In the morning she'd call Trevor and explain the recent events. No more emotional outbursts or worrying about how he'd react. Rosie needed her son involved now the police were searching her property and asking questions whether she agreed or not.

Darcy's car pulled up outside and he climbed out, weariness in every move. Charlotte met him at the back door and his eyes lit up.

'Did Abbie ring?'

'Congratulations from me and from Rosie.' Charlotte gave him a hug. 'A little girl!'

'She's gorgeous, Charlie. Lots of hair. And Abbie is the best mum ever.'

'I can't wait to see them both.'

Darcy closed the door behind himself and glanced down, then bent. 'Drop something?' He held out a folded white piece of paper.

Charlotte's stomach lurched.

It wasn't there when she and Lachie came in. She'd been here, with a little boy in her care, when someone slid it under the door. It wasn't only Rosie's house which wasn't safe.

'Charlie? You look like you saw a ghost.'

'Um. No, thanks for that. I'll put it…here. Thanks.' She took it by one corner and placed it in the middle of the counter. 'Lachie fell asleep getting a book to read. I think I exhausted him with card games.'

'He wasn't any trouble?'

'As if. Through here.' She led the way to the bedroom. 'I've loved spending time with him, to be honest.'

Lachie stirred as Darcy collected his bag and packed his clothes into it. 'Hey, mate. Time to go home.'

'Dad?' His eyes flew wide open and he sat up. 'Where's Mum?'

Darcy sat beside him with a grin. 'She's staying in hospital for a couple of days. With your new baby sister.'

'Aw…a sister. I was right. I said that, didn't I, Charlotte?'

'You did.'

'Can't we go visit now?'

'Bit late. Besides we should go lock the chooks up and check the house. We'll head down there first thing in the morning.'

'I have a present for you and Mum and our baby. I packed it already.'

Darcy stood, casting a questioning look at Charlotte. She zipped across her lip and Lachie giggled.

'Say goodnight to Charlie. And a big, big thank you.'

Lachie repeated his earlier action of throwing his arms

around her waist with a muffled 'thanks, Charlotte Dean' against her stomach.

'My pleasure, Lachlan Woodland.' She squeezed his shoulders.

When he let go and followed his father, she was cold inside.

She called goodnight as they took the steps. Once she'd locked the back door and double checked it, her attention turned to the paper on the counter.

chapter
twenty-two

Laptop open, Charlotte scrolled through her photographs of Octavia's house.

She reached the first one she'd taken—Octavia's body—and enlarged it to the full screen view. But all she searched for was the date and time stamp.

Nobody had revealed Octavia's time of death yet. If Charlotte was correct in her estimate, then the photo was taken between one and three hours after she died. That made it between eleven thirty and one thirty, give or take. Not time for Glenys to walk all the way there from the bookshop with her bad knee and cane and commit murder.

Sid came to get Charlotte around three thirty after being waved down by Glenys, who'd been at the bookshop just before Rosie returned from her lunch date with Lewis.

Which was when?

Sometime around one thirty. It was easy enough to check because the shop was busy for at least an hour and Rosie's first sale was only minutes after coming back.

Charlotte sighed and wrote on a piece of paper destined for the cork board.

Rosie out from 12.30-1.30pm approx (check)

Octavia's time of death 11.30-1.30pm approx (check)

Glenys left shop on foot 1.30pm approx (check)

Lots to check. If, and it was a big if, Octavia died as late as two in the afternoon, Glenys might have got there in time. Charlotte estimated it would take her, at a normal pace and with two good legs, twenty minutes to walk to Octavia's house, so how would Glenys have done so? If Glenys only found Octavia so late, where was she all that time?

She sat back in her chair, eyes on the screen. Octavia was face down and all Charlotte could focus on was the mark on the back of her head. And now, the timestamp. Three thirty-nine. She bit her bottom lip, her mind racing. Somebody hit Octavia. The blow may not have killed her, but it contributed to her falling forward and hitting her forehead so hard she died. Manslaughter at the very least.

Charlotte picked up the paper slipped under her door tonight. Now inside a plastic sleeve, it was a photocopy of three photographs, not one. Each photo was time and date stamped.

The first showed Rosie leaving the bookshop at a bit after twelve thirty.

The next was of Lewis, through the window of his shop, serving customers. The same day, at one o'clock, the time he was supposed to be enjoying a park lunch with Rosie. According to Rosie.

Then another of Rosie. This time she was on a footpath, the garden centre behind her. She was intent on the ground in front of her which Charlotte recognised as typical of when she was moving fast. The garden centre was only a couple of blocks from Octavia's house. The time stamp was one twenty.

'Where were you, Rosie? Why aren't you telling the truth?'

Charlotte rubbed her eyes, exhausted. This photographer

was either setting Rosie up as a suspect or had stumbled upon a terrible truth. And she couldn't say a word to Trev until she'd worked out what was going on.

chapter
twenty-three

Tossing and turning all night, Charlotte couldn't get her brain to relax. She was up before dawn, wrapped in her dressing gown and sipping coffee. She missed Lachie, which was ridiculous. He wasn't her son, and she'd only known him and his family for a few months, but his presence in her home brought a happiness to her heart. And stirred up dormant questions which she didn't want to think about right now.

What she wanted was to go to the waterfall. Watch the sun rise as kangaroos drank from the pool. See the resident kingfisher if he deigned to show himself. Or herself.

But fear held her back. Fear of being followed and photographed again. Of being alone in the deep bushland where the person responsible for putting those photocopies under her door, even when she was home, might trail her.

She needed motion. Before the anxiety kicked in and buried her. Charlotte finished her coffee and locked the sliding door on her way inside. After dressing for walking, she took her phone and keys and ran down the steps. The sky was a little lighter now but the driveway was dark, making her hesitate.

Stop letting him control you.

Yesterday, she'd met with both security companies and was expecting quotes. She'd asked for cameras around the building as well as inside, and motion sensors. But it wasn't an immediate solution and she shivered despite the warm air forecasting a hot day. Nothing moved. But she had to.

Charlotte forced herself along the driveway and around the corner, stopping in front of the bookshop under the outside light. If the photographer was around, then let him take as many images as he wanted right here. She shook her head. He wasn't just photographing her, so why think he'd be watching her every move?

She glanced at her watch. Five thirty. Time to see how long the walk to Octavia's house took, at least for someone without a walking cane.

Charlotte crossed the first street, following the pavement past the frame shop, then at the roundabout, took a left. More shops including another supermarket and a petrol station, and then houses. There was a fork ahead, one way leading to the Christmas Tree Farm and the other to Octavia's. One of the town's several sportsgrounds was deserted apart from someone walking their dogs. At least there were some stirrings now. A couple of bakeries were already well lit as their bakers did their magic for the day ahead.

Around a curve, the road narrowed, and the houses were larger, with more expansive gardens. Charlotte had noticed this when she'd walked to the garden centre once. Speaking of which, Veronica's business loomed on the left. Set on a corner, there was a long, narrow shopfront behind a dirt carpark. Beyond the shop was a sprawling outdoor nursery, including a massive greenhouse and a mix of open and covered areas. The place was in darkness.

Charlotte made her way to the opposite side of the road,

surprised at the lack of a footpath. This part of Kingfisher Falls was what she'd heard people call "old money town". Streets named after the founders of the town, houses built a century ago, residents living here for decades. But no footpath.

At this time of year, with a lack of regular rain, the grass verge was little more than a dusty track. It slowed Charlotte down. Glenys would have found it uncomfortable with a cane unless she'd walked on the road.

She recognised Octavia's property with the graceful silver birches along the driveway leading to darkness. It was five fifty. Twenty minutes from the bookshop at a normal walking pace. Charlotte made a note in her phone of the two times along with observations from the walk.

From here, little was visible of what Charlotte knew was an expansive English-style garden. A formal one. Hedges, roses, oaks, and birches rather than gums and wattles. She'd love to take a proper look and not just at the garden. If only she had taken a little more time to photograph more of Octavia's living room and kitchen. Perhaps she could peek through the windows?

A dark sedan without headlights nosed along the kerb from further up the road. Not fast but coming her way. The photographer? Charlotte pressed herself against bushes lining the frontage, glancing either way. There was nobody around. The houses weren't close together so if this was an attempt to scare her, she'd need to run fast.

The car stopped and the passenger window opened.

'Doctor Dean, you're visible.'

She sighed a quick breath of relief at Detective Bryce Davis's voice and crossed to the car. He leaned across the passenger seat.

'Get in.'

'I'm going home for breakfast. What are you doing here?'

'Watching for criminals.'

'Find any?'

'You tell me.'

Charlotte looked in his back seat. 'Can't see anyone arrested back here, so I will say, nope.' She thought she'd gone too far at the expression of frustration on his face. Best not to alienate a homicide detective. 'I'm out for a walk. I do it most mornings. When I saw Octavia's place, it reminded me of coming here the other day. That's all.'

'You're not on our radar. Not for what happened in that house, anyway.' He turned off the motor and got out. Rather than coming around the car, he closed his door and leaned his arms on the roof, stretching. 'Too long sitting.'

'What time did Octavia die?' Charlotte asked, before thinking.

'Why.'

'Trying to work something out.'

'Not for me to divulge.' Bryce stared.

'My estimation is between eleven thirty and one thirty in the afternoon.'

The corners of his mouth flicked up for a second.

'So, it wasn't Rosie.'

'I'm not discussing this with you, Doctor.'

'Charlotte. Or Charlie. Nobody calls me doctor. Have you looked inside the dishwasher?' She stared back, hoping her gaze was steady and calm. Which she felt the opposite.

'You don't give up, do you?' Bryce laced his hands behind his head and rotated his torso. 'We did. Just as well because some bozo broke in a few hours later and rummaged through it. Couple of plates broken. No fingerprints though.'

'What about the teacup?'

'We have that.'

'What does Veronica say? Has she admitted to being in the house that morning?'

He rolled his eyes and shook his head. Not much help at all.

Did Veronica break in, looking for the teacup stained with her lipstick? Her DNA? Why not acknowledge her visit with Octavia if she was innocent?

Or is she?

'No more questions?' Bryce reopened his door.

'What was stolen?'

He shrugged. 'Hard to know when she lived alone.'

'Let me look. I was in the house.'

'How many times?'

'Once. Mrs Morris wasn't fond of me, so I missed the invite to her dinner parties.' Charlotte clamped her lips shut to keep herself out of trouble. Got to work on the sarcasm.

Bryce laughed. 'Do you want a lift home?'

She shook her head and he closed the door after himself. Charlotte stayed put until he'd driven away. The minute his taillights disappeared, she followed, this time on the road.

At the garden centre, she hurried by, fighting a sudden urge to look through the windows. Who knew what was going on there?

Almost a block further on, Charlotte stopped and gazed around in the increased light. This was close to where Rosie was in the image. Her wheelchair was lightweight and fast— Charlotte knew from experience having had to run for short distances to keep up with Rosie. She noted the time.

Then ran. All the way to the edge of the shopping precinct, where she dropped to a normal walk until reaching the front of the bookshop. Again, a glance at her watch. And the sharp clenching around her stomach wasn't from the run. Rosie might have been at Octavia's house when the other woman was alive.

———

Under the shower, Charlotte released a long, low wail of despair. She would never believe Rosie responsible for Octavia's death, even by accident. But how could she raise the subject with the person she'd grown to love and trust, without sounding suspicious? And Trevor couldn't find out. Not yet.

Charlie, you need his help.

She let out another cry, willing the sound to carry the emotions away.

It didn't.

After turning the water off, she stood for a while, staring at her reflection in the shower door. Slumped shoulders, large, tired eyes. Had moving to Kingfisher Falls been the biggest mistake in her mistake-filled life? Letting people past her carefully constructed and guarded barriers until their pain became hers?

'Stop being melodramatic and get some coffee.'

She dressed for work, pulled her damp hair back in a tight bun, and slathered makeup on to mask the exhaustion. Whatever the day held, she would appear in control and that was half the battle. The other half was working out a plan of action.

Kettle on, she opened the fridge. And closed it again to hide the eggs and mushrooms. Lachie had been going to help her make breakfast. Help her cook something new.

She took her coffee into the third bedroom and stood before the corkboard. She'd added her most recent thoughts, plus comments from her conversation with the detective.

Detectives watching Octavia's house following break-in

Teacup probable target: plates broken

What else was taken?

I'm not a suspect. Does this mean Rosie is? Who else?

Until Rosie told her about the meeting with the detectives at her house, there was little point in speculating. She was only guilty of not being honest about where she was that lunchtime. Terrible timing to be caught in a lie.

Charlotte sank onto the bed, staring at the board as she finished the coffee. Was Rosie at the garden centre for some reason? Maybe she didn't want Charlotte to misunderstand why she wanted to see what Veronica had in stock? And she didn't want Charlotte to know she had gone there.

More likely she was following Charlotte's sleuthing lead and doing her own investigation. She had mentioned mysteries intrigued her. That made sense.

Charlotte closed the door on the room. She had no idea what to do about Trevor. Every instinct hammered her into phoning him. Spill every bit of information so he could help. It was the logical and sensible thing to do.

Refilling her cup, she considered what would happen. First, she'd phone and make small talk. He'd ask about the latest news around Octavia. Charlotte would explain, in clear, calm terms, that two homicide detectives spent the afternoon at his mother's house the day after it was broken into. By this point, she'd be speaking to white noise because he'd be on his way here. Right into the middle of what?

For all she knew, the detectives might find nothing. Nobody to arrest. Not Rosie. With them gone, the photocopied papers would stop being slid under her door and the phone calls would cease. Life would return to normal. It wasn't her place to go over Rosie's head. And it was in everybody's best interests if Charlotte Dean didn't over-react and bring the world crashing down on an innocent party again because of her appalling lack of good judgement.

chapter
twenty-four

Rosie arrived before the shop opened. She had bought coffee and pastries at the café and joined Charlotte in the kitchen for a talk.

'I was so happy to hear that Abbie and baby are well,' Rosie said. 'How was your afternoon and evening with Lachie?'

'Good. Too good.'

'Too good?'

'He is smart and kind. Made me wish I'd had his parents growing up.'

'You'll be a wonderful mother when the time is right. You know that?'

Not one bit. But Charlotte forced a smile and nodded. 'We went to India Gate House for dinner. He eats everything! And, there was an interesting thing going on at Italia.'

Rosie pursed her lips as Charlotte filled her in about Veronica, Jonas, and Terrance. 'Something is not right.'

'Agree. However, I want to know about your afternoon. What happened with our friends from homicide?'

Fingers tapping on the sides of her wheelchair gave away Rosie's turmoil. 'Oh, not a lot. They were very kind and checked the new locks were all good, after the break in. They spent a bit of time in the shed…it is still such a mess, Charlie.'

'I'll help.'

'I wasn't allowed in with them. And they went through the garden. We talked a while about Octavia, her disagreement with me and you, the town. And so on. None of it seemed to bother them but I imagine they are accustomed to dealing with liars and killers.' Her voice rose.

'I'm sure they are. But you are neither. Are you?' Charlotte kept her voice light. Neutral.

Rosie's face paled as her eyes flicked sideways and her mouth dropped.

'Rosie, you can say anything to me. Anything at all. I love you and will never judge you.'

Instead of replying, Rosie bit into a pastry.

'Have you spoken with Trevor yet?' Charlotte asked, already knowing the answer. He'd be here if she had.

Once she swallowed, Rosie shook her head. 'I decided there's no point dragging him into this. He can't do anything apart from make coffee in this situation, so it is best he's not bothered with silly details. And I don't want you calling him either, darling. Okay?'

'Not okay.'

For a moment, Rosie looked ready to burst into tears. She gulped some coffee.

Talk to me, Rosie.

'Trevor believes you know when to call him. To ask for help. He told me this as an example of how I should learn to trust, I think.'

'He said that?'

'He worries about you.'

'And that's the problem. There's nothing he can do about the break-in, or detectives and all of it. Nothing but hold my hand. Better to wait until there's something concrete to tell him.' Rosie collected the rubbish from the pastries and coffee cups. 'I need you to trust me, darling.'

'Why wouldn't I?'

'I can't talk about some things. Not yet. But your trust means everything.'

'I do trust you. Always.' And Charlotte did. The photograph of Rosie at a time and place she shouldn't have been was a puzzle. But almost certainly one with nothing to do with the untimely death of Octavia Morris.

————

The security camera quotes arrived by email, one straight after the other. Rosie and Charlotte went through them as customers permitted, with Charlotte walking around the shop pointing at potential camera points each company had suggested during their visits the previous day.

'I know the first company is cheaper, but they also want to install three less cameras on the property.'

'Where are the extra cameras from the second quote?' Rosie watched from behind the counter, peering over her glasses with a pen in hand. 'Do we need those extra three?'

'I think so. One was here...' Charlotte stood in the back corner of the bookshop facing the window, 'to catch movements from outside, even at night if they install the motion sensor kind. It will mean anyone looking in will be seen. And the one here...' she hurried back near the kitchen and gestured toward the front door, 'will record every customer as they come in. Or people like Kevin.'

'And outside?'

'Yes. Two at the front, pointing toward each other from either end of the brickwork. Two in the driveway doing the same. And one at the top of the steps, over the landing. Plus, they'll install motion sensor lighting.'

Rosie gazed at Charlotte. 'I'm all for this. But I feel there's a reason you want the extra cameras around the side of the building and upstairs.'

Charlotte nibbled on her bottom lip. So many secrets. Rose was keeping some and so was she. But hers were to protect Rosie. And lead Charlotte to the murderer and whoever was behind the calls and photocopies.

Except, you're not a detective. And you're protecting yourself.

With a smile, Charlotte pushed the annoying truth away. If she could bring herself to be honest about what was happening, she'd need to reveal some of the awful facts of her past life as a psychiatrist. Perhaps even further back, to her mother and childhood. Not happening.

'Charlie? What kind of smile is that?'

'One to say it is more than time to stop stressing about what might be going on in Kingfisher Falls. I want to pay for the security cameras and before you refuse, consider this.' Charlotte joined Rosie and sat on a stool. 'Not long ago you told me I'll be running the bookshop one day so unless anything's changed, you are happy to sell to me at some time. If so, then this will be my liability anyway.'

'And I am. Well, I will be soon. There's a couple of things I need to get straight in my head about retirement, but if you want the bookshop, then once I sort those out, we can begin the legal side of the sale.'

A sense of quiet joy spread through Charlotte. This meant everything to her, hearing those words of belief about her suitability to be Rosie's successor.

'You're certain I'm the right person?'

'With a full and happy heart. Yes.' Rosie squeezed Charlotte's arm.

Nothing in Charlotte's life had been a gift. She'd worked for everything she got and wore her mistakes as her own. Now, she was embarking on a life based on little more than friendship, a mutual admiration, and trust. A stab almost undid her resolve to keep silent. Rosie didn't need the extra worry.

'I'll tell you what we'll do.' Rosie tore up the first quote. 'We'll go forward with the other one and I will pay. This is something I should have done ages ago and it isn't fair to expect you to be on your own here so often, dealing with people like Sid and Kevin. This way you get a bit of protection.'

'Thank you.' Charlotte's stomach unclenched. 'Shall I call them to arrange installation?'

'Please do. Sooner the better.'

Rosie wheeled to the middle of the bookshop, staring at the back corner. Charlotte picked up the phone and the quote and joined her.

'And should I ask them to come and look at your house?'

Rosie frowned and shook her head.

Charlotte sighed. 'Rosie, you need to protect yourself. Protect your home. Security cameras will help. We need to let Trev know what happened the other night. Please.'

'I'll think about it.'

'No, Mum, there's no thinking about it.'

Not believing her ears, Charlotte swung around. Trev stood in the doorway in his police uniform, arms crossed and with an expression she'd never seen on his face. Anger. And he was staring at her.

chapter
twenty-five

'Trev? What on earth are you doing here?' Rosie covered the space to her son in seconds and held her arms wide open. He knelt beside her chair and they hugged, Rosie gripping Trev but his eyes never leaving Charlotte's.

'I'll leave you two to catch—' Charlotte began.

'I think you should stay here.' Trev gently unwrapped Rosie's arms and stood. 'Time to get a few things sorted, don't you agree?'

Nope. Not at all. Didn't ask for any of this.

Charlotte lifted her chin but kept her mouth shut for once.

Maybe Trev recognised how difficult it was for her to do so, because there was a shadow of a smile on his lips, then he leaned his hip against the counter and refolded his arms, turning his attention to Rosie.

'Why do you need security cameras at the house?'

'Oh. You overheard? What else did you hear?'

'Enough to know something is going on. Spill it, please.'

'Darling, there's not much to tell and I'm certain you have more than enough on your plate without worrying about my little issues.' Rosie wheeled back around the counter.

'Which are?' Trev turned so he could look at his mother, giving Charlotte a small break from his scrutiny.

Her heart had jumped at his voice, which annoyed her no end even though she knew it was the sheer surprise of his arrival.

Sure, Charlie. Tell yourself that.

Ignoring her inner voice, Charlotte stayed as much out of this as possible. Somebody passed the window and stepped through the doorway and with no thought but to get busy, Charlotte shot across to meet them with a bright, 'Good morning.'

It was Glenys, who stopped dead and turned an even deathlier shade at the sight of Trev.

Trev nodded to Glenys. 'Mrs Lane. How are you?'

Glenys' eyes widened.

'How may I help today, Glenys?' Charlotte looked from one to the other. Whatever was going on? The other woman was still pale and there was a slight tremor in her hands.

'Actually. I have to be somewhere. Else. Good day.'

With that, Glenys left the bookshop at an impressive pace in the direction away from town. No more leaning on her walking cane or shaking as she walked.

'What was that about, Mum? What's wrong with Glenys?'

'She's all out of sorts after Octavia's death. Thinking of selling up and moving. She even purchased all the copies of the book she and Fred published all those years ago. Would you like a coffee? How long are you staying, and why are you in uniform?'

Charlotte wondered the same thing.

Trev glanced at Charlotte, then back to Rosie. 'I had an early meeting in Kyneton at the division station. Can't say why yet. But the CI mentioned you were interviewed at home, Mum. About Octavia. Why not at the station?'

Rosie removed her glasses and gazed up at Trevor. 'Very

well. Somebody broke into the house the other night and rifled through your father's filing cabinets.'

In an instant, Trev was around the counter, reaching for Charlotte's stool to perch on, hand on Rosie's. 'I'm listening.'

'Well, there's not much to tell, dear. I came home and went to the shed to get some gardening tools and found the cabinets on their sides and the files all over the place.'

'What did you do?'

'I phoned Charlie and she was there in minutes.'

Trev's eyes were back on Charlotte. She joined them at the counter, staying on the customer side in case she needed to retreat. Her flight or fight response hummed away in the background and she gripped the countertop where Trev couldn't see her hands.

'Did the police come?' he asked.

'Yes, Sid arrived a bit later.' Rosie said.

'A bit later? What aren't you telling me?' He directed this at Charlotte although he kept hold of Rosie's hand.

'Charlie was wonderful, Trev. And she's been telling me to phone you ever since, so don't blame her, please. And she has arranged quotes for cameras for the bookshop and her apartment.'

Was Rosie planning on telling Trev anything about the intruder in the house? Or how she'd had to force Sid to help? And there was the matter of where Rosie was when poor Octavia was meeting her end.

Trev hadn't spoken. His head was tilted, and eyes narrowed as though trying to fathom Charlotte's thoughts. She'd forgotten how intense those eyes were. And the strength of his jaw and width of his shoulders. There was a kindness about the man she'd recognised at their first meeting and it still drew her to him. To trust him.

Don't hate me, Rosie.

'I'm sorry in advance, Rosie, but you know I love you and want you safe. Trevor, yes, there is more to it.'

'Charlie.' But Rosie's voice reflected resignation, not anger.

In short sentences and clipped tone, Charlotte ran through the events of the night in a few minutes. She kept herself under control despite the growing frustration on Trev's face, and wasn't brave enough to look at Rosie.

'I stayed the night and Rosie had the locks changed within hours.' She finished.

Rosie put her glasses back on and offered Charlotte a small smile. She didn't appear upset. There was less tension visible in her body. But Charlotte's muscles ached with holding the panic in. As a psychiatrist, her emotions never came into play as she dealt with another human's darkest moments, but in confrontation with people she cared about? A thousand little butterflies in her stomach implored her to flee.

'When were you going to tell me? Either of you?' Trev stood and stretched. He did what Bryce had earlier, lacing his hands behind his head and rotating his torso. Something they teach at police academy perhaps.

A family wandered in and Charlotte excused herself to attend to them. By the time she carried their purchases to the counter, Trev and Rosie were outside the shop, deep in discussion. Charlotte rang up the sale, handed over the books with a smile conjured from somewhere, and flopped onto the stool vacated by Trev with a sharp exhale.

The phone rang and Charlotte stared at it with suspicion. But it was one of the book wholesalers checking on an order, taking Charlotte to the back of the shop to answer their query. That done, she stayed in the corner to watch as Trev leaned down to kiss Rosie's cheek. They smiled at each other. Such love between mother and son. And respect.

'I wish…' she whispered.

What? That your mother was like Rosie? How could you deserve her?

Charlotte's fingers curled into her palms, nails digging into the flesh until she cleared her mind. Nothing would move the lump from her throat and when Trev glanced her way with his typical broad smile, she nodded, frozen in place. Any attempt to smile in return would have unleashed the tears sitting behind her eyes.

———

Rosie wheeled inside as Trev strode toward town. Charlotte mumbled something about the bathroom and fled, unable to trust herself to speak. Locked inside, she didn't bother with the light but leaned back on the door, eyes closed, breathing deep and slow.

Trevor was here. And it must be for longer than a quick hello or he'd have come in to say a proper goodbye. Unless he was too disappointed in Charlotte.

He'd smiled. Trev didn't hold grudges.

Within a minute or two of his arrival he'd got her to tell him about the break-in at Rosie's house. If he spent any further time with Charlotte, how much else would she reveal? All her speculation and theories? What were the pros and cons of laying it all on the line?

As a police officer, his experience outweighed her amateur attempts to unravel the mess of recent days. He had access to information she didn't. Ways to trace calls, perhaps. Track down the source of the images. He might have means to identify the person she'd photographed on the steps at the falls.

He could also dismiss this all as over-active imagination, or much of it. Hand over her hard-won stash of clues to other police and make her stay out of it. Even check into her past to understand why she had such need to keep secrets, even in the face of danger.

He must be so tired of asking you to trust him.

'Darling, are you alright?' Rosie was outside the door.

'Um, out in a minute. Fine, thanks.' Charlotte flicked on the light and ran the tap, splashing water on her neck to cool herself. Her eyes were wide, startled, in the mirror, and her colour high. If this was the effect Trevor had on her, she needed to avoid him.

Rosie was behind the counter with two cold bottles of water and a look of concern. 'I am sorry to have upset you, Charlie. You did the right thing.'

'No, I'm not upset. Promise. Where did Trevor go?'

'Meeting with the homicide detectives.'

'But what can he do?' Charlotte opened her water. 'Thank you.'

'You're welcome. He only said it is something to do with the meeting he had earlier. I'm wondering…well, I'm sure I'm wrong.' There was a little spark in her eyes.

'You think he's moving back.'

'Well, I don't know how he can, not with Sid here. But what if he did?' Rosie smiled and turned to the computer to finish some work.

Trevor living closer was something Charlotte had never considered. He belonged in Rivers End, his home for most of his police career and the place his friends were. Here, there was only Rosie, and some of his older friends.

And you.

No. Not happening. She'd already left one town to avoid dealing with her feelings for the tall, good looking and far too nice police officer. Kingfisher Falls may not be big enough for them both.

chapter
twenty-six

Glenys cupped her hands against the glass to look inside the bookshop from the furthest corner of the window. Charlotte waved to her. Was she checking Trev had gone?

'Is Rosie here?' Glenys got as far as the doorway and stopped.

'She's out for lunch. Can I help?'

'You must have thought me mad earlier.' She came to the counter. 'Rushing off like that. I was so surprised to see young Trev here.'

'He came to visit Rosie. Why is that a surprise?'

'Town's overrun with police, thanks to…her.' Glenys glanced at the wall behind Charlotte, to the photographs. 'I'd like that taken down, please. I'll pay Rosie for the frame, but I wish to take it with me now.'

Surprised by a sudden hardness in the other woman's voice, Charlotte followed Glenys' line of sight to the photo of Octavia and her ex, and Fred and Glenys.

First every copy of her husband's book, now his photograph. Had finding Octavia's body stirred up deep feelings of her own loss?

'Were you able to locate any further copies of *Perfect*

Photographs of Kingfisher Falls?' Charlotte hoped to distract Glenys.

'I didn't. Do you have a ladder to get the photograph down?'

'All I can do is speak to Rosie about it.'

Glenys' face and neck reddened, then her eyes locked onto Charlotte's with a disappointed stare. 'Very well. I shall be back.' She raised her chin, turned, and stalked out, again in the direction away from town.

This was odd behaviour. And why was she going that way for the second time today? Charlotte hurried to look out of the doorway. No sign of a car parked further along, just Glenys stomping, as much as someone with a limp can, toward the falls. But it was a place of remembrance for her. Grief—even long-buried grief—did strange things.

The ringing of the shop phone took her attention. This time it was the security firm who'd provided the successful quote. They had a last-minute cancellation and could begin the installation later today. Charlotte said yes. At last, some positive action.

————

'Lewis is concerned about me, Charlie.'

Rosie was about to leave for the day to meet Trev for an early dinner. There'd been no mention of Charlotte joining them and although most of her was pleased, a tiny corner felt excluded. But after her near meltdown in the bathroom, staying away from Trev was in her best interests.

'Why is Lewis concerned?'

'I told him about the break-in, and—'

'Wait. Sorry to interrupt, but he didn't know?'

'Of course not.' Rosie frowned. 'Until today, only you and

the police knew. Mind you, I'd expected Sid to spread the news, as he normally would.'

'I didn't tell you but Henry ran in the other morning, when you were changing the locks at home. He'd overheard Terrance ask Jonas if he'd heard about it.'

'Heard about my home being invaded? How would he know?'

Charlotte shrugged. 'I assumed Sid told him. But I can't work out where Sid belongs in all of this. Terrance, Jonas, and Veronica are up to no good and I wonder if Sid is kept out of it unless they need something.'

'Or he's laying low. Having other police in town.' Rosie still frowned.

'When I was making my statement to them, he barrelled in and made a fuss because Bryce was roughing up the photocopier. Anyway, you were talking about Lewis being concerned.'

'He asked if I'd like to go on a short…well, holiday with him. Just while all this upset is going on, to give me a break.'

Hands full of notes she'd counted, Charlotte stopped. 'How do you feel about that?'

'Unsure.' Rosie's lips curled up. 'He's so sweet to suggest it. Perhaps if the timing was different…'

'I can look after Mayhem and Mellow. Water the garden. Run the shop.'

'Thank you, darling. And I may take you up on the offer at another time. Something about this whole mess is telling me I need to stay right here. I should head home, if you're all good to finish up?'

'Two secs, let me throw the money in the safe and I'll let you out.' Charlotte folded the money bag as she dashed to the kitchen and opened the safe inside a bottom cupboard. No security risks anymore. She glanced at the newly installed recorder and monitor.

'I'm going!'

'Sorry!' Charlotte reached the front door as Rosie opened it. 'Have a nice dinner. It will be good for you to catch up.'

A flicker of uncertainty crossed Rosie's face, but she smiled. 'I'll see you in the morning, darling.'

Charlotte locked herself back in the bookshop. Rosie wasn't happy. On any other day, Trev being home, and Lewis wanting to care for her would have her singing with joy. Instead, her friend was dealing with intruders, police visits, the death of a former friend, and something else. Her secret, whatever it was.

True to their word, the security firm had arrived just after lunchtime, two young men working together to set up the surveillance system of cameras leading to the monitor in the kitchen. They'd also installed the cameras around the apartment and Charlotte had an access code to use on her phone or computer anytime she wanted to check them. They were returning the next day with new lighting along the driveway and top of the stairs, but this went a long way to giving Charlotte a much-needed sense of security.

Back in the kitchen, she spent a few minutes watching the monitor. It was strange seeing the bookshop from the bird's eye view of a camera. One by one, she double clicked each of the cameras to a full screen. The clarity was astonishing, to the point of noticing a couple of spots she'd missed when last cleaning the windows.

The camera facing the counter provided clear vision of where she and Rosie spent a lot of their time. And the wall behind them, with its photographs.

'Why do you want it, Glenys?'

Rosie had been as puzzled as Charlotte by Glenys' request. Demand. But she'd shaken her head and said no. As far as she knew, the newspaper would still have copies to buy, or if not, it wouldn't be hard to get Harpreet to replicate it.

'This copy was framed by Graeme, along with the others. Besides, she'd have her own copy from the night. Fred was so proud of his award he'd probably kept the photo and award on show.' Rosie had said.

Another little mystery but not one worth adding to the corkboard. Glenys needed sympathy, not suspicion.

Charlotte changed the monitor back to show all the cameras and reached for her handbag. About to leave, an outside camera picked up someone approaching. Someone who stopped just far enough in range to see their legs, which were bare between a short skirt and high heels. Veronica?

It was. She walked up and down the shop front, glancing around the street. A couple of cars passed, and she grabbed her phone as if talking to someone. Or was she? Cars gone, she lowered her hand and moved to the front door. She turned the handle.

Are you kidding me?

For a second, Charlotte had a horrible thought. Had she locked the door? If Veronica waltzed in with some bad intent, Charlotte could lock herself in the kitchen and phone the police. Yeah. Phone Sid who was bound to help. Not.

No, she'd call Trev. Her fingers reached for her phone.

Veronica stepped back. The door was locked. Now, she used her phone as though taking photos of the door. After looking both ways along the pavement, she tip-tapped past the window and around the corner, into the driveway.

Charlotte scrambled to change channels. It was set up on a different line so Charlotte could keep some privacy if anyone other than she and Rosie looked at shop footage. By the time the driveway camera appeared, Veronica was gone.

She clicked from screen to screen until certain the

woman had left. All her instincts screamed to phone Trevor. Let him see her trust in action. Ask for help.

To do what? Veronica hadn't broken any laws. She might not even have gone into the driveway. Trevor and Rosie were about to enjoy a much-needed dinner together and this wasn't the time to interrupt. No, instead she'd do some shopping, then go upstairs and look at the footage from the past few minutes. Then, if there was anything worth discussing, she'd phone Trev. She would.

chapter
twenty-seven

The evening was beautiful and Charlotte considered changing her plans to visit the lookout. She had two bags of shopping and once she'd unpacked those, it would still be light enough to reach the track, enjoy sunset, and get home before complete darkness fell.

She turned into the driveway and halted. Had Veronica been here earlier? A shiver ran up her spine and she shook her head to force ridiculous fears away. It was still daylight. Nobody was here. Her feet got going, ignoring the tension in her stomach. She looked up the stairs before climbing them, but all was quiet. By the time she locked herself in, Charlotte was more annoyed than scared.

Leaving the unpacked bags on the counter, she went to the balcony, pushed the sliding door wide and leaned her elbows on the rail. The air was cool, refreshing after days of heat. People wandered along the road, walking their dogs, or with their children. The supermarket was still busy and the last of the small shops was closed. From experience she expected the traffic to ease to almost nothing over the next hour, as locals went home, and the town settled for the evening.

On the surface, nothing had changed. Though shocked by Octavia's death, other residents were not privy to the murder investigation. No, that was reserved for suspects and innocent bystanders. But a new threat emerged from the crime. A murderer was on the loose. Not a serial killer, but someone with a motive to harm Octavia. It wasn't a theft gone wrong, as nothing was missing. The threat Charlotte saw was the murderer covering their tracks by hurting someone else.

The phone calls and cryptic images might be incidental, rather than from the killer themselves.

Charlotte dropped her head into her hands with sudden realisation. She'd made a fundamental, dreadful error of judgement. If it was the killer in touch with Charlotte, then she might have the only connection to them. She'd had no right to keep any of this to herself. What if another person suffered thanks to her inaction?

Somewhere she had Katrina's card. Back inside, she dug around in her handbag. It wasn't there. She found it in a pocket of the pants she'd been wearing the other day and stared at it for a moment. This might become a fiasco with her in the centre of a storm.

She dialled and the number went to voicemail.

'Detective Mayer, this is Charlotte Dean. Would you mind calling back on this number when you can? I may have information to assist with the Octavia Morris investigation. Thanks.'

Charlotte unpacked the shopping but wasn't interested in eating. Despite the closeness to nightfall, she needed to walk for a while. Phone and keys pocketed in her shorts, she ran downstairs and out onto the street with no thought of direction. She crossed the road and took the shortcut through the alley to the plaza.

The fountain was off. Not a trickle emerged from the myriad of spouts and only a little water pooled in the base.

Charlotte strolled around it, surprised how cracked parts were. It must be empty for repairs.

'Like our little fountain?' Jonas appeared from nowhere.

Well, not nowhere, but Charlotte hadn't seen him until he stepped in front of her.

'Down for repairs?'

'Down until the traders pay what they owe us.'

'For?'

'What do you think? Replacing the Christmas tree council provided when it was stolen. We told you all we'd need a contribution to buy the one from Darcy Woodland.'

Yes, Jonas and Terrance had waltzed into the bookshop with a pathetic attempt to strong-arm Rosie into paying council for the second time. She, and most other traders, refused. If council insisted on replacing it, that was their decision.

'Bit much asking the shop owners to pay twice, just before Christmas.' Charlotte kept her tone neutral. 'And now you're holding the fountain ransom?'

'There's a whole lot of history in this town you know nothing of. We don't need an outsider telling us how to run things.'

'I'm not telling you anything not obvious. Traders bring money into the town. I imagine that's a benefit to council. Expecting them to compete against bigger local towns with corporate stores happy to poach customers from Kingfisher Falls is bad enough. If we make money, you do too.' Charlotte resisted an urge to cross her arms and kept her voice neutral.

'If shops are too expensive, it is the customer's right to shop elsewhere.'

'Oh, I agree. But I'm fairly sure most of the little shops are competitive. Otherwise, why wouldn't the attempts to open cheap retail shops work?'

Maybe I shouldn't have gone so far.

It was interesting to see Jonas' face flush bright red and his hands clench at his sides. He knew what Charlotte meant. Why had Veronica failed three times in town when setting up shops designed to undercut the competition? Then, she'd gone the other way with the garden supplies business, thinking she had a monopoly on the Christmas tree market.

'Nice chatting. I must pop along to a council meeting one of these days.' Charlotte wasn't waiting around for Jonas to come up with a reply, hurrying toward the restaurant end of the plaza. He might have choked a bit as she left, or was it her imagination?

The nerve of the council. She clenched her hands into fists and wanted to pound them onto a table and call out these people in charge of the town and its surrounds and demand a full admission of where the money was going.

'Into their pockets,' she mumbled as she passed Italia and India Gate House. Both were busy and for the first time in hours, the delectable mingled aromas of spices and herbs whetted her appetite. She kept walking, thinking of what to make for dinner, and it was a moment before Charlotte noticed she was in the park.

This was a new part of town for her. Rosie often came here for lunch, sometimes alone, other times with Lewis. The river was not much more than a rippling creek flowing through the middle of the expanse of lush grass, beautiful shade trees, picnic areas, and a modern playground. Charlotte wandered along wide paths. If this was where council spent their money, it was well spent. Spaces for families, for those with their dogs, for anyone to enjoy. This part of town was at odds with the plaza which now had no working fountain. Why penalise a town rather than optimise its attractions?

Stopping on a small footbridge, she watched the water below. A sigh left her lips. Jonas was as much a threat to this town as Veronica, Sid, and Terrance. If not others. Thank goodness for all the good people.

Her stomach rumbled and she turned for home in the dark. She hesitated again at the end of the driveway. There was nothing to be afraid of. And yet, she was.

She glanced around. The street was quiet with no pedestrians or evening dog walking in view. No couples holding hands or families enjoying the cooler evening.

And no Sid, or Veronica, or anyone else.

Tomorrow the lights would go in and make all the difference. Charlotte planned to ask the security firm to link the camera along here to those in the bookshop so she could easily see if anyone was around the side of the building.

The driveway stretched far and a shiver went up her spine. Charlotte frowned. Something wasn't right. Her nostrils twitched. There was a smell of aftershave. Someone was here. Waiting.

For an instant she paused. Back to the pavement or run up the steps? Safety was inside her home. Keys already out of her pocket, Charlotte drew in a quick breath and ran to the bottom of the steps.

When she was halfway up the second flight, she saw the figure at the door.

chapter
twenty-eight

Charlotte froze. The hairs stood on the back of her arms and for an instant, her heart pounding in her ears was the only sound.

In the shadows, a tall man straightened from leaning against the wall.

She took a step back, missing the step, and almost fell, her hand flinging out in time to grab the railing.

'Charlie!' Trev was at her side in an instant, his hand on her arm to steady her balance.

Her mouth opened but no sound emerged as her brain caught up. The warmth of his hand seeped through her until the fear drained away. It was Trevor, not some intruder with evil intent.

'Hi.' She managed. He was in jeans and T-shirt. And wearing aftershave.

'I am so sorry to startle you. I should have spoken when you were at the bottom of the stairs.'

'Um…I wasn't expecting anyone.' Balance restored, she moved past him up the stairs, acutely aware of a cold imprint on her arm where his hand had been.

The key wouldn't cooperate in the lock.

'Here. Your hands are shaking.' He took the keyring and unlocked the door, pushing it open. 'Who did you think I was?'

Her eyes went straight to a folded paper on the floor near the door.

Not now.

Trev leaned down to pick it up.

'No!'

Trev paused and looked up at her. Puzzled.

'You need gloves.'

If it wasn't all so serious, his expression would have made Charlotte laugh as he straightened to his full height, reached into a pocket, and removed a single glove. 'Always keep one handy. For…unusual situations.'

Glove on, he lifted the paper. 'May I come in?'

'You kind of are. But yes.'

With his gloveless hand, he reached outside the door. 'I brought beer.' He carried a six-pack in and left it on the counter. Still holding the paper from a corner, Trev gazed at Charlotte. 'You know what this is, and it scares you.'

She closed the door and locked it, giving herself time to think. He couldn't go into the third bedroom, not with Rosie's image on the corkboard. And now that he had this, whatever "this" was, Trev will not give up until he uncovered every piece of the puzzle she'd collected.

'Charlie?'

She returned to where he waited and stopped in front of him, chin raised to meet his eyes. 'Scared isn't quite the word. Frustrated and worried and angry. Before you open it… there's been a couple of others slid under the door.'

He didn't speak, but his jaw tensed.

'And I've gathered some information.' Might as well lay it all on the line.

'About?'

'I'll show you. And Rosie doesn't know.'

'Does anyone?'

'No. But I left a message for Detective Mayer before I went out. I knew it was time.' Charlotte recognised the look he was giving her. Disappointment mixed with worry. And it tugged at her. 'I've messed up.'

'Not about to make a judgement yet. Why don't we look at this?'

He wasn't asking permission. Before Charlotte could open her mouth to say no, he'd laid the paper flat on the countertop and flicked it open. One image.

'Photocopy of a copy. Original downloaded from a phone camera to a copier, then recopied. Home job.' Trev said.

It hadn't occurred to Charlotte these images were off a phone. She'd had it in her head they'd been turned into prints first.

'That's Italia's outside seating. Terrance Murdoch, Jonas Carmichael, and I imagine Veronica…?'

'That is Veronica in all her glory.'

Trev shot an amused glance her way. 'Her glory?'

'How do I explain her? She holds court. Demands attention and doesn't care if it is positive or negative. Is loud and rude and lies.'

'Lies?'

'She yelled at poor Bronnie for bringing a bottle of red to the table saying she ordered white, then when Bronnie hurried inside to replace it, laughed about tricking her.'

'You don't like her one bit.' The corners of his mouth lifted. 'Where's Dr Dean in all of this?'

'She wants to stamp her foot and tell Veronica a few home truths. Don't laugh at me.'

'I'm not. Mum told me Veronica overheard a conversation between you both about Octavia and took it upon herself to tell her.' He turned back to the image. 'Why is she with these clowns?'

'Not sure about Terrance, but Jonas is always close by. He even comforted her when her boyfriend got accidentally… um…kneed in his private bits.' Deserved it, after having his hands around Charlotte's throat. Thank goodness though for Glenys who'd whacked him with her cane to make him release Charlotte.

'Remind me not to annoy you, Charlotte.' Trevor stated.

'Too late.'

Her phone rang and it was Katrina, who asked if she and Bryce could visit now. Trev nodded at her questioning look and she agreed.

'Trevor?'

'Charlie.'

'Will you stay. I mean, with them coming over…'

Trev stopped scrutinising the paper and gave Charlotte his full attention. 'Of course, I will. Besides, we have beers so once the detectives leave, we can sit and talk for a bit. If you'd like to.'

'I would. Should they go in the fridge? Can you put them in because I'd like to freshen up?'

She didn't wait for an answer but dashed for the third bedroom, closing herself in. It took seconds to remove all reference to Rosie from the corkboard. Then, she lifted it off the wall and left it near the door. Two minutes to throw off her shorts and replace them with jeans, and brush her hair and she was ready, or as ready as she could be, to deal with this. At least they weren't about to arrest her.

———

'I've half a mind to arrest you. This is police business, not amateur detective hour.' Bryce stood in the middle of the living room, arms crossed, glaring at Charlotte. 'What if this board includes information leading to the arrest of the murderer?'

The corkboard rested on the sofa. Katrina squatted in front of it, taking photos and ignoring Bryce, who'd been carrying on for the past five minutes. Her calmness kept Charlotte's stress levels down, but she'd have liked some support from Trev. He leaned back against the counter, saying nothing but intent on every word spoken.

'And as for your speculation about Leading Senior Constable Browne? Keep out of it. Our interest in him is none of your business and any further comment will result in my revisiting your poor choice to withhold this information.' Bryce pointed at the corkboard.

I have a history of poor choices. Let's add some more.

Charlotte clamped her lips together and met Trev's eyes. Nothing. No sympathy or encouragement or even anger.

'Bryce, ease up.' Katrina straightened and slipped her phone into a pocket. 'Obviously somebody is watching you, Charlotte. I'd suggest you move in with someone else for a bit or have somebody stay.' She tilted her head at Trev with a slight smile. Before she and Bryce arrived, Trev mentioned that he went through academy with Katrina and she'd recently moved from the city to raise her family in a rural environment.

'I don't think they mean to hurt me.' Charlotte gestured at the board. 'These are images with purpose. Each has a question in it, or a prompt, although I haven't worked out the latest one. The lookout. Frames. That dinner. What do they have in common?'

'Nothing except you are in the vicinity. I've got the photos you've texted me now.' Katrina tapped her pocket. 'We'll see if we can identify the man on the path and get fingerprints, although paper is tricky.'

'Can we get a trace on Charlie's phone?' All eyes turned to Trev. 'Cover all bases.'

'Will talk to the CI. But we're managing a murder and there's nothing to connect any of this to Octavia Morris.' Katrina removed the photocopies from the board, leaving them in their plastic sleeves. 'Coming?' She headed for the door.

Bryce rolled his eyes but followed, pausing beside Charlotte. 'Don't get in the way again.' He shook Trev's hand and joined Katrina at the door. 'Investigation's finished for now. Body's been released so the funeral can be arranged.'

'But, what about Veronica and—'

'And I can still arrest you.' Bryce closed the door with a loud click.

chapter
twenty-nine

An uneasy silence filled the space between Charlotte and Trev, who'd not moved from his spot against the counter. The way he looked at her created waves of nerves in her stomach, a bunch of butterflies flapping away. Did he agree with Bryce?

'That went well!' Charlotte declared on her way into the kitchen. She retrieved two beers, opened them, and offered one to Trev, whose expression hadn't changed. 'Balcony?' Without waiting for a response, she marched to the sliding door and pushed it wide open. Cool air brushed cheeks she'd not known were overheated as she leaned on the railing, staring below.

As a psychiatrist, Charlotte had helped patients through all manner of complex and distressing situations. She was good at it. Really good. But when it came to her own wellbeing, she was at a loss. Why she'd not gone to the police with the first phone call, the initial paper slid under her door, was because of a flaw. One tied up with her failure to make good choices in the past. Each one snowballing to the next. She wanted it to stop.

'Mum said you did all the work out here. Looks fantastic.'

Trev was at her side, his voice neutral. Charlotte turned her body sideways, so she faced him. Or, his profile. Like she had, Trev leaned his arms on the railing, his beer in one hand. He stared into the night.

'Trev?'

His lips curled up. She usually called him Trevor as if it would keep him at a distance. A distance they should stay apart, for his own good. Her heart sank. This was a terrible idea.

Without changing position, he reached out his hand, palm up. He'd done this once before. After the wedding of their dear friends in Rivers End, they'd wandered away from the laughter and music of the reception and sat on a bench near the pond at Palmerston House. She'd told him she was moving here.

And kissed you. To say goodbye.

Was he saying goodbye now?

Charlotte took his hand. For a few minutes they stood together, contemplating the evening, fingers entwined. This felt good. Perfect. And undoable.

She loosened her fingers and his grip tightened as he straightened and faced her. If there was breath in her body, she couldn't feel it. Charlotte bit her bottom lip, but her gaze didn't waver from Trev's.

'Bryce was pretty hard on you,' he said.

What could she say? Yes. But it was deserved? Or, no, and you should have defended me. Her head dropped.

Trev put his beer on the railing and inched toward her, not too close, but enough that the scent of him filled her senses. Keeping hold of her hand, he lifted her chin with his other hand, his eyes now as serious as she'd ever seen. 'Better him than me.' He released her, picked up his beer, and took his first mouthful. Then he shot her a glance. 'I'd have been much harder on you.'

'Oh.'

'Yes. Oh. Charlie, you're playing a dangerous game and tonight it ends. No more secrets about threatening phone calls, people following you, or anonymous notes. Yes?'

'I didn't think any of it mattered. Certainly not as far as the investigation is concerned because I couldn't see a connection until tonight.'

'That's not an answer.'

I can't promise what you want.

Charlotte took a step back and raised the bottle to her lips without drinking.

Trev sighed. 'I don't understand you, Charlotte Dean. Why do you keep dangerous information to yourself. When will you trust me?'

'I do. But I didn't want to bother you all the time. And you can't do much here in Kingfisher Falls, can you?'

'More than you think. Obviously.' Bitterness clouded his tone and Charlotte put her beer down and gave him her full attention.

'Sid told me you have no jurisdiction here. He's not the only one. People keep hinting at some past issue between the two of you and even your mother says there's bad blood. Yet nobody wants to explain, and I have no idea what you can and can't do to help me. To help Rosie.' Her voice rose as frustration coursed through her. 'I'm so worried about her, Trevor. She's had a dreadful scare yet refused to phone you or let me do so. And I'm in the middle and yet unable to fix everything!'

Before she lost control, Charlotte spun around and stalked inside, flopping onto the sofa and crossing her legs. She folded her arms, aware of her defensive stance but too churned up inside to play nice. Trev followed her in at a more sedate pace, carrying both drinks. He stopped a few feet away as though unsure of his welcome.

'Ask me anything.' He perched on the edge of the sofa at the furthest end. And waited.

This was silly. The minutes passed and nobody spoke. Trev was a patient man, one who took his time to understand a situation and then acted with integrity. She admired this in him, always had. But she wasn't going to look at him. Not at all.

'Charlie?'

His voice was so gentle her eyes moved of their own accord to his. There was warmth and worry and strength all mingled into one in his face and with a long exhale, Charlotte decided. 'I did something terrible in Brisbane, in my psychiatry practice.'

Will you walk away once you understand who I really am?

'Go on.'

'I worked with a patient for a few months. A young woman who believed her husband was going to leave her for someone else. There was no proof. No discussion between them. Just her instincts.'

Trev settled back on the sofa, his body language open and encouraging. Charlotte had never spoken of this, not in detail, apart from at the official board hearings and the like. She chose her words to convey the facts in the quickest manner.

'I encouraged her to bring her husband along for some sessions, but she refused. Her description of the relationship and the venom which poured out of her gave me reason to believe she meant to harm him and the person she called his girlfriend. I'm used to patients venting, telling me what they'd like to do, but there's no substance or threat behind their words. Pain, anger, confusion. People who come to someone like me want help.'

'But you saw something in this woman that alarmed you.'

Charlotte nodded and unfolded her arms. 'I'd diagnosed

her with PPD, that's paranoid personality disorder, and anxiety, which is a potent mix and difficult to treat because the patient doesn't trust the doctor either. Anyway, I reported her to the police as I believed there was a high possibility she was plotting to kill her husband.'

'Sounds as though you were justified.'

'I wasn't.' She touched her wrist. No worry bracelet seeing as she'd thrown it away last year. Instead, she played with the fingers of her other hand. 'I saw those conditions in her because I'd grown up with the same narrative. My mother has those diseases, plus a host of others. I misdiagnosed the PPD.'

Sympathy flooded Trev's face and Charlotte looked away as a tide of panic swept through her body. His caring made no sense.

'The police investigation destroyed her marriage. Her husband was faithful, loved his wife, and couldn't understand. She made a complaint and I barely came away with my licence. And you know…they should have taken it.' Charlotte couldn't sit any longer and jumped to her feet. 'My poor judgement of a professional situation damaged two innocent people.' She paced the room. To the sliding door and back, over, and over, as Trev watched her. She felt his gaze but couldn't meet it.

'Was that just before you came to Rivers End?'

Why are you so calm and non-judgemental? Aren't you listening to me?

'Yes. There were legal things to attend to and I had to make sure my mother was under the best care possible.' She stopped near the sliding door and ran her hands through her hair. 'Mum has multiple mental illnesses and at least one is genetic in nature. One way or another I've cared for her since I was eight, when Dad left. So now she's institutionalised and me? I ran away.'

Trev stood and Charlotte walked out onto the balcony. He would leave now. Give up on her as a lost cause and go back to his life in Rivers End. Wouldn't anyone do the same?

'Are you done running?' He was at her side again, but this time, there was a question in his eyes. 'Why tell me this now?'

Her hands shook and he somehow knew because he enclosed them within his. She tried a smile, without success but returned his steady gaze. 'Because, you said you didn't understand why I keep secrets. You asked when I would trust you. Trev, this is me, trusting you.'

Please don't leave. Please see through my terror and insecurity.

As the silence dragged, Charlotte sensed a change between them. Her ability to read Trev was distorted by laying herself emotionally bare. But he wasn't leaving. He didn't look disgusted by her mistakes or her background.

He released her hands to cup her cheeks, and she could feel his breath on her face. 'Know this, Doctor Charlotte Dean, your trust will never be misplaced with me. You're not broken, and it is high time you see yourself the way I do.' His lips touched hers. 'Thank you.'

chapter
thirty

You're not broken.

Charlotte kept those words close. She trusted Trev and would hold onto his view of her until she could find her own way.

It was after midnight and she was alone. After his kiss, which was imprinted on her lips, they'd gone back inside and talked for a long time, holding hands on the sofa. No more kisses, but the change between them was real. Trev knew her fears and her past and he still cared for her. It didn't need saying.

Over the remains of their beers he'd filled her in on his dinner with Rosie.

'I'm staying there tonight and will help her in the morning. Get those filing cabinets upright and bring all the files into the house. Then I need to head back, so are you able to help her sort through them?'

'Of course. Keeping precious memories alive matters. I'm pretty good at cataloguing so will do what I can to make things more accessible for her.'

Trev had smiled. 'She won't know herself, Charlie.'

I don't know myself.

The lightness inside her heart stayed long after Trev left. He'd promised to see her before going home to Rivers End and wrapped her in his arms for a moment before sprinting down the stairs in the dark. Even he had a lightness about him.

Once the door was locked Charlotte realised how hungry she was. Dinner had never happened, so she rattled around in the fridge before settling on a plate of cheese and fruit.

She'd not thought to offer Trev anything other than the beer. And he'd brought those. His dinner with Rosie was at the bistro and then he'd gone home with her to survey the mess left by the intruder. Would she be waiting up to interrogate him once he got back? Charlotte giggled at the vision in her mind of Trev climbing through a window to avoid his wonderful but over-interested mother wanting a full rundown on his visit to the woman she considered his perfect match.

'Perhaps I am.' Charlotte murmured. 'He'll never be bored around me. Or short of things to remind me not to do.' She added sliced pear to soft cheese on a cracker and crunched it.

Meal finished, she cleaned up and returned the corkboard to the bedroom. From the otherwise empty wardrobe, Charlotte collected the photocopied paper targeting Rosie. She pinned it up in the centre and then glanced to the door.

What if Trev walked in at this moment? What would he say about Charlotte still keeping secrets from him, and from the detectives?

But Rosie needs help. Not more interviews and suspicion.

These images had to mean something. Why was Rosie on her own instead of enjoying lunch in the park with Lewis? Had she visited Veronica? The proximity to the garden centre made it possible, but why? Charlotte refused to believe Rosie had anything to do with Octavia's death. This was a side mystery and whoever was responsible for taking the images was someone with nothing better to do.

Pity she'd not thought to take a photograph of the most recent offering. The image of Veronica, Jonas, and Terrance together at Italia was odd. And scary, as the photographer's position was close to where Charlotte and Lachie sat that night.

'Did I see you?'

Trev had taken a photo of it. Charlotte rushed into the living room for her phone to text him, then noticed the time. Tomorrow would do. And tomorrow, she'd ask Rosie about the missed lunch with Lewis.

Sleep first. Perhaps some dreams about a better future than she'd ever considered.

chapter
thirty-one

Charlotte's eyes flew open. It was dark. There were no sounds. Not even thunder, the usual culprit to disturb her sleep. A glance at the clock offered little insight. Five o'clock. Why?

When the phone rang her feet were on the floor in a second and she stumbled to the doorway. It was on the counter, vibrating, ringing, and illuminating the area. Rosie? Trev? Mum?

The number was anonymous.

'Hello?'

A long silence. Charlotte pulled a stool out and sat, rubbing her eyes.

'I warned you.'

Charlotte considered ending the call then and there. But something about this persistence fascinated her. 'You did.'

'Why didn't you leave, Doctor?'

'Well, I did consider what you said. That you'd tell everyone about my past.'

'And I will.'

'Old news, dude.' On the other end of the phone, something like a choke. Or cough. Charlotte preferred choke. 'Let's get a couple of things straight. The people who love me don't give a flying fig about my past. Anyone else isn't important. So why would I leave here?'

She smiled to herself. Trev knew and he didn't care. Rosie would know soon enough, because Charlotte intended to tell her tomorrow. Well, today.

'And what about mummy dearest? You happy for her to rot in the hell you put her into?'

Charlotte's shoulders tensed.

He continued, now with triumph in his voice. 'Bet the local newspaper would love to hear about the new resident who incarcerated her own mother just so she can force an old lady in a wheelchair out of her lifelong business. Good luck with that. Doctor.'

'Rosie isn't old. And if you knew her, you'd never say she could be forced out of anything. You go right ahead and tell the world whatever it is you want to tell. I only know one person in the area vindictive and petty enough to make these calls, so enjoy your early morning coffee. Sid.'

Charlotte disconnected the call and glared at the phone.

Unless it was Kevin. He wasn't nice. Nor was Jonas. Oh dear, what if she'd named the wrong person?

If she could only find out who kept leaving the photocopies, she might find the caller. Instead of glaring at the phone, she played with the settings to see again if she could phone the caller back. No success, but as she put the phone down, an icon caught her eye. The new security access icon.

'Charlotte Dean, you are beyond saving.'

Last night she'd intended to check the footage from earlier in the day to see if Veronica came down the driveway, but Trev's appearance put it out of her mind.

Charlotte opened the app. It gave the option of viewing

the book shop or the driveway and the stairs. If it was working, she might see who slid that last piece of paper under her door.

She perched on the sofa under lamplight and began with the time just after closing the shop. Sure enough, there was Veronica, rushing into the driveway and then answering her phone. She was back out on the main street in seconds. Whatever she'd planned to do, somebody interrupted her.

'It is you! You are following me and taking photographs and coming to my home!'

Veronica must have returned later. Charlotte continued searching, seeing herself leave for her walk. Nothing was happening for ages, so she jumped to the time when she got home.

It was dark now. The image of a broad-shouldered man filled the camera at the top of the steps and when he checked his phone, Trev's face appeared for a moment. Reversing the footage, she watched him go back down the stairs, or at least his outline, as it was too dark to identify him. She switched cameras and saw him walk backwards down the driveway.

Please. Please show Veronica.

A figure appeared in the driveway. Charlotte took short, sharp breaths as she changed the mode to normal play. The figure hesitated, looking behind themselves but again, with little light she couldn't see who it was. But they weren't in high heels and skirt. The figure was tall, more than Trev, and leaner, almost thin. They darted from spot to spot until reaching the bottom of the stairs.

Her hands shook as she selected the other camera. The profile of someone sidled up the steps. They stopped and peered over the railing as if checking nobody was coming along the driveway and then ducked out of sight. Sliding the paper under the door?

The person was back. They rummaged through pockets, head down until a small spark of light appeared. A match lifted to a mouth puckered around a cigarette. Clean shaven skin. A long-sleeved white shirt. The cigarette lit. For an instant, a face hovered in the otherwise black footage.

'Oh, my goodness. Henry?'

chapter
thirty-two

Charlotte watched dawn rise from the balcony, letting a second coffee go cold untouched. She'd watched the footage over and over until the truth sank in.

Henry was stalking her. Or whatever it was he was doing. Taking her photo multiple times, leaving cryptic clues, and creeping to her door on multiple occasions.

Why?

She didn't know him well enough to speculate, but what she did know hadn't alerted her to him being behind this.

He'd grown up in Kingfisher Falls. One employer his whole adult life. The pub, where he started as a waiter then learned management before taking over the bistro and function rooms. Fred and Glenys owned the pub until a few years ago, after Fred's accident, when Glenys retired.

Who owns it now?

Charlotte almost knocked over her coffee as she stood, wanting pen and paper. She saved the cup and left it beside the kettle, flicking that on in a third attempt to have a hot drink. After collecting a notepad and pen, she made coffee and forced herself to sip some in the kitchen as she scribbled questions.

Who owns the pub?

Being behind a bar or waiting tables gave a person an unusual invisibility. Henry had mentioned Terrance and Jonas speaking in front of him at their breakfast about the break-in at Rosie's. Had he overheard other snippets of conversation which encouraged him to do his own investigation?

The day Rosie closed the bookshop early and they'd had lunch at the bistro, Henry was working. He'd waited on them. Charlotte bit her lip, thinking back to what they'd said. They'd discussed the possibility of Octavia's death being suspicious.

Why send clues to me?

And why so cryptic? If the man knew something concrete, he would go to the police. Except. Sid. A person whose track record did nothing to inspire confidence in anyone reporting a crime.

The warmth of the coffee was good. Or the caffeine. Either way, Charlotte was more alert now. She took her cup back outside and continued writing her thoughts down as sunlight filtered through the trees.

Who is Henry?

Married?

Children?

What do you do with your spare time?

The only places she'd ever seen him was at the bistro or a couple of times in the bookshop. He was a reader. And the shop's loyalty programme kept track of purchases, so she'd peek soon to see what he bought.

A glance at her watch reminded Charlotte it was almost time to call Trev. He was an early riser and was the only person she trusted with this information. If Henry was behind the photos, following Charlotte and sending odd messages, he might be responsible for the phone calls. And even Octavia's death. All of a sudden, Charlotte didn't want to be outside. She grabbed her cup, pen and notepad and locked the sliding door behind herself.

———

'I'm shocked, darling. Shocked.' Rosie, Charlotte, and Trev were squeezed in the bookshop kitchen around the monitor, which was paused on Henry's face. 'I've known him forever and had no idea he leads a double life.'

Charlotte's phone call to Trev not long after six o'clock resulted in his arrival on her doorstep fifteen minutes later. He'd gone through the footage on her phone and agreed with her identification.

'Your trust means the world, Charlie.' He'd said with a heartwarming smile, even as it chilled her bones, knowing the secrets she kept in the third bedroom.

Rosie met them downstairs a little later. The image on the bigger screen gave an even eerier feel to Henry's illuminated face. Rosie insisted on seeing every frame of him sneaking up the driveway and steps, her head shaking from side to side as he ducked down to slide the paper under the door.

'But how long has this been happening?' Rosie turned troubled eyes to Trev. 'You said it wasn't the first time.'

'Mum, there's been some others. Last night we met with the detectives from Kyneton and they took the three photocopied papers away. One was taken from the top of the falls looking at Glenys and Charlie at the lookout; another was of Charlie outside the camera shop, and last night's was a photo of diners at Italia.'

'Which diners?'

'Veronica, Terrance, and Jonas. It was the night I had dinner with Lachie.' Charlotte said.

'Did you see Henry?'

Charlotte shook her head.

'He must have a whole lot of interesting photos on his phone!' Rosie backed out of the kitchen.

Trev inserted a speed stick into the recorder. 'I'll make a copy if that's okay.'

'Of course. Charlie, can you help me for a minute?'

Charlotte followed Rosie from the kitchen, stomach churning yet again. There would be photos. Unexplained photos that a good interrogator might ask Henry to explain. And then he'd mention he'd dropped them at Charlotte's place. At this rate she'd need to buy shares in an antacid company.

Or tell the truth more often.

Ignoring her inner voice, Charlotte joined Rosie behind the counter. No lights were on yet, apart from in the kitchen.

'Charlie, there's something I need to tell you. I saw Henry the other day. Taking photos with his phone. It didn't mean anything to me, and I was in a hurry so thought little of it, but now…'

'Was it the day Octavia died?'

Rosie's eyes widened. 'Why, yes. How do you know?'

Without thinking, Charlotte grabbed hold of both of Rosie's hands. 'Please, please tell me you hadn't been at Octavia's house?'

'No. No, I…oh, Charlie.'

As though she was connecting the pieces of the last few minutes conversation together, the colour drained from Rosie's face. She gazed into the distance for a moment, mouth open. Then, her eyes shot to Charlotte's. There was fear in their depths.

'I may have made a terrible choice.' Her voice was little more than a whisper. 'If Henry took a photo of me, it will look bad. Really bad.'

'Why?'

'Oh, darling, I was on the road from Octavia's house. And it was where I was coming from.' Her hands gripped Charlotte's. 'How did you know?'

'Those photocopied images Henry slid under my door? There was another one. With you not far from the garden centre. Time and date stamped.'

'Then the detectives know?' Rosie's shoulders slumped.

'Nobody does.'

'I do. Now.' Trev said.

Charlotte's eyes flickered closed. She dug deep inside. This was about Rosie, not what Trevor thought of her and she stood by her choice to have kept quiet about this. Hearing his footstep behind her, she opened her eyes and turned.

He wasn't looking at her, but his mother. 'Why were you near Octavia's?'

'I had received a phone call and it was suggested to me I should visit Octavia and make things right with her.' Rosie's chin lifted and the fear was gone from her eyes. 'I was on my way to meet Lewis for lunch when the phone rang. I popped in and asked him if we could do lunch the next day and he was busy with customers and blew me a…well. It wasn't a problem.'

Trev leaned his arms on the counter. '*This* is a problem.' His voice was steady, but he still hadn't looked Charlotte's way. 'What happened next?'

'Well, I headed in the general direction, still in two minds. She'd been rather nasty when I'd called her that morning, so was surprised she'd reconsidered her position. But the phone call left me believing Octavia wanted to make amends and I hate to have bad feelings between people. Once I was closer, I became nervous and wondered again if it was a bad idea and whether I'd lose my temper with her. I stopped in the shade down the road, sort of halfway between the garden centre and Octavia's, and just thought it through.'

'Rosie, who—'

'Stay out of it, Charlotte.' His tone was calm. Too calm.

Charlotte released Rosie's hands and put her own in her lap, fingers entwined.

'Trevor, there's no need to be cross with Charlie. I shouldn't have kept this secret. Anyway, I decided the best course of action was to meet Octavia away from her house on another day. When no harsh words had been said. Somewhere neutral. Over coffee maybe. I turned for home and as I went past the garden centre, I noticed Jonas' car was there, and he was just inside the door of the shop. So was Veronica and she was flapping her arms around and carrying on. Before they could see me, I sped up and it was about a block or so further I noticed Henry.'

'And he took your photo?'

'No idea. He didn't seem to see me and didn't acknowledge me. More interested in cars coming up and down the road.' Rosie glanced at Charlotte with an apologetic smile. 'I should have said something.'

'Okay, I'm not understanding, Mum. Did you phone Octavia back to say you weren't coming after all?'

'Octavia? Oh, she wasn't the person who called me. Didn't I mention? As bizarre as this sounds, it was Veronica.'

chapter
thirty-three

The ringing of the shop phone broke the long silence following Rosie's comment. Nobody bothered answering it.

Charlotte wasn't brave enough to risk being told to be quiet although she had a hundred questions. Such as why would Veronica suggest a make-up visit when she not only had accused Rosie of conspiring against Octavia but then made a formal complaint against her? And since when did Rosie believe anything Veronica said? And what was Jonas doing at the garden centre and why was Veronica in a flap and why was Henry taking photos of cars?

'Charlotte. I think now would be good.'

Trev stared at her as she pushed through the fog of her thoughts.

'Sorry. Did I miss something?'

His expression was blank.

'Darling, Trev asked if he could see the picture of me Henry took.'

'No, that's not what I—'

'But it is close enough.' Rosie crossed her arms and levelled a look at her son which he ignored by turning away.

'Sure. I'll get it.' Anything to escape those judgemental

eyes. She stood and hurried to the back door, grabbing keys from her pocket. By the time she was at the back door, Trev was on her heels. 'I'll be right back.'

She tore out of the door and upstairs, but again, he was behind her as she inserted the key into the lock. Charlotte stopped and looked up at him. 'I don't need supervising.'

'I don't trust myself to say what I think you need.' There was a break in his voice. A vulnerability she'd never heard. Then, hardness replaced it. 'Deal with it, Charlotte. I want to see this away from Mum.'

Before the bubble of tears in her heart erupted, Charlotte opened the door and pushed it open. She glanced down, relieved not to see yet another piece of paper. 'In the third bedroom.'

'Lead the way.'

She heard the door close and lock as she headed to the bedroom. None of this was fair. Not to her, him, or Rosie. Protecting someone you love shouldn't be like this. Just deal with it. Sure. She could deal with it.

He followed her into the bedroom and stood at her side, not touching, but close enough for the heat from his body to radiate to hers. Or it might be her imagination. For a long time, he scrutinised the corkboard as the detectives had last night. He removed the offending sleeve and gazed at it, then glanced at Charlotte.

'Where did you hide this?'

'Wardrobe.'

'I understand you want to protect Mum.' He shook his head as exasperation filled his face. 'But this wasn't the way, Charlie.'

At least we're back to Charlie.

'When did you get this?'

'The night Lachie stayed.'

'Lachie?'

'Woodland. Abbie was in hospital having her baby, so Lachie spent the day with me and Rosie, then we went out to dinner. Not Rosie. She went home early to meet the detectives. Lachie and I played card games and then after Darcy collected him, I found the note. Well, Darcy saw it.'

'You're telling me Henry delivered it—for want of a better word—when you and a small child were here?' He was aghast.

'Which made it all much worse. I'd been here before when he'd done it but putting Lachie at risk…' she gulped and sank onto the bed. Would Henry have harmed them, had she opened the door at the wrong time?

'Yet you still told no one.'

He didn't appear to want a response, leaving the room, plastic sleeve in hand. Charlotte stared after him, mouth open. Since when did Trevor ever walk away from a conversation? Was he so upset with her? She jumped up, catching him near the counter.

'Trev. Wait.'

'I want you to stay out of things now.' Trev was almost at the door.

'Please. Please wait a moment.' Without intending to, her voice thickened with emotion desperate to pour out. All her barriers were down. He had to listen.

Hand on the door, he stopped, his back still toward her.

Charlotte forced herself forward, until she was there with him. She reached out but pulled back, then she swallowed and wrapped her arms around his waist, leaning against his strong back. He stiffened but didn't reject her touch. She heard his heart beating through his body, too fast.

'I am so sorry. All I wanted was to protect Rosie.'

'This wasn't the right way.'

'I've made it worse.'

'You may have. I don't know yet.' Frustration coloured his tone. 'How many more secrets do you still keep from me?'

Charlotte couldn't think of any. Perhaps there were none. 'There's no more photocopied papers. No phone calls I've not told you about. I've shared my past. But there may be something, some moment I've thought not important or speculation about someone, or—'

'I'm not talking about incidentals.' Trev rotated until he faced Charlotte, dropping his arms behind her to hold her against him. The uncertainty in his expression alarmed Charlotte. He was always in control. Always knew what to do. 'Secrets, Charlotte. Like this.' He moved the plastic sleeve behind her. 'Ones with ramifications. Do you have any idea how complicated this might get?'

'But if I explain to the detectives that I didn't think anything of it. That I forgot I had it…no. No, I won't lie. But I will take responsibility.' She lifted her chin.

'Will you both come down here?' Rosie called from the bottom of the steps.

Trev opened the door. 'Two secs, Mum.' He rested his forehead against Charlotte's and murmured. 'Bernie's back in custody, I got a call late last night. He might have killed you in Rivers End. You didn't trust me then, not even when I knew something was wrong and I asked you to let me help. I'm not sure I want to go through life wondering if you are hiding things. Wondering if I'm about to lose you.'

'What are you saying?'

He released her. 'I have to speak to Katrina.'

Without another word or look, he was gone, down the stairs, leaving the door open in his wake. Charlotte's lips parted to say something, anything, but nothing came out. In a lifetime of fending for herself and being content with her own company, she'd never felt this way. Alone. Utterly alone.

chapter
thirty-four

Charlotte closed the door and leaned against it, eyes shut, and arms hugging herself.

Why keep doing this, Charlie?

From downstairs, Rosie's voice drifted, raised. Agitated. Charlotte couldn't make out any words, but the tone was there. Rosie was upset with Trevor.

Everything was falling apart. Her safe apartment wasn't safe. Rosie's house either. The town was not the peaceful little village it pretended to be, but as Rosie once said, a den of iniquity. Bad people doing bad things. And now mother and son against each other.

She wanted to run. Let her legs carry her as far and fast as they could until there wasn't an ounce of energy in her body. To the falls where she'd seek refuge beneath the shady trees on the soft green grass beside the glassy pool and hear nothing but the roar of crystal water tumbling down.

And it wouldn't change anything.

It stops now. The secrets. The running. No more.

She took a long, deep breath and dropped her arms to her side. Rosie and Trevor weren't going to argue about her. And she wasn't going to run. Just as she'd broken her need for the bracelet, she would overcome the impulse to flee.

Checking her keys were in her pocket, Charlotte stepped out onto the small porch and locked the door. As she followed the steps down, Rosie's words became clear.

'I can't bear for you to be angry with her, darling. Charlotte has a good heart. She's a good girl.'

'Yes, she is. But her past has messed with her sense of right and wrong.'

Charlotte joined them. They jumped, too intent on their debate to hear her approach. Rosie had tears flowing down her cheeks again. Trevor's face was drawn, his eyes sad.

'My sense of right and wrong is solid. What I struggle is with trust.' Charlotte spoke quietly but with confidence.

Trev dropped his head.

'Self-trust, Trev. I have always trusted you, from the moment you pulled my car over and I dropped a road map at your feet. But I made some terrible judgement calls in my practice and it coloured my ability to trust myself.'

'Yet, when there's a crisis, you are the most level-headed, reliable, and bossy person I've ever met.' Trev met her eyes. His were unsure.

'Funny, that's how Charlotte describes you, dear.' Rosie brushed tears from her cheeks.

'Only the bossy bit, she means.' Charlotte said.

The corners of Trev's mouth flicked up for an instant.

'So, I've made a decision about getting some help with my self-trust issue. I'll find a therapist and do the work I should have done months ago. I need help with it.' It was good to say it aloud.

Rosie reached up a hand and Charlotte clasped it. 'We're here for you, darling.'

Charlotte leaned down and kissed her cheek with a quiet, 'Thank you.'

'And Trev will get over himself.' Rosie whispered.

'I'm right here, Mum.'

'You two are meant for each other.'

'Rosie!' Charlotte couldn't believe her ears.

Trev laughed. He threw back his head and laughed.

Charlotte and Rosie exchanged a glance, which became a shared smile. Then, Rosie turned her wheelchair and headed down the driveway, Charlotte at her side.

'Tell me again, Charlie, about the day you met my son. Did you like him on first sight?'

'Rosie!'

―――

The moment of silliness cleared the air, more or less. Charlotte caught Trev staring at her a couple of times as they worked together to move the contents of the filing cabinets onto Rosie's dining table. He'd already righted the cabinets with a comment it was time to replace them and keep whatever Rosie wanted in the house.

Before leaving the bookshop, Rosie handwrote a sign to affix to the door. *'Open later this morning. Sorry for any inconvenience'.*

Now, she cooked breakfast for three with Mellow perched on the back of the sofa watching her. Mayhem stalked between house and shed as if to show his irritation at the intrusion. He sat in the middle of the shed as Charlotte picked up a final armful of files.

One slid off and skidded under the shelves along the wall. She knelt to retrieve it, peering under to see where it went. There was something else under there, lengthwise against the wall and she could just reach it.

It was the axe handle.

That's not where I left you.

No, she'd put it on the higher shelf, where Rosie asked her to. Then it was gone the day forensics were here.

'Why are you on the floor?' Trev wandered in. 'What's that?'

'I dropped a file and found this under the shelf. Right at the back.'

'Dad's old axe handle.'

'Oh. Last time I saw this, it was here.' She pointed. 'Rosie was loaning me some tools and I saw it there.'

'Let's put it back.' He slipped the handle between two boxes. 'Pass me the files.'

Charlotte handed them over and scrambled up, dusting herself down. 'Thing is, between me seeing it that evening, and the day forensics were dusting for fingerprints, it moved.'

'Moved. How?'

She shrugged. 'I noticed it wasn't there when Sid was digging around. Touching everything as if he'd find some murder weapon. He said he was searching for something long and heavy, like a handle. I glanced there because I expected him to see it and accuse Rosie of using it to knock Octavia over.'

'But it was missing. You certain you put it here?' Trev peered at the handle as if expecting it to answer him.

'Quite sure. Trevor.'

He grinned, without looking at her. 'Must have slid backwards and fell between the shelf and wall.'

'No. No, that isn't what happened.' Rosie was in the doorway. 'I knew what Sid would do if he saw it. I had about thirty seconds out here before the nice forensics police arrived and Sid would have been on their tails. So, I rolled it under. Right to the back. It isn't the murder weapon and I wasn't having Sid remove your Dad's property. Breakfast is ready.'

With that, she was gone. Mayhem hissed at Charlotte and Trev and stalked after her.

Charlotte didn't say a word. Trev's jaw had dropped, and he stared at the doorway. Then, he ran a hand through his hair. 'Right. I no longer know if you are a bad influence on Mum, or she on you.'

'Bit of both? What's so special about an axe handle?'

'Dad loved chopping wood. He even competed in the local agricultural shows and won a couple of wood chopping competitions. Always said it gave him an outlet when stuff from the past bothered him. Things he saw as a journo in war zones.'

'And that was his favourite.'

'He'd taken the head off to replace. Never got around to it before his heart gave up.' Trev sighed. 'Mum has no need for an axe, but she won't let go of it.'

'And she wouldn't use it to hit Octavia with. Not something so precious.'

Trev glanced at the axe handle. 'Katrina and Bryce were out here. Did a cursory search, from what Mum told me. Guess they didn't notice that.'

'Guess not.'

He adjusted the files in his arms. 'I need to call Katrina and tell her about Henry. But after breakfast I've got to go home.'

'Does Sid need to be told as well?'

Trev shook his head. 'Sid has other issues to deal with. I'll leave the speed stick with you. Okay?'

'Okay.'

'And the image of Mum. Tell her what you know. Keep to the facts, not your speculations about who did what to whom. Got it?'

Charlotte nodded.

'Good. We'd better go before Mum wonders what's keeping us in here.' Trev led the way to the door.

'She is incorrigible. Trying to find out what I thought of you the day I arrived in Rivers End.'

'Should have arrested you, the way you were driving. Any more secrets and I will.'

'Gotta catch me first.' Before she could stop herself, Charlotte sprinted toward the house, Trev chuckling in her wake.

chapter
thirty-five

After breakfast, Charlotte headed off to open the bookshop. She wanted to give Rosie and Trev a few minutes alone before his long drive back to Rivers End. Tonight, she'd help Rosie sort the files.

Unless you've been arrested by then for withholding evidence.

Charlotte let herself into the bookshop through the back door, disarming the alarm. Katrina and Bryce would drop by later sometime to look at the footage of Henry. Charlotte left the plastic sleeve behind the counter, beneath a book, but kept the speed stick in her pocket. Her intention was to hand both over with little comment. Rosie mentioned she'd give her lawyer a ring before coming to work and run through the state of things. Just in case.

Glenys was the first customer in, impatient for Charlotte to open the door. 'What's wrong? I came earlier and you were closed!'

'Rosie and Trev and I had breakfast before he went home.'

'He's gone now?' Glenys put both hands on the counter. Her eyes went straight to the photographs behind Charlotte.

'He has. How long did you own the pub for?'

'What? Oh, that place. Too long. It was Fred's big inheritance and he insisted we live there and run it for years.' She turned her attention on Charlotte. 'It was good in the respect of holding wedding receptions upstairs because I got paid photographing the weddings. But the rest of the time, I did the work while Fred followed his passion!'

Her hands curled into balls.

'That must have been frustrating, Glenys. You love your photography, don't you?'

Glenys smiled. 'Yes. Yes, I certainly did. Not that I do much now. Everything is about digital cameras and even some phones have cameras almost as good as my old SLR was.'

'I worked in a pub to pay my way through university. Most people don't stay long.' Charlotte said.

'It is the way of hospitality. Staff come and go. Only ever had one person who was loyal. Young Henry. He was always there to give me a hand, but he didn't get along with Fred.'

'I've met him a few times. Isn't he in the photo up there?' Charlotte pointed. 'So young.'

'Came to us out of school. But why he stayed when I sold, I'll never know. He hates the owner. Says he reminds him of Fred.'

'Hello, Glenys.' Rosie arrived with two coffees in a tray. 'What can we do for you today, if Charlotte hasn't already asked.'

'I really want to have that photo of me. Happy to pay whatever you ask.'

Charlotte stepped back to give Rosie room to get to her usual spot behind the computer. What was so important about that photograph?

'Why don't I arrange a copy? Would that do?'

A flash of anger across Glenys' face said no. 'Very well. When?'

Rosie's eyebrows raised but she nodded. 'If we have time

today, one of us will go and see Harpreet. I imagine it won't take long and I'll give you a call.'

Glenys took out her purse and placed a twenty-dollar bill on the counter. 'I'll await your call.' She stomped out without another word, pausing on the street to look either way, before turning right.

'Oh dear.' Rosie put the coffees onto the counter. 'She is in a mood.'

'Grief does that. And I think Octavia's death ignited some unresolved grief about Fred.'

'He wasn't a nice man.'

'Doesn't matter. Grief can be more than about loss through death. If their marriage wasn't good, she might grieve the lost chance to have improved it. And with Octavia, she missed the opportunity to repair their long friendship.' Charlotte sat and took a sip of coffee.

'Octavia pushed us both away. I blame Marguerite for much of it.' The tinge of bitterness in Rosie's voice was unlike her usual, tolerant self.

'Things changed when she and Sid moved here?'

'Oh, Marguerite grew up in Kingfisher Falls. She went to a private school in another town, so we only knew each other through sports and parties. Later, she travelled far and wide and after meeting and marrying Sid in the city, came home with the attitude of being better than everyone. She and Octavia hit it off.'

'And Glenys?'

Rosie sighed. 'She started the book club years ago. When the other two joined, they all got close, but Glenys was more a third wheel. Being the wife of the hotelier was beneath those two.'

Charlotte laughed. 'Yup. Sid was such a catch.'

'I wish they'd never moved here. The resident police officer suddenly left the force and Trev, almost straight out of academy, was running things while applications were underway, including his. But Sid was tired of travelling to where he was stationed and wanted the job, so began badgering Trev. Turning up at the station and call outs. Anonymous complaints about him. Stuff that made Trev threaten him with a formal complaint.'

'How awful!'

'Before it came to that, Trev was offered the position in Rivers End.'

And everything made sense. The bad blood comments. Trev warning Charlotte to steer clear of Sid, a man who'd proven to Charlotte he was underhand by creating fake Face-book accounts to give the bookshop and Christmas Tree Farm bad reviews last year.

'He has a track record of anonymous calls?'

Rosie nodded and drank some coffee.

Charlotte stretched. 'I think Sid is in trouble. I hope so.'

'At this moment, darling, I'm more concerned for you and for me. Someone wants us blamed for Octavia's death. That someone is either responsible, or knows who is, and I don't believe it is Henry.'

'But—'

'No, buts, Charlie. Henry—for want of a better description—is a scaredy cat. I've never known him to step outside the narrow box he's made of his life and quite doubt he'd kill someone.' She leaned toward Charlotte and whispered. 'If anything, Henry is trying to help us.'

chapter
thirty-six

Every time a car stopped out the front, or somebody walked into the bookshop, Charlotte jumped, expecting to see two annoyed detectives holding out handcuffs. Or at least one, as Katrina was by far the nicer of the pair. As it was, she was sitting on the floor in the children's area, reading to a three-year-old, when Bryce ambled in. She was unaware of him until the little boy pointed.

'Oh. Yes. Well, that man is a nice police officer in plain clothes. How about we show your mum this book?'

A moment or so later, the little boy was back with his mother and Charlotte led Bryce to the kitchen.

'You're alone again?' Charlotte knew she should watch her smart mouth, but something about Bryce brought out her sarcastic side.

'I've only worked with Katrina for a few weeks, but already I'm seeing a pattern. Suspects think she's a soft touch.' He grinned. 'They always get a shock when they get to know her more.'

'I'm not a suspect. You already told me so.'

'Yet, here we are.' He leaned against the wall, arms crossed and nodded at the monitor. 'Care to share?'

She did. Bryce took a lot of interest in the whole recording, including Veronica's earlier appearance. He paused it a couple of times. 'Any ideas?'

'Why she was there and then left? None. I should have shown you what she did just before. Actually, I can.'

Charlotte found the recorded footage of Veronica testing the door and peering inside. 'I know we have a lovely bookshop, but between her and Sid, I'm getting tired of the after-hours inspections.'

'Sid?'

'Since before Christmas his behaviour has gone downhill. At one point he set up a random breath test station outside the shop on our busiest day of the year. But he didn't stop anyone, just made it more difficult for our customers.'

'Why?' Bryce's attention was on Charlotte, his eyes narrowed.

'He doesn't like Rosie or Trev and from the moment I arrived, he's reminded me ad nauseum how unwelcome I am and how he intends to uncover some lurid past I have.'

'Why?'

'Is that all you can say? Because my existence annoys him.'

'Can't imagine that.'

Charlotte decided she liked Bryce. There was intellect and humour under the exterior.

Bryce picked up the plastic sleeve she'd brought from the counter and spent a few minutes examining it. He tossed it onto the kitchen counter. 'Any theories about what Henry is trying to tell you?'

Be careful. This may be a trap.

'Those images make no sense. The one from the lookout makes me wonder if he saw something being thrown over that needs checking. Everything else is a mystery.'

'And you like a mystery.'

Darn, he was good.

'Would you ask Mrs Sibbritt for a moment of her time now?' Bryce had the remote and scrolled through footage.

Dismissed, Charlotte was unsure whether to relax or be on high alert. Was it possible the Rosie photos didn't interest him?

'Finished already?' Rosie wheeled toward her. The worry in her eyes tugged at Charlotte.

'He's not a bad guy. I mean, don't let your guard down, but don't be afraid.'

'Me. Never.' Rosie straightened herself and headed to the kitchen.

What would these next few minutes bring? Accusations and an arrest? Or two? Charlotte shuddered at the possibilities.

Katrina stood outside the shop on her phone. After a moment she hung up.

Charlotte busied herself behind the counter as the detective came inside. 'Hello, your partner's in the kitchen with Rosie if you'd like to go through.'

'Nah. They won't be long. I wanted to ask you something.'

Charlotte's heart sank. Was this where Katrina showed the side Bryce hinted at?

'What's your take on Henry? What do you know about him?'

'Not much. Rosie would be more helpful.'

Katrina leaned against the counter. 'But I'm asking you.'

'Okay. I've met him four or five times. Twice at the bistro, where he waited on the table I was at.'

'And how was he with you then?'

'Attentive. Rosie dropped a fork and he appeared from nowhere with a clean one. I called him a ninja.' Charlotte smiled.

'Go on.'

'He's been here the other times. Twice to buy books

before Christmas, which reminds me, I meant to see what he bought.' She sat and tapped on the computer. 'And a couple of days ago he ran in, wearing his apron, to tell me he'd overheard Jonas Carmichael and Terrance Murdoch discuss the break-in at Rosie's house the previous night.'

There was a spark of interest in Katrina's eyes.

'They were having their regular breakfast meeting at the pub. Henry was upset and worried about Rosie so came to see if she was alright.'

Katrina took out her phone and made a note. 'Do you have a professional opinion about him?' She looked up. 'Off the record.'

'Not without proper evaluation.'

There was the hint of a smile on the detective's face. 'Personal opinion then.'

'He likes his comfort zone. Managing the bistro, working in the same place his whole life, regardless of personal issues with the owners. Away from it? Bundle of nerves. Even the footage shows a frightened man.'

'Yet, he visited your apartment several times to deliver cryptic messages.'

There was nothing for Charlotte to say in return. Henry had chosen her for some reason. Perhaps because she'd stood up for the Woodlands last year. Or because of her profession. Her eyes strayed to the computer screen, to the list of books Henry had purchased over the past year.

'Are you certain you won't stay for coffee, Bryce?' Rosie and Bryce appeared from the kitchen.

Charlotte minimised the open screen and stood.

'Thanks, Rosie. I think we're going to head across and collect a certain gentleman for a chat at the station. Will be in touch.' He shook Rosie's hand with a smile. 'No more keeping concerns like that to yourself.'

Katrina nodded to Charlotte and Rosie and left. Bryce

paused at the counter and leaned across. 'No more sleuthing, Doctor. Deal?' He grinned and followed Katrina. Charlotte sank back onto the stool as Rosie joined her with a curious expression.

'What was that about?'

'More to the point, Rosie, why is he so nice to you? Last night he told me off for ages and how he should arrest me and all in front of your son.'

'And what did Trev say?'

'Nothing. Not until they left. Then he said he'd have been much harder on me!'

'I see.' Rosie smiled to herself.

'What do you see?'

'Nothing.'

'Are you a clairvoyant now?'

'Yes, darling. I see love in your future.'

Heat rushed up Charlotte's neck and face and she grabbed a bottle of water to hide it. This was going too far. To cover the sudden embarrassment, she maximised the screen she'd had open on Henry's purchases.

Rosie patted her shoulder. 'Sorry. Been one of those days and humour helps a bit. What are we looking at?'

'I'm curious about the books Henry bought from us. Look at that, Rosie.' She pointed at each title. 'True crime. Forensics. And…oh!'

'Perfect Photographs of Kingfisher Falls.'

chapter
thirty-seven

'We need to find a copy of that book. There isn't anyone you know who would loan us theirs?'

Rosie tapped on the keyboard. 'There's a couple I could try, but most buyers get these kinds of books to send to their friends or family in other places. I'll phone them, but don't hold out much hope.'

'Before you do, what happened with Bryce?' Charlotte asked.

'Such a nice man. He wasn't concerned about that piece of paper. He took some photographs of it, but just suggested I trust my instincts more. Mind you, he did ask about Veronica and why she'd phone me and I struggled to answer. Looking back, I wonder if she knew something happened to Octavia and wanted me to be seen nearby. But how could she, unless she was involved?'

As Rosie attended to making phone calls, Charlotte fetched the step ladder from the kitchen. The timeline wasn't right for Veronica to have killed Octavia. The teapot was cold from their shared cup of tea. Veronica had an alibi for the time of death. Who? Jonas? Pity Katrina and Bryce weren't forthcoming with the information Charlotte needed.

She grinned at her silly thoughts as she climbed up to remove the photograph from the wall behind the counter. The police should fill her in on the details of their interviews. Hand over their notes. Or she could sit in on their investigation.

Would make my job easier.

Back on the ground, she folded the step ladder and left the photograph on the back counter.

'Well, thank you anyway, dear. I'm so pleased your daughter in England enjoyed the book.'

Rosie sighed as she hung up. 'That's two negatives so far. Are you taking the photo to Harpreet?'

'If you are okay with it. Before Glenys checks up on us.'

'Take the money she left. If it costs any more, I'll cover it.'

A few minutes later Charlotte opened the door to the frame shop. Harpreet emerged from a back room with a wide smile. 'Charlotte! Would you like tea?'

'Oh, I wish. But I have to get back to the shop soon.'

'You have something for me to do?'

Charlotte showed Harpreet the photograph and explained Glenys wanted a copy.

'Easy. Can you stay for a couple of minutes while I do so?'

'That fast? Thank you.'

Harpreet removed the photograph from the frame and inserted it into a machine. 'Just one copy?'

'One is fine. Have you been busy?'

'The usual for this time of year. People away on holidays but then soon they'll be back, and I'll be run off my feet when they want prints done.' She laughed. 'Every year it is the same and I look forward to it.'

The machine buzzed and Harpreet brought the new copy to show Charlotte. 'I'll get the original so you can see.'

Both appeared the same to Charlotte, but Harpreet frowned. 'The original is quite old, and the copy lacks some of the clarity.' She peered at the copy with a magnifying glass. 'Have a look.'

She passed the glass to Charlotte.

'My goodness! I never thought to use one of these.' Charlotte got a close-up look at Fred Lane for the first time. The scowl on his face was more obvious, his eyes angry and neck red. He wasn't as well dressed as Octavia's tuxedo-wearing husband, in a worn sports jacket and red bow tie with white polka dots which matched Glenys' long red dress but was otherwise out of place for a gala event.

She turned her attention to Henry in the background. In white shirt, black pants, and long apron, he was a young version of the man who'd rushed into the bookshop a few days ago. But he stared at Fred with something akin to fear in his face. Or hatred.

'Is it okay? I can redo it.'

'No need. This will be fine, thanks. I do love the magnifier and might buy one to look at some images I have at home.' Charlotte said.

'Take that one. I have so many.'

'Are you certain? I'll return it tomorrow.'

'Whenever. When we have that tea. Okay?' Harpreet reframed the original. 'I'm hearing rumours and I don't like it.'

'About?'

'Poor Mrs Morris. And someone in Kingfisher Falls being responsible. Mrs Wheemor told me Rosie did it and I admit, I did laugh at her. She wasn't happy with me.'

'Rosie didn't. But who is Mrs Wheemor?'

Harpreet gave Charlotte a shocked look. 'You know. High heels and bright orange lipstick?'

'Veronica?'

'Veronica Wheemor. She told me she descends from the Somerset Wheemors, or something. And don't forget the 'H' when writing her name.' Harpreet's lips quivered. She snuck a glance at Charlotte, and both burst into laughter.

As funny as she found it, her walk back to the bookshop was consumed with the images of Fred and Henry. So much tension in one photograph. Poor Glenys looked uncomfortable and upset. Had Henry been privy to the problems of the couple? Witnessed Fred being unkind, or worse, to Glenys?

She stopped in the middle of the footpath.

Did Henry kill Fred?

Nervous demeanour or not, a person could be pushed hard enough to carry out the unthinkable. Was it possible he was at the falls when Fred fell? Charlotte needed to look at the photos of the man on the track that day. He'd been confident of his footing so was likely to be a local, someone used to the terrain.

But why send clues to me?

Charlotte got going. Some personality types needed to be noticed. Do something terrible then draw attention to it. She needed to find her reference book to refresh her memory

Rosie was hanging up the phone as Charlotte hurried in. 'Darling, no luck at all yet, but I found something interesting.'

'Me too. You go first.'

'I didn't notice until I was going through the list of buyers, but one of them was Octavia.'

'Octavia bought Fred's book? When?'

'Ages ago. I can't be exact because we only put the computer system in four or five years ago and I transferred as many of the paper records across as I could. Never thought to include purchase dates, so it may have been straight after it came out.'

'Do you mind if I look at photos on my phone? Ones I took when Octavia…you know.'

'Died? No need to tiptoe around me, Charlie. Go right ahead and tell me what you were going to.'

Charlotte placed the photo frame on the back counter and handed the copy to Rosie. 'I'll get the step ladder in a minute. Harpreet loaned me this.' She removed the magnifying glass from a pocket. 'Have a look at Henry's expression and tell me what you think.'

As Rosie pored over the photograph, Charlotte searched the gallery in her phone for the images from Octavia's house. She scrolled past those of the body. Kitchen, no. View to the window with the sofa and some expensive looking art on an easel. No.

'Aha!'

'What?' Rosie's eyes shot up.

'I took a photo of Octavia's bookcase and look what is there!' Charlotte enlarged the picture to show a fuzzy but recognisable book.

'Fred's book. And displayed on a stand.'

'I never noticed the subtitle. "One man's perfect view". Must have hurt Glenys for the publisher to add it, given she contributed.' Charlotte said.

'They used a vanity publisher.'

'A what?'

'Paid for it to be published. Fred provided the images and text and the so-called publisher turned it into the book, printed a hundred or so copies—most of which Glenys had to buy because Fred was gone, then did little more but sell to a couple of their friendly bookshops. I bought quite a few because we get asked all the time for local books.' Rosie returned to the copy. 'I've never seen Henry so upset as this. I wonder if he'd overheard Fred telling Glenys to stay out of the photo. He's quite fond of her and even helped her move to her property when she sold the pub.'

'Who owns it now? The pub.'

'Did this never come up before? I thought you knew. Kevin Murdoch does.'

'Oh. I had no idea, Rosie. And he was Octavia's man friend.'

'Surely you don't think Henry killed her?' Rosie's eyebrows shot up.

'I don't know what to think anymore.'

Should I tell you my latest theory?

'No more sleuthing, doctor.' Bryce's earlier warning intruded. He could get her into Octavia's house to borrow the book. Or go himself. She must have his number somewhere.

'I'll let Glenys know this is ready. Are you still up to helping me after work?' Rosie asked.

'Happy to. It will be good to do something unconnected to all of this. Octavia, and Henry, and Veronica Wheemor—'

'Oh, that's her surname! I knew it was something…well, odd.'

'She descends from the Somerset Wheemors.'

'A well-known family, no doubt.' Rosie handed the magnifying glass to Charlotte. 'I agree. From now on we'll leave the police work to the detectives and tonight we might order pizza and eat as we sort. At least I know there's no mysteries hidden among Graeme's files.'

chapter
thirty-eight

'Do you have a theory on who broke in? And what was taken?' Charlotte spread files in date order across the dining room table, while Rosie sorted their contents one at a time. To her side was a large box where she placed anything she found which was not suitable to re-file. So far, it was copies of newspapers, old work letters, and books on journalism.

Nothing was being thrown away yet, but Charlotte's recommendation of separating what was of true value to Rosie from the rest made it easier. Once Rosie had everything she wanted, then their attention could turn—on another day—to the box.

'I'm stumped, darling. So far, there's nothing missing I can see. Of course, I don't recall everything Graeme kept, but nothing stands out.'

'We'll keep looking. I can't believe some of these incredible treasures. You must get Harpreet to frame some of the photographs and articles!'

Rosie beamed. 'Graeme was so talented. And so brave and kind. Even in our later life, when his health wasn't what it used to be, he'd be there for anyone who needed him.' She held out an article from a newspaper. 'This is the piece he wrote in tribute of Fred Lane. Well, perhaps not tribute, as he didn't like the man much, but as an overview of the lovely photographs he took over the years. The habitat is important, and Fred had highlighted the need to protect the area around the falls to encourage the kingfishers to repopulate.'

Charlotte skimmed the article, more interested in its two photographs. One was of Fred at the lookout in a casual pose. Two cameras were draped around his neck. He stared at the falls.

'Graeme took that a few weeks before the accident and I recall him saying how difficult it was to get the shot. Fred kept scowling at the camera so Graeme asked him to look away.'

'He liked his bow ties.'

'Don't believe I ever saw him without one. Glenys joked that she always knew what to get him for Christmas.'

The second photograph was familiar. An image of the pool and river from the top of the falls. She'd taken a few of these herself, but this one was from a professional camera, with clarity only marred by the ageing paper it was printed on.

The caption beneath credited it as from *Perfect Photographs of Kingfisher Falls* with Fred Lane as the copyright holder.

'How long after Fred died was this article published?'

'Oh, let's see.' Rosie dropped some papers into the box. 'At least three months. Could be longer because the book was released the same week the paper came out, which is why Graeme included the photograph from it.'

Charlotte pulled the magnifying glass from her handbag and searched the photograph.

'Darling, whatever are you doing?'

'No idea, but I wish I had the book to look at! Black and white on old paper is hard. But here, is that something in the water?' She passed everything to Rosie. 'A duck bobbing along?'

'Or a piece of debris. All manner of things ends up in the river so it could be anything. And I just had an idea about where to borrow the book.'

———

Charlotte peered through twilight for the entry to Glenys' property. Unlike the big sign leading to the Christmas Tree Farm it abutted, this entrance was almost impossible to see. Not even a letterbox marked the property with just a narrow gap between unkempt bushes. The driveway wound down a hill through bushland before opening to a sparse garden around a small house.

There was an empty carport to one side, no lights on at the house, and no sign of movement. Charlotte turned her car and parked it where she hoped it wouldn't be in the way if Glenys arrived before she left.

Rosie had rung Glenys' on both her landline and mobile with no reply, and neither number had a voicemail. 'I'm sure she wouldn't be far from home and won't mind you dropping by. If she still has all those books, surely she'll loan us one for the evening.'

'Right. Looks inviting.' Charlotte muttered as she climbed out of her car, phone in hand for its flashlight. Gum trees surrounded the house with a backdrop of pines from Darcy's farm. Perhaps in daylight it was pretty, but Charlotte got a sense of isolation and sadness from this place. She shivered, despite rising humidity warning of another storm on the way.

She tapped on the front door, not expecting an answer, and not getting one. Deciding to wait for a few minutes in case Glenys returned, she wandered around the perimeter of the house. Every curtain was drawn. At the back, she shone her flashlight around. A clothesline. Nothing else.

Charlotte's nose screwed up. Smoke. She followed the smell to an open firepit near a row of trees. Charlotte couldn't think of another word to describe the crudely dug hole lined with old bricks.

There was no fire alight, but the remains of burnt papers and boxes almost filled the space. And books. Charlotte leaned in and gasped. Most were past saving, but to one side, a scorched but identifiable copy of Fred's book. The rest of the books were the same shape and size, what was left of them. Glenys had bought them and set them on fire.

Charlotte plucked the intact book out of the pit and shook the charcoal off it. The edges of the pages were black but otherwise, the copy was fine. And if Glenys was destroying these—as a kind of cleansing of her grief—then she'd never miss this one.

An abrupt change from dusk to night heightened the seclusion of the house. Charlotte straightened. She wasn't willing to wait for Glenys.

She hurried to her car and slid behind the wheel, locking the doors with a small laugh at her foolishness. The coldness down her spine increased with every second she stayed here, and she sighed with relief as her car started and the headlights came on. As she navigated the driveway, her hands clenched the steering wheel. What if there was something hiding in the undergrowth?

'Like what, Charlie? Get a grip.'

Back on the dirt road, Charlotte picked up speed but watched every movement on the sides in case kangaroos were out and about. At the turn-off to the road to town, another car cut the corner and she slammed on the brakes to avoid a collision.

Heart racing, Charlotte glanced over her shoulder at the departing tail lights. It was Glenys' car.

———

Back at Rosie's house, Charlotte locked the book in her car and hurried inside. All she wanted was to go home and investigate every inch of the charred book, but with the magnifying glass and without Rosie being involved.

'Did you see Glenys?' Rosie met her at the front door. 'Come in. Pizza arrived a few minutes ago.'

Pizza. Darn. She'd forgotten about food.

'I've got it in the oven on warm, so shall I get it out now?'

'I'll help.' Charlotte locked the front door and followed Rosie. 'I saw Glenys, but only after she nearly collected the front of my car by cutting a corner!'

'Oh dear. She's never been a brilliant driver, but I fear age is making her careless. What did she say?'

'It was near the turn off and I'd already been to her house, so wasn't about to go back. Have you been there?'

Rosie pulled a pizza box from the oven, steam clouding her glasses. 'Um…'

'Hang on.' Charlotte took the box and closed the oven door. 'Perils of wearing glasses.'

'Annoying it is.' Rosie took her glasses off and wiped them. 'I have visited. It is a bit out of the way, isn't it?'

'A bit creepy at night, with no lights and all those huge trees watching me.'

'As Lachie would say, trees don't watch people.'

Yes, he would.

Charlotte smiled. 'I wonder how Abbie is. And all of them.'

'I'm sure we'll hear soon. I've put plates on the outside table.'

The pizza was delicious and filled a need Charlotte had ignored all day. The cats hung around as though hopeful for a morsel, which Rosie catered for with tiny pieces of meat.

'Glenys phoned earlier.' Rosie announced.

'Earlier, when?'

'You'd been gone for a while and she said she'd seen a missed call on her mobile. That she'd been praying at the lookout and hadn't heard the phone ring.'

'Did you ask her about the book?'

'I did. And I barely got the words out and she snapped at me. No! They are mine! So, I explained you'd gone to her house and she hung up on me.'

'Speeding to tell me to stay away from her fire pit.'

'Fire pit?. Well you'll be driving so can't have a drink, but I'm not, so I will. There is juice in the fridge.' Rosie disappeared inside. 'Then tell me everything.'

chapter
thirty-nine

'Let's see what your secrets are.' Charlotte took the book onto the balcony, switching on the overhead light and then sipping from a glass of wine.

It was late. She'd filled Rosie in on her strange discovery and they'd speculated on the state of Glenys's mind. Although Charlotte wasn't practicing psychiatry now, she wanted to help Glenys manage her grief. Tomorrow, Rosie would call her again and see if she'd meet them for coffee. If so, Charlotte would offer some coping techniques as a friend. Assuming Glenys was willing to listen.

Before opening the book, she wandered back inside to plug her phone in and left it charging on the counter. Magnifying glass in hand, Charlotte sat and turned to the first page.

Weeks ago, soon after she'd begun working for Rosie, there'd been a day when Glenys wandered in and showed Charlotte the photographs she'd contributed to the book. Her pride in the handful of images she'd taken was immense, but back then, Charlotte knew nothing of the difficult marriage or how disliked her husband was.

The first few pages were the usual ones in books such as the copyright information. All images were attributed to

Fred, other than those on six named pages. They were Glenys'.

A dedication from Fred.

To my beloved mother and father for believing in me.

What a slap in the face for his wife. Charlotte's heart went out to her. Always in the shadows.

Another page listed the flora and fauna photos in the book. The kingfisher got a whole paragraph, with the comment that Fred had only ever photographed one.

'Ha. I've seen it once already and photographed it.'

She drank some wine. The day had caught up with her. All the stress from the early phone call, Trev's anger, and the detectives visiting. And the house wrapped in trees. Shuddering, she turned more pages.

There was an interesting full-page photograph of the falls, taken from the grass beside the pool. Such a beautiful shot. The water was crystal and the sky a perfect blue. Anyone seeing this would long to visit. She knew so well the softness of the grass and the sound of the tumbling water.

The glass was empty, so she refilled it, checking her phone as she passed. There were messages there. Two from Trev. One from Katrina. And one from Bryce. So, now she did have his number. More intrigued by the book, she didn't open any, leaving the phone to continue charging.

Page after page kept her interest and then, toward the end, the beautiful photograph from the newspaper, but in brilliant colour on glossy paper. This was attributed to Fred and dated.

Charlotte flicked to the previous page where one of Glenys' photos was also attributed and dated. The same date. She must have misunderstood Rosie the other day, who'd said Glenys and Fred would not have taken photos the same day as they couldn't work together. Either that, or somebody had mixed the dates up.

She raised the magnifying glass and followed the river from the bottom of the falls until it disappeared around a slow curve. The tiny beach was to one side, the one she wanted to visit by boat. Willows overhung the furthest part of the river, almost meeting across the narrowing channel of water. Somewhere here, she'd seen a discrepancy in the newspaper image but now it evaded her.

Except…close to the beach, swept along with the current, was something red. Something small and hard to identify in the shade of the trees. Her earlier idea of it being a duck was discarded. Nor was it a branch or anything natural.

Charlotte took the book inside, under the brighter light over the counter. She unplugged her phone and took a close-up photo of the photo, then sent it to her laptop.

As she waited for the laptop to boot up, she got around to reading the messages. Trev's were short.

Safely home. Stay out of trouble.

And one half an hour ago.

Always here if you need to talk.

Did *he* need to talk? By the time they'd eaten breakfast this morning, the earlier tension was gone. Charlotte had a lot to digest. Thoughts to unravel and emotions to explore. She checked Katrina's message.

Henry is staying in custody tonight. Would like to discuss some information he has divulged if tomorrow at ten suits.

What information? If the detectives were keeping him behind bars, was it possible they considered him a murder suspect? Charlotte responded to the text with a quick agreement about the time. Then moved to Bryce.

Please photograph and send image of Mrs Sibbritt on footpath near garden centre. ASAP.

'Really?'

She'd pinned it back on the corkboard so took the photo in the bedroom. Sending it off to him, she added a word.

Why?

A moment later her phone beeped. Bryce.

Stop sleuthing. Goodnight.

Charlotte grinned and forwarded the image to her laptop. Might as well take a closer look if this was in his sights though what it would show other than Rosie heading back to work was beyond her. Thunder boomed overhead, and Charlotte jumped, almost dropping her phone. She closed the sliding door, then saw her wine glass on the table so retrieved it before a sudden wind knocked it onto the floor.

Charlotte pulled up a stool at the counter and loaded both images as rain pelted down.

She zoomed in on the red article in the water. Too close and she lost the focus. Further out, it was hard to identify. Maybe if she used the magnifying glass and a moderate zoom…much better.

It was a bow.

Rosie was right. Debris. A ribbon from a gift had found its way into the river upstream. Nothing more.

Red. With white dots.

Charlotte grabbed the keys to the bookshop, and house keys and threw on her trench coat. Then, she rushed downstairs. Lightning helped her find the lock on the bookshop's back entrance and she flew inside, pulling the door closed. A beeping sound confused her as she reached for the step ladder. The alarm.

She tapped the right sequence into the keypad a second before it went off. Her phone and Rosie's were set up to receive a call should the alarm sound and Rosie didn't need waking.

From the wall behind the counter, Charlotte removed a photograph. She slid it beneath her jacket, returned the step ladder, and reset the alarm. The climb upstairs left her soaking wet as rain pummelled her from the side.

Charlotte left the photograph by the laptop and hung her jacket to dry, then found a towel for herself. There was a missed call on her phone. She glanced at the time, a bit shocked that it was almost midnight.

She returned the call.

———

The storm passed but the rain continued, less now than when Charlotte was outside, but loud on the roof of the bedroom. She pulled the sheet around her chin, staring out at the black sky as she stretched tired legs to the end of the bed.

A red bow with white dots.

Like the one Fred wore in the photo she'd retrieved from the bookshop.

'Glenys always knew what to buy him for Christmas.' He loved his bow ties.

But was the fabric in the photograph a bow discarded from a gift, or Fred's bow tie, after he'd fallen to his death?

'It isn't possible.'

The dates were wrong. She'd checked his obituary. And how could he have taken the photo if he was dead?

Charlotte covered her head with the sheet and forced her eyes closed.

In a few hours she was meeting Sid at the lookout and she'd need her wits about her.

He'd admitted being the anonymous caller when she'd rung him back.

'Why?' She'd echoed Bryce's favourite word.

'I'll tell you. But not on the phone. We need to meet.'

'Great, I'll be at the police station at—'

'Charlotte. Please.'

What on earth?

'Please, give me a chance to explain.' Sid's voice pleaded.

'There's stuff I know. About council. Jonas and Terrance and even stuff about Veronica. But I need you to help me get out of trouble first.'

'I don't understand.'

'There's a conspiracy to force me to retire. I'm willing to share what I know if you put in a good word. Tell them you'll help me sort myself out.'

Charlotte had rolled her eyes. 'When and where?'

'The lookout. If you're okay with that. I just want to meet away from prying ears.'

'If you haven't noticed, it is bucketing down outside.'

'Yeah. Well, if so, then the carpark. In your car if you prefer.'

Sid's intentions from their first meeting were loud and clear. Send Charlotte packing. Maintain the comfortable life he'd made. But he had problems he needed to fix and if there was a way to get some intel on the darker side of Kingfisher Falls, this might be her only chance.

chapter
forty

The rain was little more than a drizzle when Charlotte set out. It was not long after daylight had forced its way through low clouds and although the meeting with Sid was about an hour away, she planned to climb to the top of the falls before it.

Underfoot, the ground was soggy and slippery. Her runners were ruined in minutes as wet mud caked the sides and soaked through to her socks. Although the air wasn't cold, she'd grabbed the trench coat on the way out to offer some protection against the weather.

Water-filled potholes and fallen branches slowed her progress but as always, reaching the top of the cliff made the climb worthwhile. She rested her hands on her knees, panting until her heart rate was back to normal. Below, a fine mist covered the river like a layer of cotton wool curling as far as the first line of trees along the banks.

The pool overflowed across the grass as the swollen top part of the river dumped water over the edge faster than Charlotte had ever seen. The day Fred died was after a night of rain. Along with his obituary, she'd checked the weather. Common belief was he'd fallen from the lookout into a fuller than normal river. And perhaps he had. Or, was the place he'd fallen where she stood?

Charlotte crept as close as she dared to the edge. The descent was abrupt. To each side of the river, rocks and bushes growing in crevasses might catch an unfortunate faller but from this spot, the water would carry the body straight into the pool.

A shiver shot up her spine. This might be the last place Fred ever stood. Why would he fall though? The reports she'd read and conversations with Rosie revealed little. The official finding was accidental death. A misjudgement of how close he was to the edge or a loss of balance.

Or were you pushed?

Had Henry hated Fred so much he'd followed him up here and waited for the perfect moment? Charlotte was convinced it was Henry she'd photographed on the path, heading her way, so he knew the territory.

Something drew him to her and the attention both repulsed and scared her. She'd had enough of obsessive patients and clinging parents to last a lifetime.

Weak sunlight cut through the clouds and the drizzle stopped as Charlotte took more photographs with her phone. She concentrated on the river where it wound out of sight, near the beach, where the bow was in the book. As the mist lifted, it drifted toward the lookout. She followed its movement with her camera, capturing some pretty images of treetops peeping through the swirling white cloud.

Small rocks tumbled through the air beneath the lookout and Charlotte lowered the phone.

A person knelt there, leaning through the rails, arms outstretched.

Glenys! No, don't do it!

Charlotte ran for the steps.

———

Did Glenys mean to harm herself?

The recent events around Octavia's passing had affected Glenys. Her actions added up to deep seated grief. Buying all of Fred's books. Wanting his photograph from the bookshop. Talking of leaving town.

She goes to the lookout to pray for Fred's soul.

Rosie had said so. Glenys was a church-going woman.

Last year, Charlotte saw her doing this. Or at least, remembering her husband by tossing flowers one by one over the edge on the anniversary of his death.

But she wouldn't...no. She wouldn't follow him.

Charlotte grabbed an overhanging branch as a step gave way beneath her feet. She steadied herself, taking more care of her footing.

I must help her.

The day after Octavia died, Charlotte found Glenys at the lookout, her arms outstretched. Glenys insisted she wasn't about to jump, taking offense at Charlotte's concern. But why now?

The book.

'I explained you'd gone to her house and she hung up on me.' Rosie was surprised by Glenys' reaction last night.

Was Glenys so private a person—or so grief-stricken— that the idea of an uninvited person at her home would push her over the edge?

Great use of words, Charlie. Not.

Did she realise one of the books was missing? If she'd recognised Charlotte's car, might she have gone looking in the fire pit and counted what was left of the once beautiful books? And would it be enough to send her, distressed, to the place she believed her husband died?

In a moment or two, Charlotte would reach the lookout. Was Glenys still there? If she'd fallen…

'Glenys! Glenys, I'm almost there. It's Charlotte. Please wait for me.' It took most of Charlotte's remaining breath to call out. Her lungs hurt from running but she had to reach Glenys.

One final turn and the lookout was in front of her.

Empty.

————

No, no, no!

Charlotte flew to the railing where she'd seen Glenys. In a semi-circle around the edge of the lookout, horizontal rails attached to steel uprights. Would Glenys have managed to squeeze through the rails to jump? She'd been on her knees. Why would an elderly woman kneel?

Were you praying for Fred? Or even Octavia?

Did Charlotte have it wrong? No attempt to throw herself over. Nothing more than an early morning visit to a place of importance to her.

She had to look though. The dread of seeing Glenys' body at the bottom of the cliff turned her stomach. Holding her breath, Charlotte gripped the top rail and leaned over enough to see the river below.

Through the dispersing mist the pool forced water into the river, flowing fast and carrying small branches. Bit by bit she released the air from her lungs. No sign of Glenys. It wasn't a sheer drop from lookout to water, with rocks and bushes poking out in this place and that.

Her legs shook from running and adrenaline and Charlotte sank onto the ground of the lookout. In the minutes since leaving the top of the falls, Glenys had finished her prayers and left.

That was all. Calm down.

She closed her eyes for a moment, visualising what she'd seen. Glenys on her knees, arms through the railing as though reaching for something. Just as she had the day after Octavia's death. Arms through the rails.

'And the photo!' Charlotte's eyes opened. Henry's image had an arrow drawn in. One pointing over the rail.

Back on her feet, Charlotte leaned further over the top rail and scanned the cliff. Not far below was a ledge of sorts. Not wide enough to stand on, nor stable enough, but an odd little bush grew at an angle beneath it. Between bush and rock face, a long, narrow and polished piece of timber was stuck fast. It was close enough to reach if Charlotte lay on her front.

She shrugged out of her trench coat and hung it over the furthest rail after dropping her shoulder bag onto the ground. With a bit of luck, she'd retrieve the stick and be back on her feet in a moment. And if it was nothing more than someone's unwanted rubbish, she'd dispose of it.

On the ground, she turned onto her stomach and wriggled beneath the bottom railing. One hand around the base of the upright post for support, Charlotte reached down. Her fingers extended and she almost touched the stick. With most of her torso still on the concrete, she could afford to go a little further forward. Another wriggle.

This time, her fingers brushed the stick. With a sickening jolt, she recognised it. A walking cane. Not just anyone's either. She'd seen Glenys use it often enough.

But not since Octavia died.

Where was Glenys? Charlotte shifted her weight to go back under the rail.

'No, you don't!'

Off balance as she twisted her neck to glimpse Glenys'

enraged face, two hands slammed into Charlotte's back with enough force to push her body to the very edge.

'You little busy body. Die. Just like the others. Die.'

Another hefty blow to her back and now her legs were pushed under the railing on the wrong side and Charlotte was falling.

chapter
forty-one

Bang.

Bang.

Silence.

A long, loud wail. Glenys. 'You made me do it. You people always make me do it.' The wail tapered to nothing.

Only the pounding of Charlotte's heart.

Her feet had slammed into the ledge and although the cane and the bush remained, the rest had pretty much crumbled.

'Help me! Help!'

Clinging to a post at the edge of the lookout, her body dangling over the side of the cliff, Charlotte risked a glance at the drop. If she was lucky enough to miss the jutting rocks on the way down, the river would do little to cushion her fall.

She willed her aching fingers to stay gripped, but they hurt. Her shoulders screamed from holding her weight.

Think.

Her hands were around a metal post. It was bolted into concrete and wasn't about to come loose. Could she lift herself enough to get an arm around the post? She sucked in air and tightened the muscles in her forearms. One foot found a gap in the rock face just big enough for her toes.

Up. Her gaze picked a spot above her hands. That's where she had to be. Up.

Fire in her arms.

One. Big. Chin-up.

Pounding heart. All she could hear. Or was it the waterfall behind?

Her eyes levelled with the ground of the lookout. Her bag was there, its contents strewn across the lookout.

Rain began.

Her fingers slipping again, she forced her muscles to work harder than they'd ever worked. One elbow was over the edge, then the other. She rested on them for a long moment. If she let go with one hand, she'd fall.

Pushing up with her toes in the little gap below, she leaned all her body weight forward and then kicked the air. Just enough to get half her body to safety.

Don't let go. Not yet.

From the waist up, she was on solid ground again.

'Aaa!' She dragged one leg, then the other to the top. Panting, she lay on her side.

'Well, what have we got here?'

No. Not you.

Charlotte released the post and rolled under the rail, back to the relative safety of the lookout. On all fours she crawled away from the edge through mud.

'Looks like you've got yourself on the wrong side of the railing, missy.' Sid stood cross-armed at the entrance to the path. To safety. 'Couldn't believe my ears when I heard a cry for help.'

'Keep…away.' Charlotte blinked the rain from her eyes, scanning the ground for a stick. Or anything. Any weapon.

'You don't want to do that.' Sid sneered as he uncrossed

his arms and put one hand on the police belt. On the holster of his gun. 'Time to finish what we started.'

'No more sleuthing.' Bryce warned her it would lead to nothing good.

He might be right, but now it was Trev's voice echoing through her head. Trev who loved her, even if the words were yet to be spoken. And she'd let him down. 'I'm not sure I want to go through life wondering if you are hiding things. Wondering if I'm about to lose you.'

'It was Glenys.' Her voice sounded fragile. Broken by the blows to her back and abrupt fall. 'She killed Fred.'

'And?' Sid shrugged. 'Common knowledge but no proof.'

'And Octavia.'

'I don't believe you. No proof.'

'You know she just tried to kill me.'

The smirk disappeared and he reached out a hand. 'No idea how a little old lady would do that. I'll talk to her. But you and I need to have that chat.'

Charlotte let him help her up, releasing his hand to stumble back to the rails to lean on the top one, wanting to throw up. Instead, she wrapped the trench coat around herself. Everything hurt. 'Go on. You said you know things about Jonas and Terrance and Veronica.'

He joined her at the railing, glancing at the river below. 'Long way down.'

If there was a threat in there, Charlotte no longer cared. 'What do you know?'

'More to the point, missy, what do you know? I'm being investigated and I reckon you've had a hand in it.'

'I don't. Rosie doesn't. And we have every right to have complained with the crap you've put us through, but we haven't. Why target the bookshop with nasty Facebook reviews? And phone me anonymously, warning me you'll reveal my past to the town? Why, Sid?'

For once, he didn't correct her use of his first name. Friends now?

'Never liked Trevor but he's not around so you and Rose are the next best thing.'

'What? To harass? Damage a local business? You should be ashamed.' Charlotte put her hands on her hips and raised herself to her full height, wincing as her back spasmed. 'You need to put things right.'

'Yeah, and how? Burnt too many bridges and now Marguerite is freaking at me because she'll no longer be married to the law keeper here.'

The rain increased. Charlotte's hair was plastered to her scalp. 'Tell me about the others and I'll give you some ideas.' She dropped her arms to hold the rail for support.

Sid stared at her for a long moment with his beady eyes. 'Need more than that.'

'Then I'm going home.'

He grabbed her shoulder. 'You want to know? You go talk to Kevin. He's the one pulling all the strings.'

'Leading Senior Constable Browne, release Charlotte and step back.' Katrina emerged through the deluge with her gun drawn.

Bryce circled in from the opposite direction. 'Do it, Browne.'

Sid raised both hands, his eyes not leaving Charlotte's. 'Watch yourself.'

'Charlotte, are you able to step away? As far as you can.' Katrina kept her gun on Sid as Bryce approached him.

'He wasn't going to hurt me.' Charlotte had no idea why she bothered defending him. Her body didn't want to move but she made some distance before slumping onto the ground. Bryce handcuffed Sid and told him to stay put, then squatted beside her.

'We should have been here earlier.' He took her hands.
'You're shaking.'

'Did you hear what he said though?'

'Plenty. Enough. But next time stick to the plan. Ready?'
Upright again, he supported Charlotte as she stood, pain in
every movement. 'Kat, I'll take the idiot if you assist our
sleuth here.'

'I'm fine.'

Bryce escorted Sid away.

'Sure, you are.' Katrina's gun was holstered. 'Trev will
have words with me for leaving you alone for even a minute
with Sid.'

'Better he has words with you than me.'

Charlotte accepted Katrina's arm and they followed
Bryce, but much slower.

'You need to find Glenys,' Charlotte said.

'Glenys Lane? Why?'

'We have to go back to the lookout.' Charlotte stopped.
She should have told Katrina and Bryce what happened.

Why is my brain foggy?

'Her walking cane is there. Over the side. My guess is it is
the murder weapon.' It all came out in a rush. 'She tried to
kill me. Pushed me over the side as I was reaching for the
cane which is why I hurt so much.'

Katrina's jaw tightened. 'Then Henry was telling the
truth. Come on, let's get you in the car.'

'What did Henry say?'

'Tell you later. You need to see a doctor.'

Charlotte shook her head as they continued after Bryce
and Sid, who was arguing about being cuffed. 'I need a
shower. Kind of muddy if you hadn't noticed.'

'Did you hit your head at all? Have internal pain?'

'No. Back hurts.'

'Well, at the least I'm driving you home. Bryce can

manage Sid. I'll just need a minute to get Bryce onto forensics and the CI. Have you got your car keys?'

In the passenger seat of her own car, Charlotte was numb. Glenys was the killer all along. She had missed every sign and almost died for her mistake. Even arranging for Bryce and Katrina's presence to eavesdrop on Sid's conversation wasn't enough to protect her from a woman with murder on her mind.

Will you never get it right, Charlie?

Leaning back, she closed her eyes.

chapter
forty-two

The steps to the apartment were too much for Charlotte. Katrina took one look at her struggling up the first one and bundled her back into the car.

'House keys, please. What would you like me to collect for a change of clothes?'

Katrina ran upstairs with a list while Charlotte rang Rosie to ask if she could borrow her shower.

A few minutes later, Katrina backed the car out. 'I'll get Bryce to pick me up.'

'Thank you. I'm sorry to put you out.'

'Got to earn some goodwill with Trev.'

'Sid was going to tell me more. He said Kevin Murdoch is behind whatever dirty deals are being done.'

'And we'll uncover any link with the death of Mrs Morris, if one exists. In the meantime, stay out of it. Not sure why I said that, but, if anyone asks, I did.' Katrina laughed. 'I'll phone you this afternoon and arrange an interview.'

'I should have known.' Charlotte muttered more to herself than Katrina. 'The clues were all there.'

'Good. Then you can fill us in with an official statement.

Here's Rosie, already waiting for you.' She pulled up outside the gate. 'Would you like me to call Trev?'

'No.' That sounded abrupt to Charlotte and she forced a smile. 'Sorry. I'll talk to him later, once I'm dry. And stuff.' She opened the door and slowly pulled herself out as Rosie wheeled across the wet grass.

'Oh, Charlie. What on earth happened?'

Katrina carried Charlotte's bag of clothes, locking the car behind herself.

'Here, detective, I've got those.' Rosie put the bag on her lap. 'Please, come in.'

Bryce's car drew up behind Charlotte's.

'Ride's here. Call you later, and Charlotte? You did good.'

'Good at what? Charlotte Dean, you need to explain this to me.' Rosie turned the wheelchair. 'Grab onto the handles and we'll take our time going in.'

'Thanks. I'm okay walking. And I need a shower if you don't mind?'

'Shower. Coffee. Breakfast. And then a talk.'

———

'Glenys was always fit.' Rosie brought a second cup of coffee to Charlotte, who rested on the sofa, feet up, Mellow watching her from the arm. 'She was a gymnast. Strong. And her using a cane was strange but I believed her story about hurting her knee.'

'But was hitting Octavia premeditated?' Charlotte sipped the coffee, savouring the warmth and heat. Mild painkillers and a long shower had minimised the pain.

'And how can anyone even prove it, unless there is some forensic evidence on the cane?'

'There's more than just that.' Charlotte shuffled her body to sit more upright. 'The photo Henry took of you near

Octavia's house?' She reached for her phone from a side table and tapped until she found the image in question. 'Look behind you. Zoom in on the car passing you.'

Rosie stared at the phone, her fingers enlarging the picture. 'Oh. Oh, I think I will use a very bad word now.' Rosie did, with force, and Charlotte giggled, earning her a stern look. 'Explain why Glenys is driving past me. Away from Octavia's.'

'She'd just killed Octavia. This photo was taken at one twenty. She must have parked somewhere close to the bookshop and came in to get an alibi. And had the cane with her!'

'I saw her leave the bookshop and go toward town. And you told me she said she was walking to Octavia's to talk to her about the delivery of books.' Rosie handed the phone back. 'Where was she all that time and where was her car?'

'She mentioned something about it being serviced. And the next morning, if you remember, I found her at the lookout. My appearance rattled her, so had she just thrown the cane over? Henry was somewhere around there taking photos.' What a shame he hadn't come forward with whatever he knew. 'I am curious how Veronica fits into all of this.'

'Beginning to wonder who we can trust in this town!'

'Lots. And lots. I need to open the shop.' Charlotte swung her feet over and groaned.

'Did you bump your head?' Rosie tilted her head. 'It is Sunday. Lay back down and have a sleep for a bit. The cats and I will watch over you.'

'But Katrina will call to do an interview.'

Rosie took Charlotte's phone. 'Later. For once, child, do as you're told. Okay, darling?'

Sleep sounded nice. Her stomach was full of Rosie's cooked breakfast. Charlotte closed her eyes.

―――――

The afternoon sky was blue with no sign of rain. Charlotte clambered out of her car, still sore despite her three hour sleep. She wandered around the garden for a few minutes, hoping the quiet would help her mind settle.

The gate in the fence was open. Hadn't she'd left a shovel against it? After shutting and latching the gate, Charlotte gazed around to find the shovel.

Your head's been fuzzy for hours. Look tomorrow.

Carrying the bag that Katrina had got for her, which was now full of wet clothes, Charlotte got as far as the steps before a sound took her attention. The tap of a shoe on concrete which came from near the back door to the bookshop.

A chill swept through her. She knew before turning it was Veronica.

'What do you want?' Charlotte dropped the bag.

Veronica held the shovel from the gate. The blade was up near her shoulder. 'Time for a little chat. Open the door.'

'I've had a difficult day, Veronica, so if you've something to say, do it now. Out here. And I'll have my shovel back.'

'Do you ever wonder what's out there.' Veronica nodded to the back fence. 'Out in the wild bushland? I'll tell you. Lots of places to hide…things.' She waggled the shovel. 'Inside.'

'If you insist.' Charlotte unlocked the door and pushed it wide open. Without waiting, she headed for the main part of the bookshop, toward the front door.

'Uh uh! Stay here. Something bad will happen to Rosie if you don't.'

'Jonas? Terrance? Or is it Kevin? Which one will harm her?' Charlotte swung around, regretting her swift action as pain radiated across her spine. 'Why did you phone Rosie and tell her to go to Octavia's? Did you know Octavia was dead?'

'Of course.' Shovel still aloft, Veronica narrowed her eyes. 'What on earth is that beeping sound?'

'Refrigerator. Must have left it open by accident.'

Five, four, three, two, one. Better work.

The beeping stopped.

'I want to make a deal with you, Doctor. Thanks to Sid, we know all about your past, and I do mean all of it. Let's agree to keep each other's secrets.'

'I need to lean against the wall. That's all I'm doing.' Charlotte positioned herself so she could see both front and back doors. 'You don't want me telling anyone about Octavia blackmailing Glenys over the death of her husband, Fred.'

Veronica pouted. 'Didn't think you knew that. But yes. Octavia's nasty ex-husband sold that land to Glenys knowing full well Octavia planned to turn it into a state-of-the-art training centre for track and field. She had the permits and everything.'

'And she wanted it back. Why not just offer to buy it?'

'Are you stupid? She tried. And when Glenys refused? Let's just say the book club presidency was a simple warning shot.' She simpered. 'But how nice of you and Rosie to make a threat against Octavia just as I walked past. Couldn't wait to tell her.'

'Octavia?'

'O.M.G. With your lack of intelligence, how did you ever get to be a doctor? If you are one.'

'Thought you knew my whole history.'

A car stopped outside. Veronica stepped further back, tossing the shovel into the kitchen. 'Did you text someone? Show me your phone.'

Charlotte handed it over to Veronica as a woman stepped out of the driver's side and approached the front door. 'Not everyone knows we close on Sundays. She'll go once she realises.'

'Can she see us?'

'We're in the dark.'

For a few minutes, the woman window shopped, even taking a photo of the display of books at the front. Then she lit a cigarette and smoked it. Veronica's toes tapped and she fidgeted with her clothes.

'Can I have my phone again?'

Veronica shoved it at her and hissed, 'why is she still here?'

'Shall I ask?'

The woman tossed her butt onto the road, much to Charlotte's annoyance, then returned to the car and drove away.

'Who did you tell, Veronica? About us threatening Octavia?'

'Enough questions.'

'Was it Marguerite?' A movement near the far corner window caught Charlotte's eye.

'For goodness sake, no. Do we have a deal?'

'Nope. Never.'

Veronica's mouth dropped open, but no words came out. She retrieved the shovel from the kitchen and held it aloft.

'Wouldn't do that.' Charlotte opened her phone.

'Gonna arrest me with your phone?' The sneer from the woman was as good as Sid's.

'She doesn't need to. Veronica Wheemor, lower the shovel and turn around with your hands in the air.'

From the still-open doorway, Katrina grinned at Charlotte. 'Can't leave you alone for a minute.'

chapter
forty-three

'He's crossing the road. Do I look presentable?' Rosie fiddled with her tidier-than-normal bun as Lewis headed to the bookshop.

'Beautiful. As always.'

'No, really. Tell me.'

'You are fine. Enjoy.' Charlotte smiled to herself as Rosie pretended to be busy behind the counter. 'Good afternoon, Lewis.'

'Ah, my favourite sleuth.' Lewis kissed Charlotte's cheek. 'Are you mending?'

'Much better now, thank you.'

'Oh, Lewis! Didn't hear you come in.' Rosie collected her handbag and came around the counter. 'Is it already lunch time?'

'Better be, my dear. Our reservation is in ten minutes and I'm rather hungry.'

'In that case, we'd better get a move on. Charlotte, you'll be alright?' Rosie was almost out of the door, with Lewis close behind.

'Have fun, kids.'

Charlotte loved seeing them together. Rosie might be nervous and even overwhelmed at times by her growing attachment to Lewis, but Charlotte kept telling her it was a good thing.

Today marked one week and a day since the events at the lookout. After sleeping for almost twenty-four hours following Veronica's arrest, Charlotte visited the local doctor and accepted some more powerful pain relief medication. The doctor also took photos of the bruising which Charlotte provided to the detectives during a long interview.

Rosie refused to let her work again until mid-week but being just upstairs meant lots of visits to the bookshop for coffee and books. And in between, she texted or spoke with Trev. He'd listened as she told him everything. Everything factual.

In her heart, she'd wished he'd been here. The detectives were allies now, supportive, good people with jobs to do. Rosie was her dearest friend, concerned and cross in equal measures. Esther and Doug dropped in, sometimes with meals, until she made Doug promise to give her cooking lessons later. But none of them were Trev and she didn't trust herself to gauge where things stood between them. So, life went on.

There was much to do in the shop today. A new window display to create and books to unpack. Charlotte was busy and only noticed Lewis and Rosie over the road after finishing with a customer. They were talking and laughing as they waited for the traffic to clear.

There was a goodbye from Lewis, and as he went to leave, Rosie put her hand on his arm. He stopped with a smile, then leant down and kissed her on the lips.

'Oh boy. Oh, whoops, shouldn't be watching!' Charlotte tore off to the kitchen. She eyed the monitor until Rosie was back behind the counter before pouring a glass of water to carry out.

'You're back. How was lunch?'

Rosie's cheeks were red and there was a twinkle in her eyes. 'Delicious.'

'Was it India Gate House?'

'Hard to go past. Mind you, so is Italia.'

'We're lucky here with the quality of restaurants and shops.'

By now, Rosie was almost back to normal. 'Speaking of which, we, well, Lewis and I, were talking about the shop around the corner. The empty one.'

'Where Veronica set up her shoe shop last year?' Charlotte wondered if she'd made bail yet.

'Yes. Here's some local news, otherwise known as gossip,' Rosie said, 'somebody is moving in.'

'And, why is this a secret?'

'The windows are blacked out and there's been no talk about what kind of shop. Until Lewis found out.'

'Are you sharing?'

'I am.' Rosie leaned closer to Charlotte. 'Do you believe in… other things.'

Had one kiss sent Rosie into madness?

'Other what things?'

'The future. Or the past. Or both.'

Time to add some gin to Rosie's drink. Or check there isn't any there already.

'Rosie Sibbritt you are not making much sense.'

'Remember our conversation about me seeing into your future?'

'Rosie!'

'You're no fun. The shop is called *Harmony's House of Mystique* and the owner—Harmony Montgomery—is a clairvoyant. A *real* one.'

'Could have used her last week. Might have avoided almost being thrown off a cliff.' As soon as the words left her lips, Charlotte wished them back. Until now, she'd managed everything. Kept the terrifying moments to herself. Her eyes filled with tears and she shut them tight.

Two arms embraced her, held her close. 'You are safe, darling.'

Charlotte drew in a deep breath and opened her eyes. 'Thank you. Sorry. Must be tired.'

'Where is the alien tree and how is it faring under your doubtful care?'

Charlotte's head shot up at the welcome sound of Lachie's cheeky voice. He peered over the counter.

'Are you well, Charlotte Dean?'

'I was. But then a certain person… let's call him Lachie… questioned my ability to raise a tree. Considering the terrible beginning the tree experienced, it is unlikely it would have survived. Without me.' Charlotte kissed Rosie on the cheek as she extracted herself and got to her feet—still a little tender—to crush Lachie against herself.

A moment later, Darcy ushered Abbie in. Safe within her arms was a tiny bundle.

Rosie was around the counter in seconds. 'When did you get home?'

'A day or two ago. And now we are out and about. Charlie. Care to hold her?'

'Me? Oh, um…'

Before she knew it, Lachie had stepped away and the tiny bundle was snuggled against her. Copious dark hair topped the sweetest face she'd ever seen.

Darcy put an arm around Abbie. 'You're a natural, Charlie.'

'I don't hold babies often. She's asleep.' Charlotte whispered.

'For once.' Abbie touched Charlotte's arm to get her to look up. 'We've chosen her names. Sophie Charlotte Woodland.'

Charlotte's eyes misted and a swell of love filled her heart as she gazed back at Sophie.

Sophie Charlotte.

'What a pretty name!' Rosie smiled up at Charlotte. 'I would love to meet her.'

With great care, Charlotte lowered Sophie into Rosie's waiting arms. She straightened with a small wince, but the others were all intent on Sophie, with Rosie making strange cooing sounds. Nobody saw her brush away an errant tear.

Except the man who'd stepped into the bookshop unnoticed. His eyes told Charlotte he'd seen her guard down. The corners of his mouth flicked up and she couldn't help but respond in kind. Trev was back.

————

Rosie went out with Lachie and Abbie to put Sophie into her car seat. Darcy lingered, talking to Trev about greenhouses and his plans for the farm as Charlotte answered the phone. By the time she'd finished, the men were by the counter and the subject was Glenys.

'Knew her and Fred my whole life growing up. And she stayed in our house, Trev.' Darcy shook his head and his gaze moved to his family. 'I put them at risk.'

'Nobody knew her terrible secrets.' Trev patted his shoulder. 'You did nothing wrong.'

'Still… anyway, looks like we're set to go. Good to see you.' Darcy shook Trev's hand, then grinned at Charlotte. 'Lachie wants to come visit you again.'

'Anytime. And Sophie.'

Darcy stopped to speak to Rosie outside.

'Henry knew Glenys' secrets,' Charlotte said.

'And they were safe with him until he overheard Veronica tell Glenys about the conversation between you and Mum.'

Charlotte leaned against the counter. Trev was in his uniform and had yet to say why he was back. 'I made Veronica believe I knew Octavia was blackmailing Glenys and it turns out I was right. But how did Veronica know Glenys killed Octavia?'

'Surprised Katrina hasn't told you. She seems to be quite fond of you.'

'I like her too. And she hasn't.'

'Veronica saw Glenys drive past the garden centre at speed, so decided to follow and look through the living room window.'

'She's known all along.'

'And has been charged accordingly.'

Rosie returned, happiness radiating from her. 'That little baby! And now, you're visiting again.' She grabbed Trev's hand and kissed it, then wheeled to the other side of the counter. 'Are you here helping now everyone is under arrest?'

'Slight exaggeration, Mum.'

'Veronica Wheemor. Love saying that. And Glenys. Henry. Now who did I forget? Plain old Sid. Nothing Leading Senior Constable about him.'

'He has some explaining to do. And so do I, but not yet.' Trev tilted his head at Charlotte. 'If I arrange everything, are you up to a picnic by the falls tonight?'

'Of course, she is. I'll close up so she'll be there by six.' Rosie's smile couldn't get any wider.

'Charlie?'

She couldn't read his eyes. Her stomach tensed. This was

a proper goodbye. No more chances. She'd taken one too many risks.

Be a grown up for once.

'I'll be there at six.'

chapter
forty-four

At six o'clock on the dot, Charlotte reached the bottom of the steps to the pool. With no rain since the last time she'd been here the water was back to its usual levels, lapping against the low banks and the ground was once again firm underfoot.

She stopped when her feet touched the grass and slipped out of her sandals. Trev stood at the water's edge, staring up at the waterfall. He'd changed into a T-shirt and shorts, as she had. His feet were also bare, and his sandals placed beside a picnic blanket and basket.

How do I say goodbye to you?

Trev turned and caught sight of Charlotte, his smile breaking her already sad heart. He held out a hand and she joined him, the warmth seeping into her the minute their fingers touched.

'I'd forgotten how beautiful this place is.' His other hand gestured to the falls, but his smile stayed on her face. 'So beautiful.'

'Have you had many picnics here?'

'A few. Mum and Dad came here a bit and I tagged along, but then I got older and picnics became boring. Hungry?'

Not waiting for an answer, Trev led her to the picnic blanket, and they sat, legs crossed, facing the water. He opened a basket and took two glasses and a bottle of wine out. 'Care for a glass?'

'Would love one. Did you make the picnic?'

'Sure.' He busied himself opening the bottle. 'No. This is all the work of Italia, I'm afraid. Although I do make nice picnics, it's hard without a kitchen.'

When he'd filled the glasses, he handed one to Charlotte. 'Before making a toast, I have a question.'

Why did I put myself at risk again? How long will it take me to pack to leave town?

Charlotte loved Kingfisher Falls. She didn't want to run again. To leave her job, Rosie, the town. A rift opened in her heart.

'Where are you, Charlie?' His voice was soft, and her eyes flew to his. 'You're miles away.'

'I realised how much I love this town. What is your question?'

'Katrina and Bryce have done more than track down a killer. They've had Sid Browne in their sights. And what they overheard him say to you up there,' he pointed to the look-out, 'was enough to open a formal investigation. He won't be in the force for long.'

'You want to come back.'

He nodded.

'What about Rivers End.'

'I'll miss it.'

'Rosie will be so happy.'

'I haven't asked my question.' Trev took Charlotte's hand again, playing with her fingers. 'How do you feel about me living here.'

'Beside the pool? It might get cold in winter.'

The corners of his eyes crinkled. 'Somewhere in town.'

'What I think shouldn't matter.'

'It is all that matters, Charlie. If you want more space, tell me now. Before I accept the job. If you don't want us… ' His head dropped.

'But my past, Trev. The risks involved in being with me.'

He raised his head and laughed. 'Risks? Sweetie, everything about you comes with a risk. Some bigger than others.'

This is true.

But he didn't understand.

'If I wasn't clear that night about my family history. The possibility of genetic illness—'

'You were. And you said there's a test. You take it, when you want to. And either way, I will be at your side.' Trev clinked his glass against hers. 'To Kingfisher Falls and those who love it.'

There was no talk for a while as they drank their wine, Trev's arm around Charlotte. If there was a word she would use, it was contentment. And hunger, as the delectable smells of an Italia feast wafted from the basket.

'Trev, on the branch.' Charlotte whispered and nodded toward the kingfisher. The tiny bird stared back. 'Do you think he's hungry?'

'I think he's telling us we are welcome to be here.'

Yes, welcome. And wanted. Faults and flaws included. Charlotte leaned against Trev. The future wasn't clear yet. She had to discover who the mysterious 'Z' was who'd signed those cards in the box in the bedroom. And find a way to help her mother.

But for the first time in her life, Charlotte wasn't facing the future alone.

Next in the series…
Cold Case Murder in Kingfisher Falls

next in the series

COLD CASE MURDER IN KINGFISHER FALLS

Hidden in a trunk was a new wedding dress, unworn baby clothes, and a teddy bear...

Charlotte's first winter in Kingfisher Falls should be filled with crackling fireplaces, hearty soups, and brisk walks to the waterfalls. Instead, she discovers what looks like an old grave in the bushland behind her apartment. Could this be the resting place of a young woman who ran away from home years ago?

When a new clairvoyant sets up shop in town, Rosie is excited to have a reading. Charlotte is uneasy about the motives of the stranger, who seems to know an awful lot about Charlotte's past. And why is she determined to spend time with Rosie?

A trunk hidden in the back of Charlotte's garage by past residents might hold clues to finding the runaway. But will Charlotte's investigation - against her police officer boyfriend's wishes - solve the sad mystery, or put her directly in the sights of the killer?

about the author

Phillipa lives just outside a beautiful town in country Victoria, Australia. She also lives in the many worlds of her imagination and stockpiles stories beside her laptop.

She writes from the heart about love, dreams, secrets, discovery, the sea, the world as she knows it… or wishes it could be. She loves happy endings, heart-pounding suspense, and characters who stay with you long after the final page.

With a passion for music, the ocean, animals, nature, reading, and writing, she is often found in the vegetable garden pondering a new story.

www.phillipaclark.com

also by phillipa nefri clark

Detective Liz Moorland

Gripping Australian Police Procedurals

Rivers End Romantic Women's Fiction

Temple River Romantic Women's Fiction

Charlotte Dean Mysteries

Daphne Jones Mysteries

Bindarra Creek Rural Fiction

Maple Gardens Matchmakers

Sweet Contemporary Romances

Doctor Grok's Peculiar Shop Short Stories

Feel-good short fantasies

Simple Words for Troubled Times

Short non-fiction happiness and comfort book

Printed in Great Britain
by Amazon